On Fluent Haunches

Fox Emm

Interior designs by mgsdesiigns

Cover by Fox Emm

No AI was used in creation of this book.

ISBN: 978-0-9970841-5-3

Content Warnings

Protect your peace above all else.

This book contains: Parent Death. Adoption. Self-harm. Mental health hospitalization, treatment, and medication. Suicide mention. Suicide attempt. Substance use. Addiction. Religious themes and iconography. Disparaging talk about mental health (From someone with a mental illness). Homophobia. Non-related sibling (adoption) romantic relationship. Open door spice.

If you find that I've missed a trigger warning know it was not intentional. Please email foxemmwrites@gmail.com with the missed warning and I'll add it to subsequent editions.

"The black marauder, hauled by love
On fluent haunches, keeps my speed."
~ "Pursuit", by Sylvia Plath

For Janet Reedy - without your encouragement and support I wouldn't be here.

~

For Linds - without you this book would never have happened.

~

For Ana - aside from your editorial contributions, you gave me the most precious gift. You read the first draft and saw as much potential in this story as I did. Thank you.

1

CHAPTER 1

Philip was average height for his age, a rambunctious ten-year-old, but he was gangling. He was crouched by a tiger cage. The big cat was lying on the far side of the pen and was taking great pains to stay opposite of Philip. The animal studied him warily with bright amber eyes. The boy took a few steps away from the enclosure. His attention moved carefully over the edges of the tents he could see. His sharp hazel eyes were on the lookout for a very specific prey.

As he hunted, a slight breeze blew off the hills to the west. The forecast on the radio at breakfast called for rain, but so far, the sky had been all sun. The storm clouds in the distance warned of poor weather just as the radio had, and the air felt thick and humid. It was likely the rain would come and ruin the performances scheduled for the afternoon and evening, but that was of no concern to Philip.

Right then, he was looking for a tiny pair of white sneakers in the grass. Finding his younger sister Melissa was never a challenging hunt. She always hid near the animals. *Always.*

Usually, all Philip had to do to find her was see which animals seemed skittish and search for her shoes. That day, he was having a harder time than usual. He crept past the lion enclosure and turned his head from left to right, ensuring he didn't miss anything.

The breeze picked up again, and Philip closed his eyes as the wind kissed his cheeks. Perhaps the rain wouldn't hold out for the afternoon, after all. He took a deep breath through his nose. All he could smell were the animal pens. Though he and his sister had just bathed that morning, he couldn't smell the rich lavender soap their mother used on them both. Not like he usually could. All he could detect were the rich, earthy musk of the creatures and the stench of their leavings. It was too early for popcorn to be popped for the show.

When he opened his eyes again, his vision felt sharper and he thought he could hear every creature on the grounds. As he snuck between the elephant and the fortune teller's tent, he crouched lower, as if being sneakier than his sister would allow him to find her more easily. It was not altogether unreasonable. He had tiptoed up to her without her hearing him before. She was a social creature and easily distracted, though catching her because she had gotten swept up in a conversation wasn't nearly as satisfying as tracking her when she was meant to be concealed.

This time she was proving to be a worthy target, though. His sneakers were all but silent on the grass beneath them. The blades were almost in need of mowing, and the lush turf bent easily under the soles of his shoes.

Philip caught movement in the corner of his eye and quickly turned to face it. It was just one of the sword swallowers—not Melissa. The man smiled at the boy, and Philip nodded at him before he ducked beneath a flap of the big top.

The tent was dark inside. The lights wouldn't cut on until much closer to the first exhibition. Philip squatted on his heels behind the bleacher-style seats beside him. He put his fingers on the earth between his spread knees. He closed his eyes again. He took a deep breath through his nose, and then another. He smelled stale popcorn, dropped beneath the seats by audiences past—but no lavender. He listened carefully for any sign of her, his eyes still closed.

She wasn't normally this difficult to find. Either she was getting better at hiding, which she ought to after years of practice, or someone was helping her. It wouldn't be the first time. The pair of them were the only children in the circus, and they tended to be spoiled by the host of sideshow acts and performers.

Once, Philip had found his sister hiding in the leather trunk the bearded lady kept her corsets in. That had been on a Sunday, though. Performance days were different. No one had time for them on show days. Even their parents were scarce when a full house was expected.

Philip slunk to the end of the bleachers. He looked to another set of seats across the ring, and his lips curled into a small grin. He saw a tiny set of white sneakers peeking out from beneath the bottom row.

The boy lowered his chest closer to his knees, his hands spread wide at the end of his outstretched arms. Silently, he slipped around the outskirts of the ring. He kept bleachers between himself and his sister in the hopes she wouldn't see him stalking her.

Philip grabbed her waist and squeezed, tickling her. The girl shrieked, surprised joy catching her off guard before she descended into giggling.

"Got you!" he announced, even as she thrashed on her belly on the bench.

"Letmegoooo!" the girl begged, only breaking from laughing long enough to plead for release.

Philip relaxed his grip and let her roll over onto her back to look at him. He grinned mischievously and mimed like he meant to grab her again. She squealed, which made him laugh in turn.

"Philip, you're wicked!" Melissa teased, sitting upright.

"And you are bad at hiding," he teased. He offered her a hand to help her to her feet. She took it gratefully and let him pull her up.

"Race you home!" she shouted, taking off like a shot.

Philip sprinted after her. With his long legs, he would have caught her in a few strides if he hadn't tripped. His foot caught on a length of rope, and he pitched sharply forward.

Before his hands and knees hit the earth, he jolted awake. He blinked a few times, adjusting to the sudden darkness around him.

It took him a few moments to realize where he was. It always did. Instead of sleeping on the bunk bed he'd shared with

Melissa in his family's caravan, he was in a bedroom. He looked across the room to the other twin bed, where his adoptive brother Kam slept. Seeing his older brother's silhouette in the dark brought reality down with jarring clarity.

He wasn't at the circus anymore. He didn't live with Melissa anymore. Their parents were dead. He might never see Melissa again.

The realizations kept crashing down on him, and his throat clenched. He felt his eyes begin to tingle, his only warning before the tears came. They were followed almost immediately by deep, hopeless sobs. They wracked his body, even as he clung to a stuffed bear his adoptive parents had given him. It had been one of Kam's cast-offs, but Philip kept it close every night.

Kam stirred and woke, jarred by the noise. His blue eyes found Philip in the darkness with some difficulty. He rolled onto his side.

"Bad dream?" He asked the question, but he already knew the answer. Philip had come to live with them roughly six weeks ago. He had nightmares several times per week. The family doctor had suggested this was normal for ten-year-old boys who had been through as much as Philip had.

He sniffled, quieting enough to answer Kam's question. "Yeah," he replied, his voice rough from the effort of the response.

"You want to come to sleep with me?" Kam asked. That had not been a suggestion offered by the doctor, but Philip had shared that when he was younger and had nightmares, his parents had let him crawl into bed with them. Kam had taken it upon himself to offer a similar comfort.

Philip sniffled again, seriously considering the offer. "Yes," he replied finally, his voice still quiet.

He kicked out from beneath the blanket and got to his feet. He left the bear in his bed—if the bear was in the wrong bed in the morning, that would give them away. Their adoptive parents insisted Philip should be strong and independent, and he didn't like to disappoint them.

Philip slowly crawled onto Kam's bed and snuggled in close to his makeshift sibling's side as Kam settled onto his back once again. He smelled clean, like minty toothpaste.

"It was just a dream," Kam reminded Philip softly.

Philip nodded, but the fact made his eyes well up all over again. It *was* just a dream. He'd likely never see his circus family again. His parents were gone. He didn't know what had happened to Melissa.

Philip buried his face into Kam's side, and the older boy put his arm around his new brother's shoulders.

"It'll be okay," Kam reassured the younger boy. "You're getting better."

Philip nodded, but he didn't raise his forehead from where it was pressed into Kam's ribs. The older boy kept his arm around Philip's shoulders, and together, they took a few controlled, deep breaths.

Held against Kam, Philip felt himself begin to cry again. This time, his tears flowed silently. He wrapped his arms around his own torso and squeezed tightly. He stayed cuddled up next to his new protector and tried to take comfort in his presence.

As he finally drifted off to sleep a few hours later, his thoughts swirled around his sister. Of never seeing Melissa again. Of worrying she didn't have someone to look over her without him there. That she'd grow up thinking Philip had left her deliberately, like their parents had.

2

CHAPTER 2

In the two years Philip had lived with the Gardners, he'd
learned a lot by watching. He saw his new parents attending
church and Bible studies. He observed as they took part in
bake sales and volunteered for the community. When he was
young, they didn't expect his participation so much as
expected him to pay attention, and that suited Philip just fine.
He learned they were a peaceful, devout couple, which made
for a similarly inclined family. They had a remarkable amount
of patience for Philip, and he believed they cared for him,
even loved him. Still, there were some things about him that
they didn't understand. They knew he'd been the one to find
his parents when they died. They knew he'd wept daily during
the first few months in their care, but then all of a sudden,
he'd just... stopped. They didn't understand how the boy had
gone from crying every day to never crying at all. They
certainly didn't know what to do once they realized he'd begun
hurting himself.

He'd started small. The first time he'd cut himself, the wound had been an accident. He'd simply been careless with the cuticle nippers. It was a mistake, he swore, cutting down too close to the nail bed. He had slipped the bleeding tip of his finger between his lips. While he'd sucked in the stinging digit, he'd found it difficult to focus on anything but the sensation and the salty, metallic flavor.

That had been the spark. The next time he'd felt his emotions building tightness in his chest, he'd grabbed a pair of scissors, the sharpened pair Mother used for her quilting. He took the blade to his shoulder, where the wound wasn't likely to be seen. He found that he felt immediately better, like all the tension building in his body had been released. He tested the experience a few times more after that, but it didn't take long for a habit to form.

The Gardners didn't catch on for a long time. He tended to focus on his shoulders, upper arms, and chest. It wasn't until a late summer lake trip that they'd spotted his scars and questioned his fresh wounds. Philip had known they'd ask, so he had held off on getting undressed as long as possible. Unfortunately, Father wouldn't tolerate him wearing a t-shirt in the water, so he'd eventually needed to disrobe. That had been six months ago.

In the new school year, all the razor blades, scissors, and pocketknives in the house were gathered up, and Philip had begun regular counseling sessions with Pastor Andrew at their church.

The removal of his usual implements and introduction of counseling didn't stop Philip, though. It had simply made him more creative. He got his hands on an old sewing kit. The kit had a tiny pair of scissors which were too small to do any meaningful damage, but the main prize was a selection of vicious little needles. What was more, he found that scratches from the needles were easier to hide, even though the Gardners were on alert for wounds.

Philip didn't like hiding his self-harm from them. It felt like lying, and the only way he knew how to lie well was to keep very quiet.

When Philip finally got his hands on a small pen knife, he was elated. The pin pricks had held him over, but they were nothing compared to the biting slice of a blade, even a short one. When he finally worked up the courage to use it, he was a little overzealous. It had been the first time he'd used a knife on himself in a while, and afterward, his watch wasn't as helpful at hiding the deep wound as he'd hoped.

He tried without success to convince his parents that the wound had not been an attempt on his life. They took him immediately to the hospital, where he was given a few stitches, and the attending physician was all too happy to admit him to the psychiatric ward.

"Please don't leave me," he'd begged, holding tight onto his adoptive mother's blouse. "Please! I'll never do it again." He knew as soon as the words left his lips that they were lies to protect his habit. He was addicted to the pain and the release it brought, but his fear of being left was more powerful than his fear of being damned.

"We only want what's best for you," his mother replied. She wiped tears from her cheeks, and then used those same hands to pry his fingers from her clothing.

Once they were gone, Philip was silent. He didn't speak for three days. Not to his therapist. Not to his roommate in the ward. Not to anyone. His dark curls were in disarray and his hospital-issued clothes were disheveled, a mess after just a few days. Despite his appearance, he hadn't forgotten his manners. He gave nods of thanks to the nurses who brought him medication and the orderlies who brought his meals, but that was all they could get out of him, aside from complaints about the medication he was given. He found the medication made him drowsy, so they allowed him to take it at night.

After his medication was changed, he found the days were monotonous, but the evenings were something worse. At night in the darkened hallways he felt like there were always shapes moving just outside his line of sight. When he woke up in the middle of the night he had nothing to seek comfort in but shadows. It was yet another insult added to the injury of being taken from the home he had grown accustomed to.

One morning after a particularly rough night of sleep, Philip was outside the facility. He was enjoying the warmth of the sun upon his face and the light feeling of the wind across his skin. The air had a hint of a chill and the leaves turned upside down and backward when the wind blew—a sure sign of rain. His eyes were closed and his cheeks were upturned. His vision was blurred red by the sunlight shining through his eyelids. For once in this wretched place, he was alone. None of the other boys had wanted to go outside, but Philip didn't fear a little rain.

A loud creaking jarred Philip from his moment of peace. The door to the activities room was in need of oiling. His hazel eyes fixed on the figure who'd just come through. It was an orderly.

"Have you seen Jeffrey?"

Philip shook his head.

"Can you help me find him? There's been an emergency at his home and his folks are coming to get him. They'll be here in an hour."

Philip couldn't imagine what they'd need to drag a depressed little boy home for, but he was immediately jealous. Guilt overtook him a moment later when he thought about what might be cause to beckon *him* home. Something wrong with Kam? Their adoptive parents? Only something dire would bring him home early, and he couldn't wish ill of his loved ones.

"Of course," he replied. He pushed his curiosity down, along with everything else.

The fenced-in yard was larger than he remembered seeing when he had arrived. It ran the length of the hospital and further around the building. Philip turned left to follow the chain link around the corner of the brick, and he didn't elevate his gaze to take in the razor wire. Philip looked around the yard and decided to peek behind the garden shed. At the back of the structure, there was a line of bushes that had become overgrown.

He was about to leave, to trek beyond the edge of the shed, when rustling in the bushes halted him. He locked his eyes on the leaves and the low-hanging branches. Philip's eyebrows furrowed at an all-too-familiar sound—was someone crying? It was muffled, but it wasn't distant the way it was at the hospital at night. He crouched low beside the bush and peered beneath the greenery. "Jeff?" His voice was uncertain, but the crying stopped.

A few drops of rain pattered onto Philip's bare arms and onto his dark curls. He bent lower and crawled on his hands and knees into the underbrush. The bush was denser underneath than he expected, which made it challenging. The light cotton uniform the hospital supplied caught on brambles and tore. He didn't mind—he was on the hunt. Finally, he was in familiar territory.

"Jeff, they're looking for you!" Philip called. He still couldn't see the young boy, but he could *sense* him. As surely as he had predicted the rain, he knew Jeff was in the bush. "Come on, you're going home!" The crying didn't resume, but Philip heard sniffling, which meant he was on the right track. He pushed some of the undergrowth aside and continued forward. Jeff sat curled in a ball just a foot away.

Philip scowled at him. "Why didn't you come when I called?"

"I can never go home," Jeff replied, his small voice was fragile. He wouldn't meet Philip's gaze with his red, puffy eyes.

"What? You're going home now, as soon as we go inside."

The rain pelted harder against the leaves overhead. At this rate, it would be pouring by the time they got back across the yard.

"I can't go home," Jeff repeated the sentiment. "Kam's dead."

Philip recoiled from the small boy. "What did you say?"

13

Jeff sniffled. "I can't ever go home." He stared at Philip with vacant eyes as he spoke again, "Kam's dead."

"Who's Kam?" Philip asked, his chest tight.

"Your brother."

The light seemed to dim around them, as if the sun had gone behind the clouds beneath the bush. Philip's heart sank with it. "What?"

"Kam's dead—Kam's dead—Kam's dead!" Jeff shouted the words over and over, his volume raising with every repetition so he could be heard over the roar of the howling wind.

Philip felt the world turn sideways on its axis. He fell from the earth, and when he landed on his back, he jolted and sat upright in his hospital bed. Tears were streaming down his face.

"It was a dream," he hissed to himself in the dark. "Kam is fine, it was just a dream." Without his brother to console him, he could only wrap his arms around his middle and rock slightly back and forth on the mattress. His tears flowed freely until the morning. When the orderly from his dream came to wake him, the man found Philip sitting upright in bed, his back to the wall.

The day after his dream, he finally spoke to the psychiatrist. That morning the orderly had made a few snide comments that if he wanted to get out, then he needed to work *with* the doctors. The combination of the nightmare and the idea of his captivity being permanent forced him to act.

"If you keep up not sleeping and giving them the silent treatment, they'll keep you in here forever," the orderly had insisted. Philip certainly didn't want that. The thought of being trapped in the hospital while something could happen to Kam on the outside was too much. He had to get *out*.

When Philip made it clear he was going to cooperate, the doctor chose to speak to him about his past, rather than about the self-harm that had resulted in his detainment.

"How old were you when your parents died?" Dr. Garcia asked. She studied him with fawn-colored eyes and a serious expression, her dark hair neatly tied back in a ponytail.

"Ten," Philip had answered quietly. The doctor was a professional, and didn't so much as blink when he shifted from staring blankly at her to answering her questions. Philip felt uncomfortable opening up, but he needed to get back. Again, he thought of Kam at home without him.

"Do you remember much about how they passed?"

"They killed themselves," he replied. He was still speaking softly, as if he feared being overheard. "They shot themselves when we were outside playing. I came back in to see when lunch would be ready, and I found them in the kitchen." He spoke slowly, carefully enunciating each word, as if that would make it less painful to recount. He thought about his parents' passing often, but he didn't often *talk* about it. Saying the words aloud was challenging. Discussing it out loud was like tonguing a cut on the roof of his mouth—it stung when touched.

"Who was *we?*"

"My sister Melissa and I."

"Where was Melissa when you found them?"

"Outside. I didn't let her come in once I saw."

"How did you feel when you saw your parents?"

"Sick. I threw up. Then I ran outside, screaming and crying."

"Do you feel like you want to cry now?"

"No." His voice sounded a little distant. Even as he said the word, he felt a little numb. "I'm okay now," he lied. He was getting better at lying. He had a feeling that the longer he stayed, the better he'd get.

"Do you cry often?"

"No," he lied again. "Mostly when I have nightmares." Dr. Garcia also knew from her notes that he had nightmares fairly often. She didn't know just *how* often, because Philip wasn't very accurate in his self-reports.

"What are your nightmares of?"

"Playing with Melissa," he answered, his voice still low.

"Why do you cry when you dream of Melissa?" Dr. Garcia asked, studying the boy carefully.

"Because I'll never see her again," Philip replied. His tone was still muted, devoid of any emotion despite what he was saying. Detaching from his feelings had been the only way so far he had found to deal with them. Well, that and the self-harm, but that was hardly an option in the hospital.

"Do you feel like crying now?"

"No."

"Were you crying when you cut your wrist?" the psychiatrist wondered, finally looping back to the matter at hand.

"Yes," he admitted. It was the first time he'd spoken about what had sent him to the hospital, beyond insisting that he hadn't wanted to kill himself. He didn't want to talk about it, but he wanted to stay committed even less. He knew he had to give the doctor *something* to work with. The orderly had been very clear about that.

"Do you feel like you need to hurt yourself when you cry?"

"No, but it helps."

"How does it help?"

"It's like unlocking a garden gate," he explained cryptically. "Having the gate unlocked makes going through it easier."

"That's what crying is, something to get through?" the woman asked.

Philip thought about the question for a moment. Unlike the previous questions, this felt more like she wanted his opinion. He didn't know how to provide his opinion, not on something personal like this.

"Yes," he finally said, but he sounded uncertain. His voice wavered a little.

"You know you can cry if you need to when you meet with me," the doctor offered. "This is a safe place where you can feel whatever emotions are moving through you. I won't judge you if you cry, or shout into a pillow, or pace around the room—whatever helps you. Dr. Kramer feels the same way." Dr. Kramer was the psychologist who led the group therapy and individual therapy sessions. Philip had been mute during those, at least so far.

"Okay." Philip didn't want to cry, or shout, or pace. He wanted to go home. "What if I just want to talk, like this?"

"That's fine too, if that's what you need," the doctor replied with a nod. "It'll take a few weeks for you to feel a difference with the medication I prescribed."

"What will it feel like?" Philip asked. He knew he'd begun taking a medication, but he didn't know what the point of it was supposed to be. The only thing he'd felt so far was sleepy and mildly dizzy, but surely *that* wasn't meant to help.

"You shouldn't feel like you need to hurt yourself so much, and the sadness shouldn't feel so deep."

Philip nodded. He didn't know if he believed the little white pills he took would make a difference, but he hoped they would. If the medicine worked, he'd get to go home. "How long do I have to stay?" he asked.

"Until we see how the medicine's working, and until we know you won't be a danger to yourself."

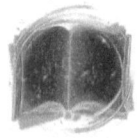

A few days after that session with Dr. Garcia, the Gardners came to visit Philip. They came as a family on Sunday afternoon, after church. They were dressed in their Sunday best, and Philip felt self-conscious in his hospital-issued clothes and grippy socks.

"How are you doing?" his mother asked.

"I'm doing well," Philip replied, smiling. "I want to come home."

His mother eyed the bandages on his wrist where he'd cut himself, and her smile looked strained. "As soon as the doctors release you, dear."

"What have you been doing?" Kam asked, blue eyes bright and his light brownish hair tousled like always.

"I have sessions with Dr. Garcia. She handles my medicine. I meet with her once a week. Then I have sessions with Dr. Kramer. I meet with her by myself, and then in a few groups." He shrugged. "Those schedules are all different. When I'm not meeting with one of them, I play with the other kids, do crafts..." he trailed off and shrugged his shoulders. "Sometimes I just sit in my room by myself or watch the other kids play."

"It sounds like they keep you busy," Kam suggested. He didn't sound too confident. "I'm glad you're not dead," was what he finally decided to add, and his mother glared.

For some reason the words, more than their mother's reaction, made Philip smile. "I'm glad I'm not dead too," he agreed. "What have *you* been doing?"

"It's just the same as before you left," Kam shrugged. He carded his fingers through his hair—it was slightly too long, so he'd be getting a haircut soon. "Schoolwork every day.

Homeschool circle twice a week. Bible studies. Church. The only thing that's different is that you're not there."

"We do miss you terribly," his mother added, glad the boys had moved to less morbid subjects. "We're really looking forward to when you're well and can come home."

"I want to come home now," Philip said earnestly. Tears welled and threatened to fall down his cheeks. Seeing him getting emotional got his mother choked up, and she looked to his father.

"We'll take you home as soon as they say you can go, son," his father said simply, in his steady baritone. He adjusted his horn-rimmed glasses on the bridge of his nose. "But we have to give the medicine time to work."

Philip nodded, but he didn't agree. He didn't think he needed medicine, or therapy, or any of it. He just wanted to go back home.

"What was today's sermon?" he asked, hoping to turn the conversation to happier things.

Over the next few weeks, Philip tried to improve. He was contributing regularly to group and individual therapy sessions, and Dr. Garcia seemed to think the medication was doing its job. He performed better on the diagnostic inventories the psychiatrists used to gauge his well-being. They had increased his medication dosage gradually, and although he felt more muted, a little more numb, he didn't feel dramatically different. He did find that he wanted to hurt himself less frequently. His emotions felt less intense. He even looked better—he'd resumed brushing his hair and he was sleeping better now that his bunk was more familiar.

The bandages and stitches had come off and out. A nurse said that if Philip didn't scratch the scab, there wasn't likely to be more than a minimal scar. Philip hadn't been especially worried about scarring, but the woman had sounded so relieved for him that he hadn't wanted to disappoint her.

"When do you think I'll get to go home?" he asked Dr. Garcia at his next appointment.

"Soon, Philip. You've made great progress," the doctor replied. "Your parents want to take you home just as soon as you're ready." That made the boy smile. It meant a lot to him that the Gardners missed him when he was gone. It even meant something to him that they had cared enough about him to have him committed in the first place, though he still hadn't quite forgiven them. He cared for them too, in his own way. They didn't feel like his parents, but they were adults he could trust and he loved them. It didn't *hurt* to call them Mother and Father.

"Just tell me what I have to say to get out of here," Philip said, eager to please the doctor.

The woman chuckled. "It's not as simple as that," she replied. But over the years, Philip learned that wasn't true.

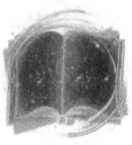

It took another two years before Philip hurt himself badly enough to worry his mother again. That time, he didn't cut himself, but had chosen to take a bottle of painkillers. He was willing to admit that it was a suicide attempt. He'd tried to kill himself rather than face life without Kam. He couldn't handle more loss.

His older brother had been planning to leave. Kam's relationship with their parents had grown strained, and an uncle a few states away had offered to take him in. It had been a last-ditch alternative before sending Kam to military school.

Philip had begged and pleaded and cried to keep Kam with him, but his parents had made up their minds. They couldn't handle Kam's defiant behavior anymore, and they weren't willing to try anything else to keep their elder son under their roof. In the face of his failure to convince them, Philip lashed out in the only way that had ever been successful for him— self-destruction.

The day the family was meant to pack up the car and start on the nineteen-hour road trip to take Kam to Uncle Adam's, they were instead waiting in a hospital hallway while the fourteen-year-old had his stomach pumped.

In the car on the way to the hospital, Kam had held Philip's hand in the back seat. The boys had sat on opposite sides of the car, and their had hands met low on the middle seat, out of their parents' line of sight. Kam's warm palm on Philip's kept him tethered to the world around him. He felt cold except for where his hand was touching Kam, and he had to fight to stay awake.

"You can't send me away while Philip is in the hospital," Kam had argued, tears streaming down his cheeks. "I need to be here in case anything happens," he insisted. "Please. I'll listen to you, I swear." Their mother had been too exhausted with worry to argue.

Father had agreed they could postpone sending Kam away to their uncle's until they were sure Philip was stabilized at the mental hospital.

For the first few weeks, Kam was on his best behavior at home. It helped, of course, that Philip flew into hysterics any time Uncle Adam was mentioned, either by the Gardners or by staff at the hospital. Kam tried to do everything his parents asked of him, but eventually, he began to fall short.

Unfortunately for their parents, it was very clear that Kam's presence was a non-negotiable piece of Philip's recovery. Kam had agreed to go, Uncle Adam had agreed to take him, but Philip couldn't handle the thought of Kam going away, even temporarily. The idea that Philip might go back to a home without Kam made him want to curl up into a ball. He wanted to pull Kam close and hold on tight so that no one could send him off.

When Philip finally came home from the hospital, his parents had been offered the guidance that he was an incredibly sensitive, traumatized boy. Although their parents weren't explicitly told they should bend to his will, they were encouraged to consider his history of loss and whether sending Kam away was critical. The Gardners took the counsel to heart. Once Philip was released, there wasn't any more talk of Kam going away. Uncle Adam couldn't be expected to handle both boys, especially when Philip was so troubled, and it was clear Philip was too fragile to handle losing someone else. In the interest of peace, the Gardners dropped the issue.

There was a small uptick in the number of shouting matches Kam got into with their parents, once it was clear he wasn't being sent away. Philip noticed the only times they didn't fight was after Kam took small, hand-rolled cigarettes into the backyard. He'd come back inside from behind the shed with bloodshot eyes and infinitely more patience for his parents. He'd change his clothes so they wouldn't pick up on the smell, and then he could take anything their parents threw at him.

Their parents never knew about the cigarettes, as far as Philip could tell, and they didn't seem to make any connection with Kam's moods. Philip never asked about his habits, and Kam never volunteered the information. This was for the best, as any interference with Philip's medication could have been dangerous. Only one of the boys could afford to self-medicate.

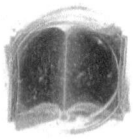

By the time Philip was sixteen, he had perfected the art of getting what he needed from institutions and of being released on his own terms. As far as Philip was concerned, it was always an accident that got him into the facilities in the first place, and so it was his own deliberate efforts that would release him.

This *accident*, as he would come to call it, was twofold. The first piece was what happened to a bully, Isaiah Frederick. Philip had begun going to a community center to socialize and play games with other teenagers. Shortly after Philip's birthday, Isaiah began harassing him every day.

He had started by teasing Philip about everything from his haircut and how he dressed to what church the family went to. Philip did what he could to ignore the taunts. After a few weeks, Isaiah resorted to pushing and shoving Philip. When he did, the younger boy snapped. He wasn't sure what made him lose control. Something about Isaiah's hands grabbing him roughly was too much. His blood boiled and he let loose a roar as a powerful animal instinct overtook him.

Philip grabbed Isaiah by the shoulders and managed to trip him, knocking the elder boy to the ground. Once he was on the floor, Philip kicked and scratched and even bit Isaiah when the older boy took a swing at him. By the end the other boy had a split lip, a busted eyebrow, and a cracked rib or two for his trouble. It had been Kam who'd broken up the pummeling.

Philip was sent away to a juvenile detention facility. The second fold of his *accident* was stabbing himself in the arm with a fork he'd stolen from the dining hall. That had been enough for the state to hand his care over to a mental hospital. Philip felt it was worth the pain in his arm. In his mind, a few months in a mental health facility was arguably better than the juvenile detention ward, and it also meant he could have more regular family visits.

"You can't keep doing this, Philip," Kam grumbled, one week later when he had made the drive to see Philip alone. His blue eyes were bloodshot and had dark circles under them; he hadn't been sleeping well. "Every time something upsets you, you can't take it out on yourself. Stabbing yourself in the arm?" Kam shook his head. "That jerk wasn't worth hurting yourself over."

"But I shouldn't have reacted that way," Philip argued. "I should have been stronger than that."

"Well, you weren't, and he deserved it," Kam retorted. "You didn't do anything wrong by teaching him a lesson. I don't care what the court said."

"I shouldn't have kicked him. I went too far. Knocking him down should have been enough. I should be better than that."

"Why?" Kam asked, inclining his head to the side. "I'm not." That got a laugh out of Philip, but it wasn't enough to sway Kam. "You can't keep hurting yourself when you get upset." Philip smiled weakly when his brother doubled down, and he shrugged his shoulders. Kam wasn't fazed. "Hurting you doesn't help anyone else, including you." Before Philip could protest, the bell chimed that indicated the visiting hour was over.

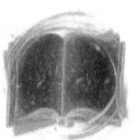

Philip had been hospitalized enough that he knew the routine and what the providers wanted to hear. By the end of the month, he had both the psychiatrist and the psychologist eating out of the palm of his hand. He didn't feel like he wanted to hurt himself or anyone else, so it wasn't that he was lying, necessarily. He was simply embellishing the truth.

As soon as they had the option, both eagerly signed off that he could be released into the care of his parents. They stipulated that he needed to continue to attend weekly counseling sessions, but they could be conducted by the pastor of the family's church, so long as the pastor filled out the necessary forms.

After his release Isaiah never so much as looked at Philip the wrong way again. Not that it mattered, Philip wasn't afraid of him any longer. Every time their eyes met Philip just saw Isaiah broken and bloodied at his feet. To be safe, for both of their sakes, Philip stopped going to the community center.

3

CHAPTER 3

After eight years with the Gardner family, in and out of
hospitals, the dreams of his old family came less frequently.
Instead of every night, he woke up crying once every few
months.

It was an improvement.

He wasn't proud of the progress he made, however. It came at
a cost. Every night he didn't remember and mourn his family
felt like a personal, moral failure. His hormones had opted to
replace them with new dreams.

The dreams weren't the first changes Philip had to contend
with. A few months prior, his stomach and chest had begun to
itch. Hair grew in wild, unruly patches. That had been his first
physical shift, years behind his peers. The peach fuzz on his
chin had followed. His voice had fortunately only cracked
once. The dreams, however, had started coming with alarming
frequency.

At least once per week if not more, Philip would wake up panting and sweating, unable to ignore the damp, sticky warmth between his legs. When his eyes opened, he could never raise them from his own body and shame. He felt heat in his cheeks if he even glanced toward his brother's side of their cramped bedroom, even in the dark while Kam was sleeping.

By the morning, Philip had always changed his clothes and stripped his sheets. He could never meet Kam's eyes. He was too afraid his glance would linger too long on his brother's lips, too worried his thoughts would flash back to his lurid imaginings. Each morning, he remembered all too clearly the way Kam tasted hours ago, in his dreams. How soft his brother's body felt in his hands...

In his imagination, he could even picture how his brother's skin would smell, clean and fresh, just before he traced it with his tongue.

Images from those dreams haunted his waking hours. Kam would move to pass the peas at dinner, and Philip would have to blink back something that made his toes curl beneath the table.

Before puberty hit, every night he hadn't dreamt of his lost family had been a blessing, but now the heartbreak was replaced by dreams of vulgar sin. He'd been too embarrassed to broach the topic with their pastor at his weekly counseling sessions, but his adoptive parents took note when Philip began taking an interest in his own laundry.

One evening before supper, his father pulled him aside. He led Philip into his study—a room typically reserved for independent reflection or his official church business as an Elder. Father looked every bit as tidy and pressed as he did for church every Sunday. His dark brown hair was neatly combed, and his shirt was tucked into his trousers around his wide middle.

"Philip," the older man began, his voice deep and warm. "I'd like to speak with you about something important."

Philip's blood turned to ice. He'd had another sinful dream the night before. He knew that as a boy, before he'd started medication, he'd spoken on occasion during his sleep. He'd even been prone to bouts of sleepwalking. He swallowed, but it didn't clear the lump in his throat. What if he had spoken again? He could only imagine what vile things he might have said or moaned the night before. What if *Kam* heard? A wave of nausea nearly capsized him.

"Don't be afraid, son." His father's lips twitched. He wasn't smiling, not really, but his expression did look a touch less severe. "I've put off this conversation for too long, but you never showed any interest— Well. We're having it now."

Philip nodded. He wasn't confident he could speak without confessing everything.

"You're familiar with Genesis?"

Once again, Philip nodded. It seemed this conversation wasn't easy for his father either.

"Genesis says that God created mankind in his own image, male and female, and that God encouraged them to be fruitful and multiply, to fill the Earth, and to subdue it." He looked to Philip over his glasses.

Philip froze under his father's direct attention. It felt like the man could see into his very soul. "Yes," he said quietly. He agreed because he didn't know what else to do.

The reply, however inadequate it may have felt to Philip, was sufficient for his father, and he continued. He couldn't recite the passages he referenced by memory, but he knew them well enough to call the sentiments to mind. "In Thessalonians, it's said that it's God's will that you should be sanctified, and that you should avoid sexual immorality." His tone was somewhat accusing, though what Philip noticed most was that this was the first time he'd ever heard his father reference sex. "You should learn to control your body, your sinful impulses, in a way that is holy and honorable—as the scripture says." Philip swallowed again, and his father frowned.

Controlling his body, controlling his mind—those ideas felt too far out of reach.

"You have it within you, Philip, to be godly. You aren't a beast filled with the passionate lust of the pagans."

Philip meant to speak then, to reassure his father that he hadn't deliberately sinned during his waking hours, but his father raised a hand to silence him before he could utter a word.

"My son, I believe the best of you, but this will require effort on your part. As Galatians says, you must stand firm and resist to submitting to a yoke of slavery. I encourage you to walk the path of the spirit, and it will keep you from carrying out the desires of the flesh."

Desires of the flesh. Even the words sounded sinful to his ears. (*And so delicious...*)

"Dreams," Philip said suddenly. He was desperate to interrupt, lest his father say something else that sounded so electrically enticing and damning all at once. "I've been having... dreams." He couldn't help feeling that his tone wasn't sufficiently apologetic.

His father nodded. Due to the frequency of the laundry, Philip was sure his parents suspected as much. "If we confess, he is faithful and just and will forgive us our sins and purify us from all unrighteousness."

John 1:9. Philip knew it almost as well himself, due to how often his father cited it. "I've never..." Philip trailed off, hesitating before he let filth spew from his lips. "I mean..." He faltered again. "Not while I'm awake." He knew that by not admitting the full extent of his sin, that he was damning himself, but it was better to do that than to face his father's judgment and his own shame.

"Sinful desires will wage war against your very soul, Philip. Fill your waking mind with scripture, with your faith, and your sleeping mind will have nothing impure to draw from. Lose yourself in prayer and God will deliver you. You should come with me this week to the men's Bible study group."

Philip bit his lips between his teeth and nodded. He knew that was a dismissal. The conversation was over. The invitation wasn't optional.

He got to his feet and nodded again at his father before he left. When the door closed with a click against his back, Philip took a deep breath. He let his eyes close, and then squinted them tightly. He took another measured breath, tears tingling just behind his eyelids.

"Are you alright, Philip?" Kam's voice cut through the oppressive silence. Philip's eyes opened and his chin angled up so he could face his elder brother. He looked handsome and perfect even during the day, and the thought made Philip swallow.

"I'm fine," he lied. (The smallest of his sins that day.)

"You don't look fine," Kam argued, his arms folding across his chest.

Philip shrugged. He couldn't dispute that. He took a step away from the door. "I'll be fine," he suggested as an alternative. That seemed to please Kam, who nodded.

"What did Father want to speak with you about?" Kam's expression suggested he didn't really expect an answer.

"Sin," Philip replied. Kam's eyebrows raised.

"Fun," he replied sarcastically. "I was just coming to tell you it's time for dinner."

It was an unspeakable relief that Kam didn't ask any follow-up questions. Philip gave his brother a nod of thanks and stepped around him toward the dining room.

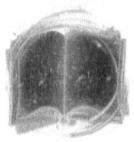

Philip took his time with his prayers that evening. He expressed gratitude for every kindness he had ever been shown. He offered requests of goodwill for those he cared about—his family, his homeschool group of friends, people from church, people from the hospitals he'd stayed in, and his long-gone little sister Melissa. He sent blessings after his poor, departed, adoptive grandparents, and even the parents who had killed themselves rather than watch him and Melissa grow up.

Philip mentally recited the various passages of the Bible that he knew. Kam went to sleep while Philip was still crouching by his bed on his knees. By the time the younger man climbed onto his mattress, he felt lighter.

He didn't even feel a pang of longing when he happened to glance across the room. He told himself he was looking out the window, the same way he always did, but that night, he didn't feel a dull ache in his belly when his eyes landed on Kam's outline in the darkness.

He slept a peaceful, dreamless sleep. When his alarm rang in the morning, he felt as though he had only just laid down. Philip worried for a moment that he was still asleep, because when he looked over, the first thing he saw was Kam pulling his t-shirt off over his head.

Philip closed his eyes quickly and began to rub them viciously with his knuckles. He knew what the Bible had to say about lustful gazes, and especially the kind one man might have for another.

"Good morning," Kam greeted Philip cheerfully. He had always been annoyingly chipper in the morning. "Sleep well?"

Philip opened one eye and looked Kam's way. He was pleased —or was it disappointed?—to see Kam was already fastening the buttons on his shirt. Philip sat up as he replied, "Better than the last few nights."

"Yeah, I noticed you didn't wake up last night."

That made Philip's heart stop. *Kam had noticed.* Everyone was noticing. He thought he'd been so careful. He was ready to make an excuse, find a way to explain it away, but Kam didn't let him.

"Your nightmares have been getting bad again lately," Kam observed, tucking his shirt into his black trousers. "I thought maybe that was what Father wanted to discuss with you."

Philip got to his feet and tugged his own shirt off over his head. He dropped it on a pile at the foot of his bed before he began to dress himself. He was glad Kam had assumed the best about him, that he hadn't somehow guessed the truth.

"No," he replied. "I did tell him about my dreams, though." He was willing to admit that, though they weren't the kind of dreams Kam imagined.

"Did it help?" Actual concern was written across his elder brother's fine features. Philip looked away, focusing on buttoning his shirt.

"Maybe." That felt like an honest answer. "I hope so." That felt more honest still.

"You know you can always talk to me, if you ever need to," Kam suggested.

Philip could feel Kam's eyes on him. He kept his face turned down, pretending he was preoccupied with his shirt and belt.

"I know. Thank you," he murmured.

When Philip heard Kam's sock-covered feet on the stairs, he exhaled deeply.

There was no way he could talk to Kam. He couldn't talk to their father, either. He had thought briefly about speaking with the pastor, but that felt just as misguided. This was between him and God.

4

CHAPTER 4

Philip's father would be the last to the breakfast table; he always was. Philip kissed his mother's cheek as he took his seat beside her, opposite Kam. She had curled her light brown hair, and the waves framed her face and accentuated her green eyes. She always made an effort to look nice for church. Their father emerged a moment later—he didn't like making his family wait.

Once they were all seated, Father led them in a brief prayer. "Dear Lord, we thank You for Your love and for this meal, and pray it gives us strength as we venture forth to hear Your divine word. May You guide us to Your teachings and lead us on the path of righteousness. We thank You for this meal and for our many blessings. In the name of Your son Jesus, we pray."

The breakfast prayer was usually the shortest of the day. Breakfast before church was the shortest of them all. As soon as the prayer was done, they began eating.

Emma Gardner loved making robust breakfasts for her family. That morning was scrambled eggs, toast with butter and jam, and bowls of oatmeal at every place at the table. There was also a plate of bacon in the center for each of them to serve themselves.

Philip and Kam—she affectionately still referred to them as her *growing boys*—would see that none of it went to waste. Kam, at 22, was tall and muscular, and Philip was lean but finally filling out in his shoulders. He had always been a late bloomer. That was likely why their father had held off on giving him his brief approximation of The Talk for as long as he had. Kam had gotten it earlier, when he was fourteen, but he'd always had an eye for the young ladies.

Philip was also more devout than Kam had ever been. He had never found the girls in his Bible study groups so tempting. Of the two boys, Kam had always been the one to find trouble, which was part of why he still lived at home.

The meal was eaten largely in silence. Father was never much of a morning person. Mother was, and on homeschool days, she often chatted with Philip about what he expected from the day's lessons. Church days were different. Somber.

That was just as well for Philip. He didn't exactly want to share his relief at his dreamless night with the three of them, and that was the closest thing he had to news.

"Is tonight your counseling session at church?" Mother asked. It was every other week, and she had a hard time keeping track. "I'm working on cupcakes for the women's group bake sale, and I won't be able to pick you up."

"I could pick him up. I'm not doing anything," Kam interjected. Philip thought the words were harmless enough, but he noticed they earned Kam a glare from their father.

"How kind of you to offer, Kam. Thank you," Mother replied before Father could make a harsh remark. "Thank your brother, Philip."

Philip nodded, his mouth full of eggs.

Kam grinned at him. "Don't mention it. I'm sure I'll need a favor one of these days."

Father looked at his watch. "Kam, help your mother clear the table and load the sink. You can wash when we get home." That was what Father usually contributed to the housework—delegation.

"I'll help too," Philip volunteered, and he got to his feet. His mother seemed grateful for the extra hands, and if their father minded that Philip had offered, he didn't say as much.

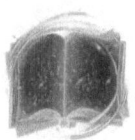

Once they were at the church, the Gardners and their sons spread out. Father and Mother had a usual spot on the right side of the wide-open worship space, just a few rows back from the pulpit. They liked to sit underneath a beautiful oil painting of a dove in flight.

Kam and Philip usually sat with one another, away from their parents. When the boys were younger, the family sat all together, but as the boys grew up they were treated to some independence.

Philip was always partial to the right side of the room, so their mother had to crane her neck more obviously to look at them. Kam preferred the very back, so they chose that more often than not.

Philip and Kam left the very back row of folding chairs for those who were running late to the service. There were always more than a few stragglers, since Pastor Andrew always started promptly at the top of the hour. The boys took the end of the row by the wall, beneath the stained glass window that depicted the tongues of fire from the book of Acts. As the morning light filtered in, it covered both brothers in beautiful shades of red and orange. Philip watched the way the sun leaked through the glass and painted Kam just a little too long.

Kam took the seat beside Philip and put his Bible in his lap. Philip noticed the way the book was cracked open, even though it was sitting flat on Kam's thigh. Philip couldn't be sure of what exactly his brother planned to read during the service, only that the small dime-store paperback was thick enough to keep the Bible's pages from touching. Philip glanced away from Kam, the smile lingering on his lips. He would keep his brother's secret.

Philip was always impatient for the service to start. He found the sound of large groups of people overwhelming when they were all talking. Thankfully in a sermon setting, when all the voices weren't bleeding together, he didn't mind being around so many people. It reminded him of the circus crowds, a happy memory so long as he didn't dwell on it too long.

That morning, after the day's hymns, Pastor Andrew spoke with great reverence. His graying brown hair was slicked back with gel, polished as he stood in front of the room.

"The fortieth Psalm," he began, "starts with a testimony. David shares how the Lord delivered him from what felt like impossible circumstance." The pastor looked around the room as he spoke, trying to catch the eye of those who listened in his own gray-eyed gaze.

"It begins like this, if you can turn to Psalm 40, verse 1. *I waited patiently for the Lord; and he inclined unto me, and heard my cry. He brought me up also out of an horrible pit, out of the miry clay, and set my feet upon a rock, and established my goings. And he hath put a new song in my mouth, even praise unto our God: many shall see it, and fear, and shall trust in the Lord. Blessed is that man that maketh the Lord his trust, and respecteth not the proud, nor such as turn aside to lies.*

"David says, let me testify as to the goodness of God. He says he waited on the Lord. He admits he felt as though his circumstances were getting worse. He speaks of the horrible pit that God drew him from because he was patient. That doesn't sound like it was easy.

"Now let's be honest. We hear that *patiently I waited* and some of us think it sounds simple. Many of us know how to wait on God, because in many situations, that's all we can actually do. But there is a difference, I assure you, between waiting for the Lord and waiting patiently.

"I would argue that most of us don't know how to wait patiently. We want to take action. We want to do something. At the very least, we want to react to our circumstances. We want to plead our case, whatever that looks like. We want to take back what we've lost, but the Lord says *wait*.

"Have you ever felt impatient? You get annoyed by waiting. Why is that? Because it feels like we have to be doing something. We think that if we don't act, that nothing will happen.

"Well, I'm here to tell you that the lack of patience is a lack of faith. It takes faith to believe, ladies and gentlemen. The Lord never stops working on our behalf.

"Remember again the plight of David, who waited patiently. He wrestled with his doubts. He struggled with his insecurities, as many of us do. Even when he questioned his place in the sight of God—he waited.

"Though it looked like nothing was happening, David kept waiting. His waiting was not wasted, no matter how he may have felt in those moments. It took time for things to change on the outside and on the inside, but something was happening for David. David was not forgotten. God heard his cries. Every day that David trusted in God and waited patiently, his faith grew. David reminded himself of His goodness and His promises, and when the time was right. God brought David out.

"Remember, this is David's testimony about what God has done. He is on the other side of his trial. He is sharing his story because he has seen the outcome and he wants to strengthen your faith here and now.

"It's important to remember David found himself in a pit of miry clay, a muddy, horrible pit. The more he struggled, the deeper he sank. In Jeremiah 38, the prophet was thrown in a miry pit, and it took thirty strong men to free him from the muck. The Bible says without intervention, he would have died there.

"David was in just such a situation. He could not free himself. This is much like the pits that plague us today, though these days, they are blessedly more metaphorical.

"Our mires are often pits of sin. It always starts small, but one small sin often leads to another. You tell yourself that this time will be different, but the mud of sin is so slippery. Once you've started down that path, there's often nothing you can do but slip and fall further from grace.

"You may struggle with yourself, thinking you can get out of the mess, up out of the pit, but like David, you can't lift yourself out. That's the nature of sin, folks. No man or woman born has what it takes to break free of that pit alone.

"Despair is another pit we face. Hopelessness. In the pit of despair, you begin to believe that what has always been must always be. The darkness of your past failures and defeats overshadows the rest of your life.

"Despair is a mental and emotional pit, not only a spiritual one. You see only the worst in everything, even yourself. It makes you believe that your current struggle defines your whole life. The Deceiver tells you that you will never be anything more than what you are right now. Despair is a vicious pit that clouds your view. It denies you the promise of God.

"There are other pits along the way. Bad choices, unforeseen circumstances and other obstacles can turn into slippery pits you can't climb out of by yourself.

"But in these times, remember David. David waited. The Hebrew makes it even clearer. It literally says: *waiting, I waited*. And that's what it feels like, doesn't it? While I'm waiting, I'm waiting. My waiting is compounded by even more waiting. It's the feeling you get when you've been waiting for a long time, but you're still stuck in the muck. In those moments, remember David.

"Waiting, I waited.

"Remember that feeling was the beginning of David's testimony—not the end."

Kam gently closed his Bible with its paperback concealed within, and glanced at Philip. The younger man noticed the attention out of the corner of his eye, but didn't make a move. As the pastor preached on, Kam got to his feet and crept to the back of the room, slipping into the hall.

Philip paused a minute or two before he got up and followed. He found his brother standing outside in the morning sun with his face upturned. Philip stood silently in the door frame, staring. All thoughts of murk, mire and horrible pits were gone. In their place were Philip's thoughts on how magnificent Kam looked. Philip swallowed and shifted his weight between his feet.

When Kam opened his eyes, he grinned at Philip and waved his hand to beckon him closer.

"I needed some air," Kam explained. "All that talk of waiting on God... I couldn't wait anymore." He cracked a grin at his bad joke, and Philip mirrored the expression.

"Maybe if you'd *waited* around, you could have learned more about patience," Philip teased.

Kam rolled his eyes and gave his brother a shove. Philip tried to ignore how even the slightest of touches sent a shiver down his spine. He was still destined for the sin pit, it seemed. He had a feeling he'd be smiling as he slid.

"You know, if you smoke out here, they'll smell it on your clothes."

"I wasn't planning on smoking."

"There's a first," Philip teased again, pushing his hands into his pockets. "It hardly feels like church if I don't have to talk you out of a cigarette."

Kam laughed. "Maybe I've finally learned a lesson."

"What were you reading instead of paying attention?" Philip asked, reminding his brother that he hadn't learned *too* much.

"Nothing important," came Kam's reply. He never went so far as to tell Philip something was none of his business—this was about as close as he ever got.

"I'd better get back in there," Philip said, an olive branch for prying.

"I'll be back soon. I just needed a palate cleanser."

Philip nodded, though he knew Kam was done with church for the day. It didn't make sense to Philip. He couldn't imagine not wanting to hear as much of the service as he could, but Kam had always been independent like that.

When Philip returned to his seat, it was like he'd never left. Pastor Andrew was still preaching about David and his testimony. Philip turned to the appropriate page in his Bible when the pastor began reading, but his attention kept drifting. He couldn't shake the thought of sin as a pit he couldn't crawl out of. If that were true, then he wondered if his plan to follow his father's advice would be in vain. Still. It had worked the night before, hadn't it? There was no reason to think it couldn't work long-term. It was maybe a sort of waiting, wasn't it? It was a little more active process than what the pastor had been describing, that was all.

Philip ran his tongue over his lower lip. It felt rough and dry. He glanced around the room, watching the other parishioners. Maxine Arden, a middle-aged woman whose husband never accompanied her to services, looked like she was half-asleep. The Jones sisters, who were about Philip's age, were smirking at each other like they had just said something cruel. Philip rolled his eyes. The twins were always trouble. With his keen hearing, if they had actually said something aloud, even in a whisper, he would have heard them.

He turned his attention back to Pastor Andrew, and the holy man met his gaze. Piercing gray eyes locked on deep hazel ones. The man's lips twitched with a hint of a smile, but he never lost his pace or his cadence.

When the sermon was finally over, Philip gathered his Bible and made his way to the front of the room to meet his parents. Kam hadn't returned, so the odds were good that he'd turn up smelling like cigarettes or weed or both by the time they made it back to the car. It would be a tense ride home.

Philip approaching alone made his father frown. Before he could speak, his mother piped in. "Let's head outside to find your brother." That was enough to quiet Mr. Gardner's disapproval, at least until they got into the car.

5

CHAPTER 5

Philip knocked on Pastor Andrews' office door. "Be there in a minute," came the voice from behind it.

Philip stuffed his hands in his pockets as he waited. He was wearing jeans now, a far cry from the suit he'd worn to service that morning. Still, his white, buttoned shirt was freshly pressed.

When Andrew opened the door, he was dressed similarly. He wore a black leather belt with a large silver buckle. "Welcome, Philip. Come in." He stepped back and went to sit behind the cherrywood desk. Philip followed to take his seat across from him.

"How are you?" Andrew asked, his hands clasped in front of him on the table.

"I'm fine," Philip replied quickly. "Good service this morning," he added. It never hurt to suck up a little.

"Thank you," the pastor accepted. "What struck you most about it?"

Philip hesitated, deliberating. "I never thought of sin as a pit," he said finally. "The idea that you can't climb out by yourself really struck me."

"Why's that?"

"I always thought of sin as more of a personal failure. You're succumbing to the desires of the Devil, and it's something you get into on your own. I always thought it would be up to you to get out of it. You'd have to pray and repent and atone or whatever, and God would help, but I thought you'd be... I don't know..."

"You thought God would make you do it alone?"

Philip nodded.

"Is it better or worse that you don't have to do it by yourself?"

That wasn't an easy question to answer.

"It's better that you don't have to take on everything alone, but you really have to let God in and accept His help." Philip hesitated. "That's not easy to do."

The pastor smiled, approving of the answer. "Has there been a time when you needed God's help, but didn't want to let Him in?"

Philip's immediate thought was Kam. He couldn't say that, though. God may forgive, but in Philip's experience, man was far more judgmental. He wasn't prepared to face Pastor Andrew. "Haven't we all?" he deflected. The answer made the pastor's smile grow a little broader.

"So what do you want His help with now?"

"Avoiding sin," Philip answered quickly. "Embracing my faith." The pastor's dark eyebrows raised. Philip was among the most dedicated members of the flock, despite his age.

"Are you tempted into sin, or out of your faith?"

"I think we all are tempted by sin, but I think if I can do those two things better, I'll be a lot better off."

"Are there any sins in particular that trouble you?" The pastor was fishing. It sounded like Philip's father had already spoken to him. That made sense. Even an Elder would seek council.

"The flesh is weak," he answered.

The pastor nodded sagely. He didn't seem surprised by the response, which was further proof.

"Prayer will serve you well in moments of weakness."

"That can help while I'm awake," Philip replied. "But when I'm asleep..." His voice trailed off and his cheeks flushed. "I'm sorry. It's hard to talk about."

"Are you devoting enough of your waking time and energy to prayer?"

Philip shifted his weight in the seat and bit his lower lip. He couldn't raise his eyes to meet Pastor Andrew's gaze. "Apparently not," he admitted.

The pastor chuckled. "Recognizing where you can improve is the first step. You are opening a door for Him. Now you just need to invite Him in." Philip swallowed the lump in his throat and nodded. "Remember you're not the first young man to be tempted, and you won't be the last."

Philip managed to force a smile to his lips. It didn't come as easily as the pastor's smiles had. He nodded again. "Right."

He still suspected he was alone in his *choice* of temptation. Another man? *His own brother?* He didn't want to imagine how much worse this conversation would be going if he'd told Pastor Andrew the whole truth. Guilt settled deep in his stomach. Lying by omission was easier than lying outright, but he still didn't like the way it hung over him.

"Is that the only thing troubling you?" Andrew asked, studying Philip. "You know the purpose of these sessions is for us to talk. I can't help you if you're not open with me."

There it was—the opportunity Philip needed to come clean. He met the pastor's gaze with wide eyes.

He shook his head. "That's all," he lied. "I'm just self-conscious about it. I feel like I'm the only one."

"It's normal to feel ashamed about something you know is wrong." Andrew fixed Philip with a reassuring smile. "Do you want to talk about your dreams?"

Philip's cheeks flushed a brighter red. He shook his head vigorously. "I'd rather forget they happen at all."

"Let's pray together, Philip." The pastor bowed his head and Philip did the same. The young man stayed quiet as Andrew recited a stirring prayer about perseverance. When they finally raised their heads and reopened their eyes, the older man was smiling again. "I have faith in you, Philip. It's important that you have faith in yourself too. The more you pray and the more you trust in God to help you move past this, the better off you'll be."

Philip glanced at his watch—their hour was nearly up. "I should get going," he said. "Kam is picking me up."

Andrew nodded. "Alright. Remember what I've said and let me know if you need to dive any deeper."

"Thank you." He got to his feet and headed quickly for the door, closing it gently behind him.

As he'd predicted, Kam was already waiting. He leaned on the hood of the car, and a quarter of the cigarette between his lips was gone.

Good. He hadn't been waiting long.

Philip greeted his brother with a wave, and Kam took a drag from the cigarette.

"Good session?" Kam always asked and Philip was always noncommittal, even when Kam wasn't the subject of the appointment. It was a practiced exchange they had performed for years.

"Yeah, it went alright." Philip smiled. "Thanks again for picking me up."

Kam smiled. "Of course. Anything for my little brother."

Philip wished the words could do anything to quell the warmth in his belly when Kam smiled at him, when he gave Philip his full attention. He looked away, back toward the church. Dark clouds had moved in during Philip's appointment. They were large, thick and a deep gray that suggested it would rain soon. The air felt heavy and full, oppressive like the full weight of

Pastor Andrew's focus. With every breath, Philip sank deeper into his shame.

Almighty God, he began, *whose praise is in the Gospel, may all diseases of our minds and souls be healed, through the merits of Your Son Jesus Christ our Lord.*

"Let me finish my cigarette and we can go," Kam said, interrupting Philip's concentration. "After the last time, I know better than to smoke in the car." Philip nodded before he climbed into the passenger seat. Kam's back was to him through the window, and Philip studied his silhouette as the sun began to descend. When the rain began to sprinkle outside Kam snuffed his cigarette and got in the car. Philip closed his eyes and took a breath before he started again.

Almighty God...

6

CHAPTER 6

In the middle of the week after his lessons, Philip went to the church to help sort donations for their food pantry ministry. His mother dropped him off with the small group of volunteers gathered outside the tall, brick building.

The efforts were led by Mrs. Oliver. She was a member of the women's Bible study his mother attended and was a well-regarded member of the church. Her husband had been an Elder before he'd passed, and she'd only gotten more involved with church activities in the years since his death.

Though she was a godly woman, she was not the most punctual. It wasn't uncommon for Philip and the other volunteers to have to wait fifteen or twenty minutes for her to arrive and unlock the volunteer room.

"Hi, Philip," Beverly Jones greeted him shyly, her brown eyes fixed on the ground. She was hiding behind her chestnut bangs as usual.

"Hello Beverly, Denise." He greeted her and her identical twin with a nod of his head. "How are your studies going?" Like Philip, the Jones sisters were homeschooled. Their curriculum, like his, was also self-paced.

"Oh, fine," she glanced to her sister before she looked back again. "Yours?"

"Fine, fine," he agreed. "How are your parents? We didn't catch them after services last week."

"Very well, thank you," she replied. She was beaming, though she still didn't meet his gaze. "We noticed you and Kam slipped out of service. Don't tell me he's got you smoking too."

Denise shot her twin a surprised look, but she kept quiet.

"No, nothing like that. I thought I'd keep him company." The Jones family detested smoking, and this wasn't the first time the girls had made a snarky comment on the subject. The rumor was that before the twins had been born, Mrs. Jones herself had been a heavy smoker. When Mr. Jones had lost his job two winters ago, she'd bummed more than a few cigarettes off Kam after a holiday recital. The girls didn't know, and it was only at times like these, when they were judging Kam, that Philip was tempted to tell them—especially since it hadn't been *only* tobacco that she'd borrowed.

"I told you," Beverly said to her sister. "I knew Philip was too good to pick up that nasty habit."

Philip forced a smile, as though he was grateful for the half-praise, but it was difficult to be sincere when the girl was insulting his brother. "I appreciate the vote of confidence, Bev." She finally met his eyes when he said the nickname.

Beverly, and by association Denise, were pretty girls in their own right. They both had long, wavy brown hair and bright eyes that seemed to see everything.

Beverly had always been the friendlier of the sisters, and Philip could never quite get a read on whether Denise approved of him or not. From the way she watched him when she thought he didn't notice, he knew she had *some* opinion on the matter.

"How late do you think Mrs. Oliver's going to be?" Denise asked. "We're almost a quarter past now."

"At least twenty minutes," Beverly gossiped, smirking.

"Last week she was almost thirty," Philip added, eager to contribute to a topic unrelated to Kam. "And it was raining. You were lucky you missed it."

"We were sick," Beverly replied, quick to explain their absence. "I babysat for the Morrises and their toddler gave me some kind of bug. I'm sure standing around in the rain wouldn't have helped."

Philip watched her mahogany eyes as she spoke. He noticed the way she avoided looking at him until she mentioned the rain, and only then she looked up.

"Sad you both got it," Philip said looking from Beverly to Denise. "I guess sisters really do share everything."

"Not everything," she replied. "But just about." The way she said it suggested further meaning, but before Philip could parse it, he heard a familiar voice.

"Evening folks, sorry I'm late!" Mrs. Oliver was hurrying down the sidewalk from the parking lot, already fumbling through her oversize handbag for her keys. She didn't offer an excuse for her tardiness—she never did. At a certain point, Philip had to wonder if the *sorry* qualified as a lie.

Beverly tapped her watch and mouthed *twenty* to both Denise and Philip. Her little grin suggested she was pleased to have guessed correctly.

"Thank you all for meeting me this evening. We had quite a few donations come in through the grocery store drives over the last month. Pastor Andrew was kind enough to collect all the items for us." She unlocked the door and stepped through.

"Because if he didn't, they'd never show up," Denise muttered under her breath. Beverly playfully swatted her sister's arm, but they smirked at each other over the jab.

They were *always* like this. Philip wondered what smarmy thought they must have exchanged during services to have prompted a similar look on Sunday.

Despite the thought, Philip smiled at Denise, gesturing for both girls to enter ahead of him. They each gave him a nod of acknowledgment and crossed the threshold into the familiar volunteer room. The colorful room was decorated similarly to the sanctuary, with doves and flames as well as the occasional cross. There was no chance of anyone missing that the space was affiliated with a church.

The twins made a path straight for a long table in the front of the room. It already had a few boxes of donations on it. While Philip collected the inventory notebook, Denise waved him over, and he approached them. The work was easiest as a group of three, but that didn't always mean the girls wanted his company. More often than not, the twins preferred to keep to themselves.

"Do you two want to inventory and I'll sort?" Philip asked, passing the notebook and pen to Denise. Beverly nodded.

"I'll pick and you tally?" Beverly asked her sister.

Denise nodded, and before long, they had settled into a rhythm. Beverly would draw an item out of a box or bag, say what it was and when it was due to expire, and then she'd pass it to Philip. He'd put the item in a pile further down the table. Like items went together, and anything due to expire soon was added to a special pile for more expedient distribution.

One thing Philip liked about volunteering was that it didn't require him to maintain a lot of idle chit-chat. The girls would occasionally make an observation about the donations or the other volunteers, but for the most part, they kept on task. Whenever his piles of resources got full, they would pause so that he could stack the goods on the food pantry shelves in the back of the room. This gave the twins an opportunity to gossip while Philip wasn't compelled to take part.

"Evening, Philip." Mrs. Oliver smiled and greeted him with a kind wave when he approached the shelves. She was putting all the soon-to-expire items into bags that could be distributed the next morning. "How are you?" she asked, fully focusing on him rather than her task. "How are your studies?" When Philip was younger, Mrs. Oliver had tutored him in English. She had been a teacher herself, once upon a time.

She had enjoyed the opportunity to use her skills into retirement.

"I'm doing fine," he answered simply, passing her the small bag of expiring items. "My studies are fine too. I'm dug deep into math right now, so nothing I need a hand with." He'd always been especially good with figures and hard sciences. "Have you talked to Estelle lately?" Estelle was Mrs. Oliver's granddaughter who lived out of state. The girl was a few years younger than Philip, but they had always gotten along well when Estelle had visited over school breaks. Asking about her was polite, and it had the added benefit that it always seemed to please Mrs. Oliver.

"I have! She's doing very well. She joined the debate team, and she's going to be in the school play this winter." Unlike most of the teenagers Philip had met, Estelle wasn't in homeschool, and they often compared notes on education and on what dealing with other students was like.

Not that the truth of their friendship had kept the Jones sisters from speculating. Neither one had taken a liking to the girl. Philip had been baffled as to why.

"Sounds like she's doing well," he agreed.

"She'll be visiting for Thanksgiving in a few weeks," Mrs. Oliver added, studying Philip. She raised her eyebrows meaningfully. "She always asks about you, you know."

"Does she?" He paused restocking the shelf in front of him. "That's thoughtful."

"Mm-hmm. You've made quite an impression, young man."

Philip chuckled. "Thank you, ma'am." Before she could say anything further, he stacked the last of the items, grateful to depart before she said anything else he didn't know how to respond to. He headed quickly back to the table where he'd left the Jones sisters.

Philip was nervous. His palms were sweating, and he kept wiping them on the thighs of his trousers. He was trying to focus on the content of the pages in his textbook, but the lines were blurring together. He had another twenty minutes until he'd ride with his father to the men's Bible study. It was effectively the Elder's Bible study, because they were the only men of the church who reliably attended. Attending the study was a status symbol, and it was an honor that his father had invited him to go.

He didn't think he would make it.

He folded the textbook on the desk and closed his eyes. With them shut, he could feel the restless churning of his stomach even worse. He took a deep breath and held it for a few counts before he exhaled.

His father's knock on the door frame startled him, and his eyes opened. He turned in his seat to face his father. Father was dressed in a black button-up shirt, charcoal pants, and dark leather shoes. The Bible study was less formal than church service, but Father always made an effort to look his best when he was going into the church.

"Are you ready to go?"

Philip nodded. "Yeah." He wasn't, but he could make an effort. He got to his feet and forced a smile. "Do you have any idea what we'll be talking about this evening?"

His father shook his head. "Not sure." He smiled easily at Philip. "Are you excited?"

Philip chuckled and nodded. "And nervous."

"There's nothing to be nervous about. You won't have to talk. Just listen."

"Yeah, alright," Philip nodded. "Let's go."

The car ride passed in silence. That wasn't unusual for them. Philip fiddled with his cuticles in his lap. He was wearing dark trousers and a dark red long-sleeved shirt that buttoned neatly up the middle. He wasn't prepared for Bible study, but he was at least dressed for the part.

When the pair got to the church, they went straight for the sanctuary. A dozen chairs had been arranged in a circle toward the front of the room. Six or so men were already seated, and Pastor Andrew was by the door greeting other parishioners as they came inside.

"Good to see you, Philip. Russell." They each nodded a greeting before they took seats next to one another around the ring.

"Philip, nice to see you." Aaron Spencer, another Elder, greeted him as he took the seat on Philip's right. He was a nice, middle-aged man. He helped with the volunteering sometimes. "I'm surprised to see you here."

"He's going to start coming to these," Philip's father explained.

"Oh, well, welcome. We're glad to have you."

That seemed to be the consensus as more of the Elders filled out the circle. The majority of men were surprised to see Philip, but were welcoming. Philip felt uneasy as they gathered around. As more men filtered into the building he felt increasingly out of place. Each of the Elders wore inky shades of monochrome and dour expressions. The Bible study had existed in its current form for several years without a new member. Any man from the congregation was technically welcome, but the fact it was composed entirely of the Elders had discouraged most from trying.

Once everyone had arrived, Pastor Andrew took his seat. The men who were still lingering followed his lead and joined them. Philip felt even more out of place once they were settled in. Eyes kept finding their way to him and he couldn't tell if it was his presence or the boldness of his clothing against the crowd's dark.

"Evening, gentlemen," the pastor greeted the group as a collective, and then made the rounds with eye contact. "Before we get started, I would like to welcome Philip Porter. Remember that this group is open to all the men who attend services here, and that we should welcome any fresh blood we can get. New members are a blessing." Again, he made the rounds with eye contact. Philip couldn't help but observe Andrew's attention lingered on two of the elder Elders. They hadn't greeted Philip when they came in. Apparently, his father had been wrong, and he did have a little cause to be nervous.

"Tonight, gentlemen, we'll discuss a challenging topic of grave importance. I'd like to discuss rebuking demons in Jesus' name."

Philip's eyebrows shot up. This wasn't exactly the pastor's usual fare.

"Now first, let's talk about what's typical. In popular culture and even in real life, you have undoubtedly heard a simple *I rebuke you in the name of the Lord Jesus Christ.*" The men around the circle nodded and Philip nodded along with them, though he had certainly never heard anyone say such a thing.

"Now it is correct, absolutely and Biblically speaking, to use Jesus' name. You're invited to use Jesus' name in healing, casting demons out, and other ministries. Jesus, our Savior, is all-powerful, and His all-powerful name should be centered in everything we do as believers. Remember, in Colossians 3:17, it says, *And whatever you do, whether in word or deed, do it all in the name of the Lord Jesus.*" Pastor Andrew smiled at a few of the men he caught in his gaze.

"The issue is with the generic phrasing, and what it means. *I rebuke you.* Where does that come from? One would think that for it to be so widely spread, that it must be Biblically based, but where do we hear it? For that, we look to the New Testament."

Unlike his sermons, Pastor Andrew didn't have his pulpit or notes in front of him. He was reciting everything from memory. Philip was transfixed, focused entirely on the holy man.

"In Jude 9, it's Michael the archangel that says *The Lord rebuke you.* He says that when disputing with the Devil. Notice he says, *The Lord rebuke you.* An archangel, one of God's holy, powerful angels, and yet he still says, *The Lord rebuke you.* The mighty warrior archangel does as we all should—he centers the Lord Jesus Christ in this moment of spiritual warfare."

Pastor Andrew made eye contact with Philip and gave him a little nod of encouragement.

"Now what's interesting is the phrase *I rebuke you.* That phrase is never actually said by a human being in any Bible I've read. Jesus himself also doesn't say *I rebuke you.* No. Jesus makes different commands of the devils. His disciples command demons, but they don't say they rebuke them."

Pastor Andrew looked serious as he surveyed each of the gathered men in turn. "So where did this come from? From the way rebuking demons is described. In Luke 9:42, Jesus rebuked the impure spirit, healed the boy, and returned him to his father. Rebuking the spirit is what Jesus *did,* but it's not what he said. So it shouldn't be what we say." Pastor Andrew raised a hand toward them.

"Think about it. *I rebuke you, devil* makes about as much sense as telling the manager of a retail store or a restaurant *I complain.* What good is it to say what you're doing? No, instead we must do as Jesus and His disciples demonstrated. We must command the devils. We must tell them what to do."

The men around the circle nodded. Again, Philip nodded along with them.

"In Mark 1, Jesus said, *be quiet and come out of him*. This sent the man who was possessed into convulsions, and after the unclean spirit cried out, it did indeed come out of the man. You have to order the demon away. In Matthew 4, Jesus says, *Away from me, Satan*, and again the Devil leaves. We, like the disciples and our Lord, must follow His example. In Acts 16, the apostle Philip said, *I command you in the name of Jesus Christ to come out of her* to a demon in a fortune-telling girl. *Commanding* demons, not scolding them or saying we're rebuking them, is how you actually drive them out. In Mark, it says, *In my name they will drive out demons*, and that is what we must do. Command demons to come out, to go, to be quiet. Only by commanding action can we hope to rebuke demons who threaten those around us, or who try to tempt us away from our walk with the Lord."

Again Philip found himself inclining forward, mesmerized by the pastor's sentiments.

"What spiritual weapons are we armed with against demons and unclean spirits?"

At first Philip, thought this question was rhetorical, but Pastor Andrew didn't answer himself.

"The name of Jesus Christ?" offered Aaron on Philip's right. Pastor Andrew nodded.

"Yes, good. What else?" There was a moment of silence around the room before one of the senior Elders spoke.

"The Word of God?"

Pastor Andrew nodded vigorously.

"With the name of God and the Word of God together, we are very powerful against devils. They allow us to put on the full armor of God, as described in Ephesians 6:11-20. The armor includes the belt of truth, the breastplate of righteousness, the gospel of peace, the shield of faith, the helmet of salvation and the sword of the Spirit. The sword of the Spirit is the Word of God and prayers and requests. God has armed us well for conflict with the Devil and all his minions."

Pastor Andrew's gaze fell back on Philip. The young man had scarcely blinked for the entirety of the session.

"I will offer you one final recommendation before you venture forth to engage in spiritual warfare with the Devil. Make the Lord's prayer a part of your daily devotions. Jesus himself taught us to pray this very thing, and the prayer speaks of Our Father in heaven delivering us from the evil one. Call on God the Father to deliver you from evil." Pastor Andrew drew his hands together in front of him. "And now, together, let us pray."

Philip closed his eyes and bowed his head immediately, his mind racing. He liked this side of ministry. He liked guidance with actionable steps to take, concrete ways to improve. It reminded him of all the advice he'd ever gotten from his father. It reminded him, too, of all the individual guidance he'd ever gotten from Pastor Andrew in their counseling sessions.

When Philip opened his eyes at the conclusion of the prayer, he found Pastor Andrew's attention on him and smiled broadly. The holy man's own smile reached the corners of his eyes. He seemed very pleased by Philip's rapt attentiveness.

"Thank you for coming this evening, gentlemen. As always, I hope you've found this meeting to be enlightening." Mumbles of gratitude went around the room. The pastor got to his feet, and so did the group.

Philip waited to rise until his father stood, but when he got up, Philip was quick to follow. No one milled about after the meeting. The Elders simply rose together and made their way to the door.

The moon was full and hung low in the sky as they went to the car. The night was cloudless, but Philip couldn't see stars thanks to the light pollution in the parking lot. Once he took a seat in the vehicle, he fastened his seat belt and focused his attention on the night ahead of them. It felt eerily dark and quiet after all the demon talk. Although he and Father were safe inside the car, he still felt uneasy.

"Are Bible studies always like that?" Philip asked.

"Like what?" His father asked, turning the key in the ignition.

"So..." Philip hesitated, struggling to find the right words, "powerful."

Philip's father nodded. "Usually. Pastor Andrew is a brilliant speaker." Philip nodded, his eyes on the road.

"Have you ever rebuked a demon?" Philip asked. His father shook his head.

"Pastor Andrew has. He'd probably tell you about it. I'm surprised he didn't tell the story tonight." Philip's eyes were wide at the thought of his kind, mild-mannered pastor facing an agent of evil.

"I'll have to ask," Philip agreed. "Thank you for letting me come tonight."

Father scoffed. "You heard Pastor Andrew. All men of the church are welcome."

"Still," Philip said, "it meant a lot to me."

The rest of the ride passed in silence. Clouds obscured the stars in the sky, and the moon was covered. Between the street lamps, the night was pitch black. He thought of the agents of darkness Pastor Andrew had discussed. Philip wondered what his father had thought of the sermon, but he didn't dare ask. His father agreeing he'd found the Bible study powerful felt like a deeply personal admission in and of itself. Typically, they didn't reflect on sermons together. His father was an incredibly devout man. Still, his relationship with his faith was a very personal, private thing. Philip knew better than to pry too far into his father's experience, and he didn't dare share more of his own.

When they got home, Kam was helping Mother in the kitchen. She was washing their dishes from supper and Kam was helping to dry them. That was usually Philip's job. If Philip had been at home, it would have been over and done with long before now.

"Welcome back," Mother greeted. "How was it?" She was beaming at Philip, her hands still immersed in dishwater.

"Great," he replied enthusiastically. "What did you two get into?"

"Trouble," Kam teased, toweling off another plate for his pile. "You know us."

Father kissed Mother on the cheek. "I'll be in my study."

"So what's the Elder session like?" Kam asked. It didn't escape Philip's notice that he'd waited to ask until the door to their father's study had clicked closed.

"Really different," Philip answered vaguely. He knew Kam wasn't as religious as he was and didn't want to incite an argument. Plus, he worried that talk of rebuking demons would upset their mother.

"Worth it?" Kam asked, not digging deeper, to Philip's relief.

"Definitely," he replied.

"Good." The reply came from their mother. She passed the last dish from the rinse water to Kam. "Do you have more studying to do tonight?"

Philip sighed and nodded. He had been too distracted earlier to get much done.

"Well, then you'd better get to it."

Philip nodded again, turning down the hall and ascending the stairs. When he sat at his desk, he spread his notebook out, but he didn't pull out the textbook. He took a pencil from the drawer and began to write.

I command you in the name of Jesus Christ to be quiet.

He wrote the sentence a dozen times on the page. He pressed hard on the paper with the sharpened lead. Philip would have to ask Pastor Andrew about the best methods for self-rebuking, but in the meantime, writing the words made him feel a little stronger. Once he'd copied the sentence onto every line on the page, he tore it from the notebook. He prayed silently as he folded it. He asked for strength, for inner peace, and prayed to the Lord that the demon who kept sending him horrible, profane dreams could be driven out.

"It doesn't look like you're getting much studying done," Kam said from the doorway. Philip was startled by his brother's sudden presence. Taking a breath to steady himself, he raised his attention from the folded paper on the desktop. Then he shrugged.

"I'll get to it."

Kam laughed. "I know you will. I'm just giving you a hard time." He took a step into the room. "Is it going to bother you if I read in bed?" Philip shook his head and pitched the folded sheet of paper into the trash can at his feet.

"Not at all." He pulled his math textbook out of the desk and opened it. It might just be his imagination, but he felt less distracted by Kam's presence after his little invocation. The thought made him smile as he turned the book to the problems he'd been struggling with.

He was going to be okay.

7

CHAPTER 7

This Wednesday was different, since Philip had an important meeting that afternoon. He had gotten up early and Kam was grinning at him in the kitchen.

"You're peppy," he'd teased.

Philip shrugged. He couldn't refute it, but he didn't want to say what had him excited. He hadn't had any nightmares that night, and he felt optimistic about the meeting scheduled for later that day with the pastor.

"Oh dear," Mother said loudly.

"What's wrong?" Philip asked.

"Bloody eggs," Mother replied, showing him her bowl. Two eggs had yolks with lines of blood running through them. She tossed them into the garbage and cracked another egg into the bowl. Her face contorted into a mask of disgust. "What are the chances?" she asked as she glared at another bloody yolk.

There were only three eggs left in the carton. When she cracked the next one, she made a soft little gasp. Philip peered into the bowl and saw that a quarter of the yolk was a dark red.

"Gross," Kam remarked, making a face.

The next egg was half red. Mother's hands shook a little when she cracked the final egg. The full yolk was blood red and it had a black, solid mass in the center. Mother stared at it before she spoke.

"Looks like it's cereal for breakfast this morning, boys. I'm sorry."

Philip's stomach clenched as Mother threw the last egg away. Suddenly he didn't feel so good about his appointment with Pastor Andrew. He had set up this meeting after a few months of men's Bible study sessions. It wasn't often that he asked for appointments outside of his usual Sunday counseling sessions, so the pastor had been quick to agree. Kam still hadn't found a steady job, so he'd offered to drop Philip off and pick him up.

On the way to the church, Kam tried to chat, but Philip was too nervous. There was a lot riding on the outcome of this conversation with the pastor, and he still hadn't shaken the eerie feeling that had hung over him since breakfast. One word here or there was all he could manage in reply.

"Thanks for the ride, Kam," he'd said when they pulled up—the most he'd said for the entirety of the drive.

"Don't mention it. I'll be back in about an hour."

Philip stood a little straighter, swallowing the lump in his throat before he knocked on the office door. The pastor called him in.

"Good evening, Philip." He smiled. "Is something wrong?"

Philip shook his head. "No, nothing's wrong. I've been thinking about the future. I've had some thoughts about what I might like to do when I finish school."

"That's prudent. You've always been smart, Philip."

Fueled by the praise, Philip pushed onward. "I feel called to do what you do. Dedicate myself to God. Spread the word. Help people. I really want to commit to the service of the Lord. What would that take?"

"That would be a fine thing, Philip, a very fine thing. You're devoted to your studies and to the church, and you need both if you're going to pursue a lifelong calling." His smile stretched slightly, reaching his eyes. "I think you'd do very well in seminary."

Philip brightened. "Yeah? Tell me more about what it's like."

The pair spent the rest of the hour discussing what kind of training Philip would have to undergo. By the end of the conversation, Philip was feeling very positive about his plan, and had almost forgotten about the shadowed mass and bloody yolks. He beamed when Kam pulled up outside.

For the first time in a long time, he felt good about what was to come.

Philip's palms were sweating. He could feel his heart beating rhythmically in his chest. He'd asked Father and Mother to meet with him in the study. He'd never been so formal, and neither had they. It had all three of them on edge. He was just glad he'd asked to meet them before dinner so that he didn't have a meal churning in his guts.

Father was sitting at his desk, his arm resting on the polished top. Mother was sitting in the chair where Philip had gotten his lecture about sin a few months ago. In that time, a great deal had changed. Philip had begun regularly attending the men's Bible study with Elders of the church. He had become more devoted to his prayers. The dreams which had upset him were less frequent, and they plagued his waking hours less.

Philip paced across the room and swallowed. He wrung his hands in front of himself, and then stuffed them into his pockets.

"What's this about, son?" Father sounded stern, the way he always did, but Philip could hear the faint inklings of concern in his tone. Mother was silent. She sat upright in the chair with her hands clasped in her lap, but worry was etched in every fine line of her features.

"I want to talk with you both about my future," Philip explained, turning to face them. "I've already spoken to Pastor Andrew, and he supported the idea. I hope you both will as well." Going to the pastor first had been a power play. Philip knew this was what he wanted, but he wasn't sure what his parents would think. By getting the pastor's approval ahead of time, he ensured that his parents would be on board, or would have to appear they were.

"What's your idea?" Father was still speaking for both of them. Mother's lips were pulled tight into a thin line. With all his mental struggles, she was clearly on edge to hear his plan, despite the pastor's alleged approval.

"I feel called to become a pastor like Andrew," Philip let the words rush out of him, and only took a breath once they were out in the open. "I want to devote myself to the Lord and help people the way Pastor Andrew has always done for me. While my mental health has wavered, my faith never has. It has been the one thing I can rely on when everything else falls away." *Well,* he thought. *Everything except Kam.* But he could hardly base the rest of his life on his brother. Philip feared he had already devoted too much of his time, energy, and attention to his perverse preoccupation with Kam.

There was a moment of silence, and then another. Both of his parents had their eyebrows arched high, their eyes widened, and their lips parted a little while they processed. It was Father who finally spoke.

"That's wonderful, Philip," Father said, and his lips curled into a smile. Philip started breathing again when the praise came. He'd been braced for a negative response.

"Pastor Andrew thinks you can do it?" His mother spoke for the first time. Her eyebrows were still elevated, and she looked more concerned than pleased.

Philip nodded. "He helped me look into a few seminary programs I can apply to once I've graduated high school."

Father reached his hand across the desk toward his wife. She raised one of her hands from her lap to take his. He gave her hand a squeeze and smiled more gently at her than Philip could recall ever seeing before.

"This is a blessing," Father said, studying her. "There is no greater calling than to serve the Lord. We should be proud of Philip." Mother nodded and smiled, first at her husband and then at her son.

"Of course." She chuckled lightly, shaking her head. "Of course I'm proud. It's just a mother's nature to worry."

Philip nodded. He had expected it to be a tougher sell for both of them.

"We should celebrate," Philip's father suggested. "Why don't we go out to dinner?" The last time they'd had a celebratory dinner on his account had been when he'd come home from psychiatric care the last time.

"Of course, if that's what you want." Mother's smile looked less strained now. "Tomorrow evening when Kam's home, we can all go."

Father's smile flickered for a fraction of a second before he nodded. "Of course. The whole family." He looked at Philip and tilted his head. His gaze was piercing through his horn-rimmed spectacles. "Have you told your brother yet?"

Philip shook his head. "Not yet." He wasn't sure how that conversation would go. Kam, like their mother, had always treated Philip like he was made of glass. Combined with his apathy for their faith... well, Philip had been worried about Kam's reaction to the news too.

It was why he'd told their parents first.

"You can tell him before the dinner," Father suggested. "Maybe it'll inspire him to do something with his life." Mother glanced quickly back at Father, her expression souring with disapproval.

She was protective of both of her boys.

8

CHAPTER 8

As he had with their parents, Philip carefully planned how he would tell Kam about his plans for the future. He waited up until Kam got home on the evening he told their parents. When Kam entered their room, he seemed to be in good humor, so Philip bit the bullet.

"You're up late," Kam said.

"Waiting for you," Philip admitted.

"Everything okay?"

"I have something to tell you."

Kam's whole body seemed to stiffen. He took a seat on the edge of his bed, facing Philip. "What's on your mind?" he asked, his shoulders rigid.

Philip swallowed. This was harder than he'd thought it would be.

"You can tell me, Philip," Kam offered. He had forced a smile across his face. "Whatever it is, you can tell me. You can tell me *anything*."

He was trying to make this easier, but Philip knew that he'd be driving a wedge between them forever. It was the hardest thing he'd ever done.

"I want to go to seminary. Be a pastor, like Andrew."

Kam seemed to wilt where he sat. Whatever confession he had believed he was in for, it apparently wasn't that. His smile was strained, and his eyebrows had furrowed slightly.

"Seminary?"

Philip nodded. "My faith has seen me through so much. I want to devote myself to God. To the Word."

Kam's lips had retreated into a thin line. He looked almost pained when he spoke. "You're sure that's what you want?"

"It is." Philip nodded. "I spoke to Mother and Father, and Pastor Andrew, they all think it's a good idea."

Kam snorted a laugh and rolled his eyes. "Yeah, I'll bet they do." Kam managed a grimace of apology when he saw Philip's crestfallen expression.

"Can you just be happy for me?"

"I would if I thought this was what *you* wanted. I think this is what *they* want for you."

"Why can't it be both?"

Kam hissed an exhale between his teeth and shook his head. He collapsed into his bed without taking off his clothes and then he rolled over to face the wall. The conversation was over.

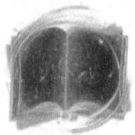

In the weeks after the awkward discussion, Kam was just as prone to slipping out during church services, and Philip didn't notice any other differences in how Kam treated him. It was almost eerie.

Their father, however, had taken to chatting with Philip more. It started small, with brief anecdotes about his work day. Then he began discussing their thoughts after men's Bible study— saying what he thought and then inviting Philip to do the same. He wanted Philip's opinion, he said. *Philip's* opinion.

Philip had never felt closer to his father.

One night, Father called Philip into his study. It was after dinner, and Mother was meeting with her women's Bible study group. Kam had started working at a hole-in-the-wall restaurant as a busboy and kitchen hand, so he was absent. The place paid under the table nightly, which made it all the better.

"I'm worried about your brother," Father said pointedly, looking at Philip over his tightly clasped knuckles. "He's never been driven. He's always lacked ambition. He's a good boy, but he oughta be a decent man by now."

Philip swallowed and shifted his weight in the armchair. What was he supposed to say to that? "He's working now." That was a new development. Philip offered, "He tried hard find a steady job for the last six months, at least."

Father nodded, but his jaw was tightly set. The facts didn't change his opinion. "How long do you think this place will keep him on for?" he asked, his tone as sharp as the reproachful look he was giving his youngest son. "He looks for jobs longer than he keeps them. You're the only decent friend he has, Philip."

It was challenging not to bloom under the praise, even though it came at Kam's expense. Philip managed to keep his reaction down to a half-smile. "What would you have me do?" he asked, genuinely curious about where the conversation was headed.

"Talk to him. Share your plans again. Encourage him to turn back to the church instead of out into the secular world. Start your calling now."

At that, Philip chuckled. He'd always tried to get Kam to come with him when he was volunteering or doing church activities. As it was, Philip thought the family was lucky Kam still went to Sunday services and only stepped out partway through. Still, Philip didn't want to disappoint his father.

"I'll try," he said quietly. "And I'll pray for him. Should I fail, it's the Lord we can depend on to bring my brother home."

That answer made Father smile. "I do think you'll be a good fisher of men, Philip. You've had your troubles, but your faith has always been strong."

81

Two compliments in one day! He could scarcely believe it. Philip nodded his thanks. "I'll do my best to make you proud."

He waited up that night. The restaurant Kam worked in had a bar attached that didn't close until 1:00 a.m., which meant the folks washing dishes and cleaning up didn't usually get clear until well after 2:00. Philip was dozing at his desk with the small lamp burning when Kam finally slipped in.

Kam reeked of cigarettes, and when he said hello, Philip could smell stale liquor on his breath.

"You're still up?" Kam whispered, surprised.

"Yeah. I had a chapter to finish." It was true, but not the whole truth. "How was work?"

"It was alright. Busy night. Busier than I would have expected for the middle of the week." Kam tugged his sweat-soaked t-shirt off over his head. Philip's eyes wandered across the room to his brother. Kam was bent over, bare-chested and rooting through a low drawer for something clean to sleep in. Philip studied the way the muscles in his back moved as he rifled through, looking for a suitably soft t-shirt.

"You can borrow one of mine if you want," he offered, his eyes still locked on Kam's shoulders. "I know you haven't had a chance to do laundry this week."

Kam looked over his shoulder and grinned. "Thanks, I owe you one." He retrieved a pair of gym shorts, closing his drawer and stepping to Philip's dresser. He opened the top drawer and pulled out a large, light blue t-shirt Philip often slept in. He pulled it on over his head. He was lucky it fit, though it was tight across his chest and shoulders. Philip had a noticeably lighter build than Kam, but he wore his sleep shirts oversized, so there was room for Kam's larger frame. Philip dropped his attention back to the book on his desk when Kam started unfastening his pants. His cheeks felt warm.

"You work again tomorrow?" Philip asked the page.

"Yeah," Kam said with a grunt as he tugged off his trousers and pulled on the gym shorts. "Every night this week. Why? Do you need something?" He collapsed back onto his bed and reclined onto his side.

"No. I'm just glad it's going so well for you. I know you've been looking for a job for a while." Philip let his eyes raise from his textbook.

Kam smirked. "If you say it's a blessing, I'm going to come over there and smack you."

Philip laughed. "I didn't say it was a blessing."

"You were thinking it," Kam teased. "When you're a pastor, you won't be able to help yourself. You'll be minding your business, and all of a sudden, you'll be saying *the Lord provides* or something. You won't be able to hold a normal conversation anymore." He was still smirking. Philip shook his head.

"I don't think it'll be that bad. Pastor Andrew can hold a conversation."

"With you, maybe. You're on his wavelength."

Philip closed the book and got to his feet. He went to his dresser and pulled out a set of pajamas for himself. "I don't know about that," he replied. "You seem to do alright with him." He started unbuttoning his shirt and shrugged it off his shoulders. He slipped one arm through the sleeve of his pajama top, and then pulled the other on. He looked down and started buttoning his pajama shirt from the bottom up. He swallowed. Kam's eyes were on his body as he dressed. He could *feel* them. His thoughts were a jumble. He stumbled over the last button. When he had his shirt fully fastened, he dared to look up. Kam was lying in bed with his eyes closed.

Had he imagined it?

"Good night, Kam."

"Night, Philip. Can you get the light?"

"Yeah, of course." Philip turned off the lamp on his desk, the only light in the room. He waited to pull off his trousers until he was back beside his bed in the dark. He tugged the pajama bottoms on and slipped under the covers.

Our Father, who art in heaven...

9

CHAPTER 9

In the spring, Philip completed the last classes he needed to graduate. When his diploma arrived, he was quick to frame and hang it. The family had gone out for another dinner together to celebrate.

Kam was still working at the same place when the end of the school term rolled around, but he was distant. He wasn't completely gone, but he was further away than he had ever been. He came home from work later and later, long after Philip went to bed. He stayed in bed through breakfast. Kam missed most mornings entirely, instead rising in the early afternoon. The only thing that remained constant about his schedule was that he didn't work on Sunday. He'd attend services in the morning with the family, and then would take Philip to his counseling sessions in the evening. Philip would have thought Kam was avoiding him, if it wasn't for his reliable transportation to his counseling appointments.

On those drives, the brothers were as close as ever. Philip had chattered excitedly about the seminary programs he was researching and applying to. Kam's smiles were strained and his tones were unconvincing, but he didn't argue or try to dissuade Philip from his plans. In turn, Philip tried to encourage his brother to go back to school, but Kam was always quick to rebuff him.

Philip suspected Kam lied about his work schedule. Some nights when he got home, his clothes reeked of marijuana smoke. Philip suspected his brother could get a drink or two from the bar while working, but a blunt was a little less believable. Still, he seemed happy and was still faithfully attending church every week, so Philip didn't have cause to complain or lecture his brother the way Father might have liked him to. Philip did miss him, though.

Philip thought it was the best he could hope for with Kam. It wasn't enough for their father, but Philip was a little more realistic.

One especially hot summer night, Philip was lying in bed in just a pair of shorts. He had a book open in his hands, but he wasn't reading it. It was too hot to read. Too hot to sleep. He had all but resigned himself to turning off the light to lay in the dark when Kam came in.

"You're up late," his elder brother observed as he closed the door behind him.

"It's too hot," Philip complained, closing his book.

Kam nodded and pulled his own shirt off. Even across the room, Philip could smell the tobacco and weed scent. "If it wasn't so late, I'd take a shower, but I don't want to wake anybody up." The bathroom stood next to their parents' room, and the thin walls meant anything noisy was off-limits after 10:00 p.m.

Kam had stripped down to his boxers, but he stood next to his bed rather than continuing to change. "How sleepy are you?" he asked.

Philip was staring straight up at the popcorn ceiling until Kam spoke. He tried to be mindful of where his eyes wandered when Kam was changing. He rolled onto his side and didn't let his eyes leave his brother's face. "Not very," he answered honestly. "Why?"

Kam grinned and pulled a pair of shorts out of his dresser. "Good. Come with me." It was an order more than a request. Philip didn't have time to question it before Kam was half-dressed again and heading back out of their room. Philip set his book on his nightstand and scurried out into the hall as quietly as he could.

Kam was waiting for Philip in the darkness. He could see well enough to get to the stairs, thanks to the light they'd left on in their bedroom. Philip followed him.

Philip thought Kam would turn a light on when they reached the bottom floor, and was surprised when he didn't. It didn't matter. Philip's eyes adjusted enough to get around after a few moments in the blackness. He caught up and was irritated when Kam moved cautiously through the dark room. There was a sliver of moonlight coming through a gap in the living room curtains. The outside streetlamps shone brightly in the night, and their glow was sufficient to guide them through the living room.

"Come on," Kam whispered, as he padded barefoot to the door where they had sandals waiting.

Philip did as he was told, a small grin spreading across his lips. He didn't know where they were going, but creeping out with Kam when the house and whole town was asleep set his heart racing.

Outside, Philip was surprised to find it felt cooler—not cool, but less sticky. He followed Kam through their yard and into the yard of the neighbors. Kam was taking care not to lead them under any streetlamps or pole lights, though he couldn't do much about the light of the half-full moon.

"Where are we—" Philip started, but Kam silenced him with a look and a wave of his hand. The pair continued quietly through the neighborhood. Philip glanced at the houses as they passed, just to see if there were any signs of life. As far as he could tell, he and Kam were the only two people awake on their street.

Kam led them over onto the next block and into the backyard of neighbors Philip only knew by sight, a small family. Philip remembered seeing the couple and their young daughter walk around the neighborhood. The Starlings, according to their mailbox.

What were they doing here? Uneasiness settled into the pit of his stomach. It didn't abate, especially not when Kam ducked through the bushes by the side of the house. He was heading to the backyard.

Philip followed, wincing as the brambles scratched his legs and bare chest.

When he reached Kam, his stomach calmed, slightly. Kam gestured in front of them, silent in the dark. He was indicating a tranquil swimming pool. The only sound, aside from the occasional frog or cricket, was the quiet mechanical hum of the pump. Kam took a few more steps forward and took a seat by the edge of the pool. He slipped out of his shoes and slowly dipped his toes into the water until he was submerged up to his knees.

He looked over his shoulder at Philip and waved at him to approach. Philip moved cautiously, his eyes darting to the dark back of the house even as he sat down.

He submerged his legs beside his brother. Kam kicked his feet silently under the water, and he grinned at Philip. "Wanna take a dip?" he asked in a whisper before he rolled onto his belly and slid quietly backwards into the pool.

It was deep. Kam was a few inches taller than Philip, and even on his six-foot frame, the water came to his shoulders. "Come on!" he whispered.

Philip mimicked the way his brother had slid in. He had to tilt his chin up a bit to keep above the water, but he had to admit it felt good. Kam was grinning at him in the darkness.

"How'd you know this was here?" Philip asked, his whisper barely louder than the pool pump.

"Remember last summer, when I was working for that landscaping company?" Kam asked. Philip nodded, careful to keep his face above water. "This was one of the lawns I mowed." Kam leaned back until he was floating on the surface of the pool. He paddled a little with his hands to keep afloat.

Philip swam next to him. He kicked hard, keeping his head high enough that they could talk.

"Better than a shower, huh?" Kam asked, sitting up so that he could tread water.

"Much better," he agreed.

"I figure we cool off for a while and then head home, back to bed."

"Yeah, alright." He held his breath and let his head sink under the water. When he reappeared, he ran his hand over his dark hair, slicking it back to his head.

They swam in silence for what felt like an eternity before they both agreed that they should return home. Philip swam to the side of the pool and climbed up over the edge. Kam followed right behind. They were quiet as they made their way across the dark lawn, their shorts dripping as they went.

Once they were back on their street, Kam grinned. "I can't believe you did that with me."

"Why?" Philip asked. "Trespassing isn't a sin."

Kam snorted a laugh. "Maybe not, but it's not something I'd

expect from you." He chuckled and gave Philip's shoulder a playful shove. "You're the good one."

Philip opened his mouth to reply, but closed it before he spoke. He couldn't deny it without admitting his secret sins.

Kam laughed again. "And you *know* you're the good one. I'm glad you didn't try to argue. It would have made you a liar."

Philip forced a laugh.

"Well, we know I'm not a liar." That was itself, neatly, a lie.

"I'm gonna miss you," Kam offered suddenly as they crossed their own lawn to the house.

Philip stopped halfway across the porch. "Miss me?" he repeated, his voice still a whisper.

Kam nodded. "When you go off to school. I'm thinking I'm gonna move out." Philip sat on the porch swing by the door. Kam took a seat beside him. Minutes of stunned silence passed, where the only sounds were the crickets in the yard and the faint clinks of the chain from the rafters. Philip was leaning forward over his knees while Kam leaned back against the swing.

"Where will you go?" Philip asked. The only time Kam had ever entertained the thought of leaving had been years ago with Uncle Adam, and he remembered how well that had gone.

"I'll still be around," Kam offered. "I have a few buddies at work who have an extra room. The house is nice and the rent'll be cheap. Plus, I think things would just get harder for me here after you leave."

"Harder how?" Philip asked, his voice still quiet.

"You're a great buffer, Philip. I don't think I can handle the full force of Mother and Father's attention. I can get by when you're here to distract them, but without you, I think it'll get really uncomfortable, really quickly."

Philip nodded. He hated that it was true, but he knew it was.

"Don't say anything, alright? We have the rest of the summer to go, and if they figure out my plan now, we'll just fight about it. I don't want to ruin our last summer together."

Philip swallowed. He hadn't thought about it like that. *Their last summer together.*

Kam nudged his shoulder.

"You good?" he asked.

Philip nodded. "Yeah. I'll keep it quiet."

Kam grinned. "Good man. You should probably keep tonight a secret, too." Philip nodded in agreement. "Alright," Kam said. "Let's go to bed."

Philip followed his brother silently through the house. He faced the wall as he slipped out of his wet shorts. He tossed them into the hamper and climbed under the sheet without putting anything else on.

Kam flipped the overhead light off and he did the same. It was too hot to sleep in clothes. Philip tried his best not to think about them both laying naked in the dark as he tried to get some rest.

When Philip stirred in the night, he was back in the caravan from his childhood. His teenage frame was crunched into the bottom bunk, facing the wall. It was night, and he could hear his birth parents snoring loudly nearby. He rolled over and was startled when he saw his sister, young as he remembered, gaping dead-eyed at him from the floor.

"Woah, hey." The girl didn't react. "Melissa?"

She was gazing through him in the dim moonlight.

10

CHAPTER 10

Philip settled into his new life in seminary after a few months. Once he wasn't trying and failing to wait up for Kam every night, he kept to an early to bed, early to rise schedule. He woke around 6:30, said his morning prayers, and then joined a small group from his cohort that went running. Running wasn't something Philip would have ever imagined enjoying. Getting hot and sweaty wasn't dignified, nor was exerting himself. Still, he found that he enjoyed pushing his body toward its limits. When he was on the trail, chasing down members of his cohort who were stronger or faster than he was, he was invigorated. Making himself stay close enough he could reach out and grab them got his heart racing. It wasn't just the exertion. The hunt was what excited him. It was a powerful way to start the day.

When he got back, he would make himself breakfast, take a hot shower, and then get off to his 9:30 a.m. lecture. He spent the rest of his day in lectures and studying until 6:00 p.m.

Each evening, he went back to the dormitory for dinner, to study more, and to get ready for bed.

His weekends were a little less regimented. He'd sleep in until 7:30 or 8:00 a.m., have a leisurely breakfast, and run errands. Sundays, he would go to church services instead. In the morning, he went to a local church near the school, but Sunday evenings, he attended a service held on campus.

Once a week, usually on Sunday afternoons, he'd call his mother. Sometimes, if his father was home, he'd get to speak with both of them.

Kam had moved out the week after Philip left, so they had fallen out of touch. According to their parents, Kam's new place didn't have a phone. Philip felt a tightness in his chest any time his thoughts lingered on his brother for too long, so his solution was to avoid thinking or speaking about Kam at all.

Thanks to friends he'd made in the program and the rigor of his studies, it wasn't too challenging to keep his thoughts on other things. Seminary had proven to be the most difficult and worthwhile thing Philip had ever done. He told his mother as much on one of their weekly phone calls.

"I'm so glad, Philip!" she exclaimed happily. "We're so proud of you, all of us—your father and me, everyone at church. Pastor Andrew has asked me about how you're doing. You might call him, or write."

"I'll be home in a few weeks for Thanksgiving,"

"I'm sure he'll be glad to see you," his mother replied.

"It'll be good to see everybody," Philip admitted. Although he was adjusting well to his newfound independence, this was still the longest he'd ever been away from home outside of institutions. He tried to avoid thinking about *those* pieces of his checkered past as much as he could. He had enough reminders the mornings he'd wake up hours before his alarm, jarred by some nightmare of his past or some fractured approximation of his future. That was as much hold over his day to day as he allowed his mental health to have. He was determined to achieve normalcy by force.

"Hey, Philip," a young woman named Eileen called from the doorway. She was a member of his program, but she wasn't in his running group. "Do you know how much longer you're going to be?" She smiled at him, but she rested her hand on her hip. "I need to use the phone when you're done."

One of the downsides of the program's simple, communal living was the shared resources, like the one phone available for public use in the lounge.

"I'm almost done," Philip replied, offering her a friendly smile. "Mother, I have to get going. It's Eileen's turn to use the phone. I'll call you next week, alright?"

"You have a good night now, Philip. I love you."

"Love you too, Mother. Tell Father I said hello."

"I will, and I'll tell Kam how you're doing if I see him."

"Alright." Philip could have gone without hearing his brother's name, but it couldn't be helped.

When he hung up, Eileen beamed at him. "Thanks, Philip." He nodded at her and got up.

The lounge was a shared space all the seminary students were allowed to use, but as a general rule, they tried to give one another privacy when they made phone calls, especially phone calls home. Philip was on his way out of the room, to give Eileen her turn, when he ran into David.

"Hey. Eileen's calling her parents."

David nodded, stopping in his tracks in the hallway. "Thanks. I wouldn't want to interrupt."

David was older than Philip by a few years. He was only twenty-four, but he already had a peppering of gray in the dark hair on his temples. He'd started in the program at the same time as Philip, after a few years of professional experience. "Have you made any progress on the essay for Hanlan?" Philip grimaced.

"Not yet. I need to do that tonight." He looked at his watch. "I might have to skip service."

David nodded. "Me, too. I started it, but twenty pages is a lot of ground to cover." David shifted his weight from one foot to the other. Philip had noticed he was prone to uneasiness like that. "Want to work on it in the library tonight? It'll help me to focus if I have someone to keep me accountable, and maybe we can bounce ideas off each other."

"Yeah, that would be great." He'd never had such an easy time making friends as he had in seminary. David was among a dozen or so people Philip felt like he was really getting to know. "I'm going to head back to my room to get my things together and have a bit of lunch, but then I'll head to the library."

David nodded, his green eyes bright. "Yeah, that's great. Do you mind if I walk back with you? I was going to call home, but if Eileen's just getting on the line, I don't want to hover."

"Not at all." The two men started down the hall. Philip put his hands into his pockets. "What did you tell me you were doing before you came here?"

"I wasn't doing anything especially interesting, so I'm not surprised you forgot," David replied. "I worked in an office after college. I had taken some time to get a little real-life experience and try to find my purpose."

"Were you always religious?" Philip asked. He was genuinely curious, but he was also trying to make conversation. He didn't like lengthy pauses—they made him uncomfortable.

"I was raised Catholic," David replied with a shrug. "Went to Catholic school and everything."

That perplexed Philip. He tilted his head to study David for a moment as they walked. "Really? How'd you end up in a Pentecostal seminary program?"

"I had an accident. A woman from work took me to her church to see a faith healer." He paused, a grimace overtaking his features before he back-tracked. "Well. It wasn't really her *church*. She was Pentecostal, and through her church, she found out about this faith healer. The healer operated out of a big tent that he'd set up at the county fairgrounds. He'd travel around to different states. It seemed like he didn't stay in one place very long."

Philip raised an eyebrow, but he kept silent. A murder of crows in a branch overhead were not so courteous. A chorus of discordant caws made both of the young men look up at the birds. The noise seemed to grow louder the longer they watched. David tried to speak over the sound, but the birds became deafening. Both men grimaced, overpowered by the volume, and quickened their pace. David kept quiet until they were long past them.

"Anyway, the faith healer was really flashy. The pageantry of his sermons really hit right after spending most of my life in Catholic mass. The snakes caught me by surprise, though."

"Snakes?" Philip had heard of snake handlers, but had never witnessed the rituals himself.

"Yes, the man said that believers imbued with the Holy Spirit could handle rattlesnakes." David swallowed. "He cited Mark 16:17-18. *In God's name they should take up serpents, drink poisons without harm, and heal the sick.*"

Philip jolted when another trio of dark, croaking birds cried out from the power lines overhead. That was two murders in a short walk. He'd never seen so many crows. David kept his attention on the sidewalk in front of them. If the birds were a sign, he did not want to see it.

"What were the services like?"

"Loud. Chaotic. Whole rows of parishioners would storm the stage, shouting in tongues and begging to be poisoned to prove their faith. I've never seen anything like it."

Philip swallowed. The whole thing sounded unsettling. "But they healed you?"

"They did. *He* did. It's easy to convert when you're touched by something like that. I *experienced* the difference. After six months in a wheelchair, I could walk again. I kept going to church with the woman who took me to see the faith healer. Outside of the spectacle, I could really hear the message and appreciate the church itself. I saw it for what it was. Then I got the call to serve. I haven't looked back."

"I guess you have a deep connection to the essay topic, then," Philip said, needing to release himself from the hold the story had on him, and the lingering discomfort it left in its wake. In the back of his mind, he could still hear the militant echoes of the crows. "Maria Woodworth-Etter did a great deal for the foundations of faith healing, if I recall correctly."

David nodded. "Unfortunately, practical experience doesn't always translate into academic knowledge. How about you? You're pretty young. What brought you here?"

Philip didn't mind telling his origin story in broad strokes. He knew he was the youngest member of the cohort. He also knew he was the only one in that year who hadn't attended an undergraduate program before he'd started his Master's of Divinity. That meant people were curious, so he'd gotten a great deal of practice sharing these details about himself. It was almost like doing introductions before a group therapy session.

"I was adopted. My birth parents killed themselves when I was just a boy. My adoptive parents raised us Pentecostal. The church was always a safe home for me. When I was graduating high school, I felt the pull towards seminary. My pastor encouraged me to apply, despite not having a degree." Philip shrugged. "The admissions counselor told me I wrote an incredibly moving essay. I'm very blessed to have been accepted. Being able to start seminary now means I don't have to wait another four years to start pursuing my goals in ministry."

"I'd like to read your admission essay sometime," David replied. "They only admit one student without an undergraduate degree per year. You must have made a compelling case."

In his essay, Philip had been open about how his birth parents had died, as well as about his mental health struggles. He'd shared how his faith had delivered him from a lifetime of tribulations before he'd reached adulthood. He wasn't too eager for any of his colleagues to read it, but he supposed if he was going to let anyone look at it, he wanted it to be David.

"Maybe one day, I'll let you," Philip replied with another little shrug. They were quiet for several minutes as they walked along the street. Philip half expected another murder of crows to descend as they walked.

"So what's your family like? Are you close?"

Philip nodded. "Very."

"Not me," David replied. "Not anymore, anyway. My parents were disappointed when I converted. They said some terrible things, and basically told me that if I went through with this program, they'd disown me."

Philip raised an eyebrow. "So who were you planning to call?"

"My sister," David explained. "She's as Catholic as my parents, but she has somehow found it within herself to be proud of me." He smiled. "Do you have any siblings?"

The question gave Philip pause. He nodded. "Yes, I have a blood-relation sister I haven't seen since my birth parents died, and I have an older brother I grew up with, with my adoptive parents. My adoptive parents were the ones who raised me, who got me involved with the church. Both my brother and I were adopted by the Gardners. Neither of us took their name, but we're a family." David nodded but he didn't say anything. Philip decided to fill the silence, again. "I haven't gotten to speak with him since I left home. He doesn't have a phone at his new place, apparently. It has been hard. We were really close before." He hesitated before he continued. "He wasn't really religious, so me coming here was hard for him. He felt like our parents pressured me into it."

David nodded in understanding as he opened the door to the dormitory building. "It can be hard for folks who don't feel the pull to understand. I lost some friends when I decided to come here."

"I don't think I've lost Kam," Philip clarified, feeling the familiar instinct to defend his brother. "He just has his own life. I'm sure I'll see him when I head home for Thanksgiving."

David nodded. "I'm sure you're right." He stopped in the hallway. "This is me. It was good talking with you, Philip. I'll see you in the library this evening."

Philip nodded and continued up to his room. He tried to ignore the creeping doubt and discomfort he felt in his belly.

11

CHAPTER 11

It was just after sunrise, and the only sounds in the dim early morning were Philip's ragged panting and the crunch of his sneakers in the gravel beneath them. He was alone on the trail, a rarity, but he could push himself further without the worry that someone would see and judge his efforts. He was running faster than his usual pace. Every step collided hard with the path and brought him closer.

Closer to what? He didn't know. He had the ominous feeling that his footfalls were carrying him *toward* something. *After* something. He was *chasing* something.

Hunting.

He didn't know why that word came to mind, but it felt right. He pumped his legs even faster and thought he saw a shape flash on the trail ahead of him. That was it! He urged his body harder, his arms swinging to propel him forward. Every turn he took, his prey was just out of reach. He'd catch a glimpse of it, and then it was gone. Philip pushed himself to the point of exhaustion, but he was still trying to see *what* he was hunting, never mind actually catching it.

When he awoke, he was covered in sweat and the sheets around him were damp from the same. He took several slow, deep breaths in an effort to stabilize his lungs. His alarm went off beside him.

The nightmares hadn't let up, lately. It didn't matter how long he slept, he still woke up feeling exhausted. He'd had tense, disruptive dreams for the last several weeks. His waking hours had also been fraught with tension. There was a great deal of work for him to do and never enough time to do it. He had been feeling more and more overwhelmed lately, and his body only had one way to deal with the pressure.

Stress had a way of creeping up his spine and settling into his shoulders. After his muscles knotted, his tendons remained tight, and since he couldn't reach his back, he'd started picking at his cuticles. It wasn't so bad as the behaviors that sent him away during his youth, but the impulses were still there. They lingered just under the surface. He feared what might happen if they returned in full force, so he did what he'd always done—he tried to lose himself in service.

It was the week before Thanksgiving, and David had invited Philip to come to a soup kitchen to volunteer. It had been a long while since Philip had the opportunity to give back, so he was excited by the prospect, and hoped it would quell his urges.

David suggested stopping for coffee at a shop near the shelter, and Philip agreed on his friend's insistence that it was his treat. They stopped walking at the corner, waiting for the light to change. Philip kept his attention on the signal, but he could feel David's eyes on him. He wondered suddenly if David *knew* somehow. Was it possible he was aware that something was wrong with Philip? Could David sense that he was plagued by nightmares? Did he know that Philip had agreed to volunteer because he needed to be distracted from thoughts of hurting himself? The idea made Philip's stomach churn, and these weren't even the most damning of his secrets. He closed his eyes for a moment. He focused on his breathing the way he'd been taught in order to let the anxious thoughts pass. Despite his efforts, they opted to linger.

"Is your whole family getting together for Thanksgiving?" David asked.

Philip swallowed before he answered. How might a *normal* person answer this question? "My parents and my brother will be there, and then two of my aunts from my mother's side and their families will come. I think my dad's brother and my cousins are coming too." Philip was counting off family members on his fingers when the light changed, and they both started forward. "How about you?"

"My grandparents still host my sister and I. I think some aunts and uncles are coming." David shrugged. "It will be a full house, I'm sure. My parents have their own celebration now, without me."

David held the coffee shop door for Philip before he followed him through. "Get whatever you want," he instructed. "I don't want you getting an extra small Americano you won't enjoy."

Philip chuckled and nodded. David was right to chastise him—
that had been his plan.

"Thank you," he said, after they'd ordered. "For the coffee, and
for inviting me. I'd like to do this more."

"Go out for coffee?" David asked.

Philip laughed and shook his head. "I meant volunteering, but
I don't suppose I mind the coffee, either." David glanced at
his watch. "We're still in a good spot for time. We're maybe
two minutes out from the kitchen." Philip took a long sip of his
coffee and nodded.

"Good. Should we get going?"

David shook his head. "We should stay here a little while. I
don't like walking in with a coffee shop cup. Let's take a seat,"
David suggested. Philip agreed and followed him to one of the
small, round bistro dining tables. After a moment, David spoke
again. "Is there anyone you're looking forward to seeing when
you go home, aside from your family?"

Philip shook his head. "Not really. I have a few friends from
church, but I'll probably be back here by Saturday evening.
How about you?"

David shook his head. "Nah. I'll be focused on family time. I
was seeing someone before I left for this program, but we
both decided long distance would be too hard." Philip nodded
as though he understood. David must have remembered what
he'd said about dating earlier, because he asked, "Have you
ever had a girlfriend, Philip?"

The fear that David knew his secrets, *all* of his secrets, came
surging back at full force. Surely David wouldn't have

innocently asked such a question. Was this the kind of thing *normal* people asked each other? Should he have asked David about *his* dating history? Philip took a quick sip of his drink and shook his head. He felt his cheeks go warm. David smiled and waved a dismissive hand at him. "Don't worry. You're young, yet. There's plenty of time." David took a sip from his own coffee. "It's important not to rush into these things."

"I'm not in any rush," Philip explained. The only person he'd ever been attracted to was his older brother, but he planned to carry that secret to the grave. Assuming, of course, that David didn't decide to out him then and there.

"What's on your mind?" David asked, an eyebrow raising again. "You look like you're a million miles away."

Philip swallowed and shrugged. "Nothing. I didn't mean to. I just made a face, is all."

David nodded like he believed Philip, which was a relief. Philip still imagined that David somehow knew all of his terrible secrets, but if the other man had actually pried, Philip didn't know what he would have said. He took a long drink of his coffee.

"How do you know when you want to date someone?" Philip asked, studying David.

"Well, you'll meet someone you like. Someone you want to spend time with. Someone you enjoy talking to. It'll be someone you find attractive and feel drawn to." Philip tried to think if anyone from his past ticked all of those boxes and tried to push down the sinking feeling in his gut as he connected the dots.

"Why?" David asked. He was studying Philip with his piercing green eyes. "Have someone you're interested in?" Philip sputtered into his coffee cup, and David passed him a few napkins from the dispenser on the table. "Are you okay?"

Philip nodded but coughed again. He was relieved when David didn't repeat his question or press for an answer, he just glanced at his watch again.

"We'd better get going."

Philip nodded. They both tossed their empty cups on the way out the door.

"Look, Philip, I'm sorry if I was out of line," David said.

Philip shook his head. He shoved his hands firmly into his pockets as they began to walk. "No, you're fine."

"I'm just nosy by nature," David explained. Philip shook his head again.

"Don't worry about it."

They made the rest of the walk in silence. When they reached the soup kitchen, Philip shot David a smile. Again, he held the door open for both of them, and once they were inside, they were absorbed into a flurry of activity.

Philip was recruited to help set up rows of clean trays, bowls, and plates, while David was tapped to help with heating food up in the kitchen. They had half an hour until the doors opened for lunch, and there was a lot to do.

Once the kitchen opened, both of them served food on the long, cafeteria-style assembly line. Their conversation shifted to greeting patrons and serving food. Time moved quickly, and for a while, it seemed that they'd never run out of hungry mouths to feed.

At the end of the shift, after everyone was gone except for the volunteers, David and Philip helped to clean up. The industrial washer made quick work of the dishes until the hall was empty. Once they were sure all work for the day was done, both David and Philip said goodbye to the other volunteers.

Once they were outside and alone again, David smiled. "See?" He asked. "I told you they were great."

"Yeah, it was a good day," Philip agreed.

"We'll have to do it again," David replied. He studied Philip out of the corner of his eyes when he said it.

"We will," Philip agreed. David's smile blossomed.

"Good. Yeah. I'm glad to hear it."

Philip smiled. He liked spending time with David, even though doing so put him on edge. It was nice having friends to volunteer with again. He caught David looking at him and renewed his smile to something that reached his eyes.

When the pair reached the ground floor of their dormitory again, it was time to part ways. David held out his arms, offering a hug. Philip hesitated, but stepped forward into the embrace. It was warm, but brief.

As Philip slowly climbed the stairs towards his room, his face fell. The brief touch had been enough to make him feel homesick.

He'd be on a plane headed home in just four days. He could make it that long.

12

CHAPTER 12

It was the afternoon before Thanksgiving, and Kam was the one who met Philip at the airport. He'd parked and was waiting in the terminal. His attention had been on the arrival boards when Philip had exited the plane. That meant Philip got several seconds to study his brother before the attention was mutual. Hazel eyes had picked Kam out of the crowd immediately. Kam's hair looked freshly cut, likely due to the impending family celebration. There were faint circles under his eyes, but he was still as handsome as ever. The realization made Philip's chest feel tight. He hadn't had an impure dream about Kam in weeks, but he had a feeling that was going to change.

Kam was wearing a light jean jacket despite the cold. That probably meant he hadn't come from their parents' house, or they'd have made him change. Though the coat was impractical, Philip liked the way it clung to Kam's broad shoulders.

When their eyes met, the pair grinned at each other, and Philip thought his heart might beat out of his chest. He was home. The guilt couldn't keep up with his thrumming pulse as they crossed the room to meet.

"Hey," Kam called.

"Hey. Thanks for coming to get me."

"Yeah, of course. Just like old times." Kam reached for Philip's duffel bag.

"Are you going to stay at home while I'm in town?" Philip asked.

Kam nodded. "I have tonight and tomorrow off work." He shrugged. "I might stay till you go back. I missed you, Philip." It was a minor confession, but it still made Philip's heart squeeze.

"I've missed you, too. You'll have to get a phone at your new place."

Kam grimaced apologetically. "We have one. I just don't want our parents to have the number—or my address. They were overbearing before, but it's worse now that they don't have you to focus on. I'll give you the number before you leave—just promise me you won't share it with them, or mention it to them."

Philip nodded. He was quite good at keeping lies by omission where Kam was concerned. "Of course. I'd just like to talk to you more than once every few months." All the tension of his rigid schedule melted away as his brother smiled at him.

"Yeah, I know. I'm sorry about that. It's been hard getting settled. I'll have to show you my new place while you're here." He looked at Philip inscrutably. "I mean, if you want to."

Philip nodded. "Yeah, sure. I'd like to see it," he agreed.

As they loaded Philip's bags into the back seat of his car, Kam watched Philip curiously.

"So what's seminary like?" he asked. "Is it everything you wanted it to be?" Kam turned the key in the ignition and looked over his shoulder so he could back out of his parking space.

"It's very challenging," Philip admitted. "Harder than I thought it would be. It feels right, though. Like I'm on the right path."

"That's important," Kam replied, his eyes on the road. "I'm happy for you, you know. Your path isn't mine, but I'm proud of you for pursuing it and really committing to what you believe in."

Philip fiddled with the collar of his shirt. It felt too tight all of a sudden. "I appreciate that. Having your support means a lot to me."

Kam chuckled, his attention still on his driving. "Of course I support you. You're my brother."

Philip murmured some noncommittal agreement in reply and turned his attention out the passenger window. He was still fidgeting with his shirt as they rode on.

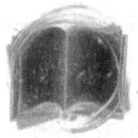

Mother met the boys at the door and swept them both into a big hug before they had even pulled their coats off.

"It's so good to see you, it's so good to see you!" She repeated the words a few times, swaying from side to side with them both enveloped in her arms.

"It's good to be home," Philip replied, and she hugged him a little tighter.

"Are you hungry?" she asked when she'd pulled away.

"I could eat," Philip replied. He knew she aimed to feed them either way, so there was no sense in fighting it.

"Me, too," Kam agreed. Their mother smiled.

"Good." She scurried back into the kitchen, where she'd already been working on a meal. "It'll be about twenty minutes. Go on up to your room and get settled in. I'll call you when it's ready."

The young men shed their coats and carried Philip's things upstairs. Kam had brought a backpack of his own.

Philip's bed, dresser, desk, and chair were the only pieces of furniture left in the room. Since he'd gone to a furnished dormitory, he hadn't taken his things, but he hadn't realized Kam had taken his belongings with him when he'd moved out. It felt like a foolish oversight now in the half-barren room.

Philip began unpacking his clothes in the top drawer of the dresser.

"It feels really empty with just your stuff, huh?" Kam asked as he plunked down on Philip's neatly made bed.

"Yeah," Philip agreed.

"If you're alright with it, we could share like the old days," Kam suggested. Philip was glad to be facing the wall. He couldn't be sure of what his face was doing, and was glad he had a moment to collect himself before he responded.

"If you'd rather just take the bed, I can sleep on the couch downstairs," he said quietly.

"That's not necessary," Kam grinned. "You're not so big that we won't fit, little brother."

Philip forced a laugh and faced Kam.

"So what have you been doing lately? When you're not working, I mean." Kam scooted over near the footboard, making room for Philip on the bed.

"One of the guys got me into this sitcom he watches. He has a VCR and tapes it for me when I'm working."

"What are your roommates like? There are a few of them, right?"

"They're good guys," Kam replied, smiling. "Steve works with me at the restaurant, and Mike, the one who tapes shows for me, is a friend of his from high school."

"I've made some friends too," Philip offered. "There's a group of us that run together."

That got a smirk out of Kam. "Like you needed to get any skinnier," he teased. Philip rolled his eyes, and Kam just pressed further. "Don't you do *anything* fun?"

"Running *is* fun," Philip argued. That earned him another skeptical look from Kam. "I've started volunteering again," Philip tried instead.

Kam snickered. "It's not your fault, I guess. You've always been bad at having fun."

"I'm not bad at having fun," Philip grumbled, petulant as he studied his lap.

Kam draped his arm around Philip's shoulders and gave him a reassuring squeeze. "It's alright, I like you boring."

Philip didn't shrug out of the partial embrace. He hated how good it made him feel. "Boys!" Their mother's shout rang out from the foot of the stairs. "Food's ready!"

Philip got to his feet quickly. "Finally," he murmured, darting across the room and down to the kitchen.

It was going to be a long visit home.

That night, Kam was the first one to head upstairs and get settled in for bed. He changed into a baggy t-shirt and a pair of sweatpants that had seen better days. He was lying on his back, on top of the blanket and near the wall when Philip came in.

"Ready for bed?" Philip asked. He hoped he sounded casual. He *needed* to sound casual. He had been dreading this moment all afternoon, and even more through dinner with their parents. The smile on his face was forced.

Kam didn't seem to notice, or if he did he didn't mind.

"Just about," Kam replied. *He* sounded casual. Unlike Philip, Kam wasn't plagued by guilt. He could sleep right next to his brother without worrying about the sinful thoughts Philip was occupied with. Kam wasn't bothered by sin *at all*.

Philip took out his own sleeping clothes. He'd brought a proper pajama set, and he felt self-conscious about the choice when he pulled his shirt off. Philip glanced at Kam as he fastened the buttons up his chest. *Kam was watching him.*

"What?" Philip asked.

"Nothing," Kam replied, moving his blue eyes to the ceiling. "I was just trying to see if you looked any different, since you're a runner now."

Philip took advantage of the moment of privacy and yanked off his jeans. He slipped his pajama pants up quickly in their place. He'd kept his underwear on—he wasn't about to let his brother see him naked.

He pulled back the blanket and sat on the edge of the bed, and then he pulled the cover up over his legs.

"Aren't you gonna get the light?" Kam asked. Philip grimaced. He'd been in such a hurry, so preoccupied with trying to get into bed without causing a fuss, that he'd forgotten. When he began to sit back up, Kam put a hand on his shoulder. "Don't worry about it, you're settled. I'll get it." Kam hadn't gotten under the blanket yet, so he crawled over Philip to get to the floor.

Philip was speechless when Kam flicked out the light, and when his brother clambered back over him to get to his side of the bed. "Goodnight, Philip," Kam said, and he rolled onto his side to face the wall.

"Night," Philip echoed. He rolled onto his side away from Kam. It was safer to sleep with their backs together. He'd learned that a long time ago.

When he finally drifted to sleep, his dreams were restless. He was a large lion like the ones he'd lived with as a child. The setting was familiar, too. He'd recognize the pens from the circus where he grew up anywhere.

Philip paced back and forth between the rows of iron bars. The cage was the length of a truck bed. It was too small for the cat, but they hadn't known better in the eighties, much less in the forties when the cage was built.

Back and forth. Back and forth. Back and forth. He paced the cage from one end to the other until the bars blurred together. No matter how long he walked, the time never seemed to pass. Whatever he was waiting on didn't get any closer.

A low growl rumbled deep in his belly. He was frustrated, and the more he walked, the more he felt constricted. Restrained. He knew what he wanted, but it was outside his grasp.

He woke up around 3:00 a.m. with his back to Kam. He was close enough to feel his brother's warmth in the darkness. He scooted as far as he could away from Kam when he realized that while he slept his body had become a *different* kind of frustrated. He tugged at the fabric constricting his revolting, disloyal anatomy. When he was on the edge of the mattress, with some breathing room, he rolled over. In the dark he could still see Kam's outline. Philip watched the way his breaths made his back rise and fall. He blinked his tears away and kept more from rising by locking his attention on the way Kam's lungs moved in the dark. Philip took long, slow breaths and tried to mimic Kam's tranquility.

Philip clenched a fist full of the sheet between them. He wanted to curl an arm around Kam's back and snuggle close. He wanted it so badly he ached for it. The tears came back suddenly—careful breathing be damned. Philip rolled back over so he faced away on the very edge of the bed. He curled his knees tightly to his chest.

By 5:00, he fell back to a dreamless sleep with tear-stained cheeks.

13

CHAPTER 13

When Philip told David and his other peers at seminary about his Thanksgiving trip home, he didn't tell them that he'd shared a room, and a bed, with his older brother. Nothing else had happened, in his dreams or otherwise—by some small miracle—but he didn't think it was the kind of thing aspiring clergy did.

Or at least, it wasn't something they should be willing to admit to. Whenever he mentioned his brother, Philip's eyes tended to veer to the side or skyward, but then again, they always had. Philip was usually cagey when he talked about his family. David didn't seem in any position to judge anyone for strained familial ties, so he left it alone even when Philip chose to abruptly change the subject.

The Monday after the holiday, the running group picked back up again. They had all enjoyed some downtime but not going for runs while visiting family had made several of the members feel restless, Philip included. If the group still planned to run a half-marathon together in the spring, then they didn't want to fall too far off course. The first several months, the group had focused on endurance. The most difficult part for members who had not run significant distances previously was running consistently for long periods of time.

Now they could all run for two hours in one session, so the goal was to build speed. Then, they could hope to actually complete the full half-marathon distance. They didn't want to *just* run for two hours or *just* finish. They wanted to finish the half in roughly two hours—an attainable goal, according to their research.

Philip still felt he had a long way to go, and his times for their practice runs did nothing to allay his concerns. Still, after the holiday break, he found he was making steady progress. He liked having something to focus on that didn't make him feel bad, or guilty, or wrong. When he was running, Philip could focus on his breathing or the sound of his feet on the pavement. He could fixate on the steady thrum of his heartbeat in his chest. Running wasn't as relieving as cutting himself had been when he was a child, but running wouldn't get him hospitalized. It was good for him. It was healthy. It was *normal*. Philip liked feeling normal. There were so few things in the world that made him feel like he was just like everyone else. Like he didn't get overwhelmed by his powerful emotions. Like he didn't still have dreams about Kam. Like he could actually contend with any of his problems.

It was nice to feel the taut muscles of his calves when he bathed, and to be able to hurry up the stairs when he was late without becoming winded. Even if he'd never had the runner's high that others reported, he always felt accomplished afterward. That was enough to keep him going. Plus, while he was running, he could block it all out. He could block *everything* out. He wasn't the fastest, but he could hold his own with the middle of the pack. While he was running, he usually picked one person who was faster than him to focus on, to chase. Trying to hunt them down was motivating.

When he wasn't running, he was in class or studying. As David had predicted, as time passed, Philip found it easier to keep up with the readings and assignments. His grades remained high, even as he approached daunting final exams. He and David became regular fixtures of both the library and the lounge. They worked independently, but both found they worked more diligently when in the other's company. Philip felt less compelled to withdraw socially when he wasn't actually expected to engage with anyone. David was incredibly patient with Philip's reclusive tendencies. He learned his needs quickly. When Philip greeted him with a nod of his head rather than a warm hello, David didn't push back. He simply took what he was offered and gave kindly smiles in return.

David made a point of asking Philip to volunteer with him whenever he went to the soup kitchen, as he'd promised to do, and Philip found time to volunteer on most Saturdays. It became a part of his regular routine, and he came to look forward to it.

David even let him pay for their coffees, sometimes. The two young men talked more openly on their treks to and from volunteering, but David didn't ask about Philip's social history anymore. Philip usually felt better, lighter, when they were headed to the soup kitchen. His chest didn't feel so tight, and his throat didn't hurt the way it did when he thought of Kam and home.

When he spoke to his parents by phone, they seemed stressed. His mother let it slip a few weeks after his visit that she hadn't spoken to or seen Kam since Thanksgiving. By then it was mid-December, and the news caught Philip by surprise. Before the holiday, Kam had been going to church regularly, and had said he made a point of seeing their parents for dinner on Sunday evenings.

Philip felt a sharp pang of guilt when the line disconnected. He had always been a good influence on Kam. His parents had said as much, but he knew it to be true. What did it mean if Kam was falling further from grace without him? Then his guilt coincided with the discomfort he felt about his own attachments to his brother. If he wasn't so attracted to Kam, maybe he could have maintained more regular contact. Maybe he could have kept him on the right path.

He swallowed the lump in his throat. Which was worse? The thought that his distance might damn his brother to Hell, or the thought that by keeping Kam close, he might condemn himself? His stomach churned as he considered the possibilities.

Kam's welfare won. Philip tried to call his brother after his phone call with their mother, but according to the dazed-sounding roommate on the other end of the line, Kam was at work. Philip got the same answer each time he tried to call over the next few days. Each evening, Kam's roommates sounded surprised to hear from him. Every time they answered the phone, they sounded vacant and far away. Philip recognized the far-off tone—they were high.

By the fourth day, Philip was growing concerned, though he tried not to let his mother hear it on their call. It had been impossible to reach Kam. He didn't like the fact that the only people who could vouch for Kam's well-being seemed barely tethered to Earth. It was simply lucky for Philip that their mother didn't want to talk about Kam herself. Philip's strategy of avoiding the subject was the only thing keeping him from worrying overtly, and that would surely have made her even more concerned.

Philip finally made contact with his brother the week before he was due home for Christmas. When Kam answered the phone, he sounded hazy. Philip didn't like how similar he sounded to his roommates, but he'd take an inebriated Kam over one he couldn't reach at all.

"You're *sure* you don't mind picking me up at the airport? I can get someone else to do it if you're too busy," Philip had insisted.

Kam scoffed loudly into the phone line. "I told you, I'll be there. I took off work. I've been working non-stop lately, so I could swing some holiday time away." The admission made guilt rumble in Philip's gut. He had assumed the roommates had been lying when they'd insisted repeatedly that Kam was at work. Philip didn't blame himself for being skeptical, though. How was he to know that the space cadets could be trusted?

"Alright, alright. I'm just making sure."

"I can't wait to see you," Kam said. Philip could hear the smile in his voice. "It's just not the same when you're away." The admission made Philip smile too. It warmed him to think that Kam might have missed him at all.

"Yeah, I'm looking forward to it," Philip had replied. "Hey, if you get a minute, you should call Mother. She's worried about you."

When Kam replied, he sounded significantly less friendly. "Yeah." His tone was frigid. "Hey, Philip, I'm going to go."

Philip's stomach clenched tighter. Now he'd done it. Why couldn't he just have a nice conversation with his brother without messing it up?

"Yeah, okay. I'll see you next week. Don't forget, I'm getting in at 3:00 on Tuesday."

"Yeah, yeah. I'll see you, then."

Philip hung up the phone and got to his feet. On his way back to the dorm, he kept his eyes barely above his shoes on the sidewalk. When he got to his room, he kicked off his shoes and peeled out of his clothes without turning the lights on. In just his boxers, he curled up under the blanket, knees tucked into his chest and arms wrapped snugly around them.

He stared into the darkness for a few hours before he finally fell asleep. When he hurt other people, he found it especially difficult to resist the urge to hurt himself.

14

CHAPTER 14

When Kam picked Philip up from the airport, he looked tired. He had dark, sunken circles under his eyes. Philip also thought his brother looked thinner than he had before. For all his jokes about Philip's new running hobby, he seemed to be the one dropping weight. The sight of him still brought a smile to Philip's features, but there was concern poorly hidden in his eyes.

"How've you been?" Philip asked when they were settled into the car.

"Oh, you know. Pretty good. I can't complain."

"I'm sure you could if you tried," Philip teased. "How are things at work?"

Kam shrugged, pulling out onto the highway. "Work's work."

Philip couldn't help but take it personally that Kam was withdrawn. He wondered if his brother was upset he hadn't kept in touch after Thanksgiving. He had tried to call a few times, but Kam had been working and Philip couldn't be sure if Kam's roommates had forwarded his messages. Kam had mentioned he'd been working tirelessly—surely he had to realize how difficult he had been to reach?

"I'm sorry for not calling more," Philip tried. He stared straight ahead through the windshield. He felt faint tingling in his eyes. "It has just been hard with school and everything."

Kam snorted a laugh. "What? No," he said dismissively. "Don't worry about it, Philip. I know you have a lot on your plate. Have you been able to keep running?"

"Yeah," Philip confirmed. "Four days a week, now. I've been volunteering at the soup kitchen every other week, too. I'm glad I've been able to keep up with it all."

Kam nodded, but he kept his bloodshot eyes on the road. "It sounds like you're doing great. Making a life for yourself out there."

"I'm trying to," Philip agreed.

Kam nodded again. He stayed quieter than usual, a lot more distant than usual. It was worse than when Philip had announced his plans for seminary. Philip wondered if something was wrong that he didn't know about. He didn't know how to broach the topic gracefully.

"How have your roommates been getting on?" Philip asked finally, grasping at any last straw of connection.

"They're good," Kam replied. "Steve got fired from the restaurant, so I've been trying to pick up the slack." That didn't exactly sound *good* to Philip, though that did explain why he'd been working so much.

"I'm sorry to hear that. Is he looking for another job?"

"Yeah. Nothing has panned out so far."

Kam took a deep breath, like he meant to say something else, but then he just let the breath slip away in a deep exhale. Philip waited for a few moments for Kam to speak, but when he didn't, Philip continued. "Has work been okay, aside from that?"

"More or less." Kam turned off the main road toward their parents' neighborhood.

"How have Mother and Father been?"

Kam seemed to hesitate over that question. *Odd.*

"They've been alright. A little overbearing. I've been working seven days a week trying to keep up with things at the restaurant and help make up for the money Steve's gonna be shorting on rent and utilities. Despite all that, I tried to start coming back around to the house for Sunday dinners. But it's never enough for them." He sighed and glanced at Philip briefly before he shifted his attention back to the road. "I'm hoping it'll be better while you're here."

"I'll do what I can," Philip said, and he meant it.

"I know you will. Thank you." Philip thought he felt the atmosphere in the car warm a little when Kam thanked him.

They were quiet for the rest of the ride, but it was more of a comfortable silence than a tense one.

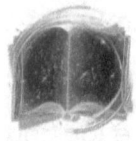

When they got home, Philip and Kam greeted their mother and kicked out of their shoes before heading upstairs. Kam flopped on the bed on his back as Philip began unpacking.

"Are you going to stay here?" Philip asked. He hoped he sounded casual, more than hopeful or apprehensive. Kam shrugged, fiddling with his rolled-up sleeves.

"I was thinking I might go home, actually. It really depends on how they act."

"How they act?" Philip asked. He studied his brother, his head tilted to the side.

"Yeah." Kam sucked his teeth. "You'll see." Kam was staring deliberately at the ceiling, so Philip couldn't meet his eye.

"Well, I'd like it if you stayed," Philip said, his attention on the bottom of the drawer. He held his breath as he waited for a response. He worried he'd overstepped, but he didn't have to worry long, because Kam chuckled.

"Yeah? I didn't hog the blanket too much at Thanksgiving?" he teased, rolling onto his side to watch Philip.

"No," Philip replied. "Not too much. Though, I always was the patient one."

Kam grinned. "Is that right? I seem to recall being pretty patient with you, growing up."

Philip slid the drawer closed, a small smile playing across his lips. "You were, but that doesn't mean I wasn't more patient than you. Do you know how many sermons, Bible studies, and lectures I've sat through?"

Kam laughed. "Yeah, but you like that stuff."

"That may be so, but the lessons and sermons can be... tedious." He'd chosen his words carefully, but they still made Kam laugh.

"I think that's the first bad thing you've ever said about church."

"Well, I attend a lot more church and church-related functions now than I ever used to..."

"So what, one day you'll be a cynic like me?" Kam teased.

"In a few years, *I'll* be the one giving the sermons. I should think that would change my perspective quite a bit."

Kam laughed. "I guess we'll find out, won't we?" Kam was still smiling, but he yawned and closed his eyes. "If I take a nap, will you wake me up when Father gets home?"

"Mother said he'd be home any minute."

"Yeah, but she's probably wrong. You've been putting your clothes away a few minutes now, and he's not home yet." Kam rolled onto his back, his eyes still closed. He'd apparently decided he was going to try for a nap, regardless of whether Philip planned to wake him.

Philip didn't want to spend time alone with his thoughts. He knew he'd spend it ruminating on having told Kam he wanted him to stay. By doing so, he'd implied that he *wanted* to share a bed with him, again.

The fact it was true didn't make it easier to stomach.

Philip took a seat on the floor and leaned back against the side of the bed. The sound of Kam's breath whistled every time he exhaled, and it was oddly comforting after spending his nights alone for the last several weeks.

After a few minutes Kam was lightly snoring, and Philip got to his feet. He quietly crossed the room and closed the bedroom door behind him. He padded down the stairs softly and met his mother in the kitchen.

"It's so good to see you," she said warmly. "How does Kam seem?"

That was a strange first question. He took a seat at the table and folded his arms across his chest. "He seems fine. Tired, overworked, but fine."

"Really?" She put a hand on his shoulder. "He doesn't look sickly to you? He doesn't sound off?"

Philip shook his head. "No. He said he's been working seven days a week, and he does look tired, but I'd expect that with as much as he's working. He wanted to take a nap while we waited for Father to get home, so it sounds like he's trying to take care of himself."

"But doesn't he look thin?"

Philip supposed *this* was what Kam meant when he'd said it depended on what their parents were like. "He might have lost a little weight, but he doesn't look unwell. He's just burning the candle at both ends."

"Just keep an eye on him while you're here." She took a seat at the table across from him. She watched Philip for a moment, as though she was debating saying something else. She fiddled with the silver watch on her wrist. "Your father thinks he might be on drugs."

"Drugs?" he asked carefully. He wasn't sure how to play this. He knew Kam smoked weed on occasion, he had for years, but he didn't know if that was something their parents were privy to. "Why do you say that?"

"He's always so out of it when he comes by, and he's stopped coming to church." Before Philip could reply, she extended a hand toward him across the table. "Don't feel bad about that. I always thought he would stop coming once you left. You have always been a good influence on him."

Philip couldn't help the slight smile that tweaked his lips at the praise. "And you think without me, that he's stopped coming to church because he's gotten into drugs?" His eyebrows furrowed. "That's a little extreme, don't you think? He said he's working a lot, isn't that more likely?"

"See what you think when you've spent some time with him." She didn't seem troubled by Philip not believing her. She already had her theory about what was going on, and she seemed determined to stick with it.

He could understand why Kam might be reluctant to hang around.

Before he could say anything else, they heard the front door open through the living room. Philip sat a little straighter at the table when he heard his father coming in. He tried to twist his expression into a friendly smile, and he didn't let it dampen when Father crossed the threshold into the kitchen.

"Hello, Father."

"Welcome home, Philip." He smiled and patted his son's back before he took a seat beside his wife. "Has your mother told you about Kam?" Philip nodded. "While you're here, I want to try to talk to him. I want to see if we can talk him into getting treatment."

Philip frowned. "You really think it's that serious? He just says he's working a lot."

"That's what he told you. That doesn't mean that's what's happening. He is on a slippery slope, Philip. We don't want him sliding any further."

As long as Kam was still getting to work and taking care of himself, Philip didn't know how much *slipping* Kam had done, but he respected his parents. He didn't see the harm in cooperating.

"Did he say how long he wanted to sleep?" Mother asked.

"He just wanted to nap until Father got home, so we could all spend some time together." His parents looked at one another. He knew the look of skepticism in their eyes. They stayed quiet, though.

"Will you go get him?" Father asked.

Philip nodded and got to his feet. His parents started whispering amongst themselves as soon as he was out of the room.

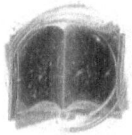

When Philip got back into the bedroom with Kam, he smiled again. His brother had gotten comfortable. Kam was rolled onto his belly and had sprawled across the bed. Philip hated to interrupt, but it had to be done. He sat on the edge of the mattress and reached over to shake Kam's shoulder. His brother made a quiet groan in his sleep.

"Hey, Kam," Philip coaxed. "Are you awake?"

Kam's brow creased, but his eyes were still closed. He rolled on his side and nuzzled into the side of Philip's thigh. The aspiring pastor felt his cheeks grow warm. He rubbed Kam's shoulder. "Hey, Kam," he called in a soft voice. He shook his brother's shoulder lightly, again.

Kam's blue eyes fluttered open. He looked up at his younger brother for a moment in confusion, and then he smiled. His cheek was pressed against Philip's leg.

"Hey," Kam greeted him groggily. "Father make it home?"

Philip nodded. It was hard not to fixate on Kam against his flank.

"He sent me up after you."

Kam grimaced. "Yeah, I bet he did. Did they tell you I'm on drugs?" He seemed remarkably cavalier about the accusation.

"They did."

Kam rolled his eyes and sighed, his cheek still pressed to Philip's pants. "I'm lucky they haven't started accusing me of Devil worship."

"They said you stopped going to church, so that's probably not too far off." Philip was trying to make a joke to lighten the mood, but Kam only groaned as he rolled onto his back. Philip missed the touch immediately.

"I missed church *twice* because they needed me to cover brunch shifts, and they decided I'm never going back. It's ridiculous."

Philip didn't have any reason to disbelieve what his brother said. He patted Kam's shoulder. "They've always been a little dramatic." He worried his lower lip between his teeth. "I can't help but notice you haven't said you're *not* on drugs, though."

Kam sighed and sat up, finally putting some real space between them. Philip regretted the words immediately, until he realized Kam wouldn't meet his gaze. "There's a difference between *taking drugs* and having *a drug problem*. They don't see it that way." He was frowning and looking at his lap on the bed. "To them, abstinence is the only way. They don't like that I started smoking openly, either." He shook his head.

Philip could make sense of the way their parents thought. If he were being honest, his own thoughts on the subject were similar to their parents' black-and-white thinking. "So you *are* on drugs?" he asked.

"Don't be like that, Philip. It's not all the time," Kam sighed. He was still looking anywhere but Philip's face. "I'm not on anything when I come here, or when I go to church, or when I go to work. I just... need help relaxing. Now that I'm working every day, I need something to take the edge off."

Philip didn't like it, but he knew arguing with Kam wasn't going to get him anywhere, especially since their parents already had. "How did they find out about it, if you're not on anything when they see you?"

Kam shrugged. "I dunno. It might have just been a lucky guess after I moved out." He smirked, finally looking Philip in the eye. "I guess they knew as soon as you left, I'd get into trouble."

Philip wasn't as amused. "You have lost weight, and you look tired. It's not normal for you to need to take a nap in the middle of the afternoon."

"I work at least six days a week, every week. I'm on my feet twelve hours a day. *Of course* I'm tired. *Of course* I lost weight from when I was living at home and sitting around most of the time." He sighed and shook his head. "Work has me stressed out and I'm going, going, going all day, every day. I get so keyed up trying to stay afloat that I take something to relax when I'm off. Is that really so bad?"

Philip found it difficult to argue with Kam. He always had, but it was especially difficult now with their parents driving a wedge further between them. He wanted his brother to know he was on his side, even if he didn't understand it. Philip shook his head, which Kam seemed to take as agreement.

"Come on. We'd better go downstairs," Philip said quietly.

15

CHAPTER 15

Philip came back from Christmas break a day before classes were set to resume, with just enough time to do laundry and read for an upcoming lecture. After spending the last week with his family around, his dorm room felt too quiet and isolated.

He glanced at his watch and frowned. The library wasn't open on Sundays, and it was too late for him to have coffee. That severely limited his options. He gathered his books and notes and headed off toward the lounge. The sky had been dark ever since he returned from his visit home. The clouds were full and gray, and although he didn't yet feel rain, he heard cracks of thunder from the darker clouds on the horizon. It made the walk to the lounge foreboding. He pulled his jacket tight as the harsh wind tried to whip it free.

A bolt of lightning flashed in the sky above him as he reached the building doors. It seemed the clouds were trying to usher him inside, because he'd barely touched the handle when they gave way to furious, pouring rain. The droplets fell, large and heavy. He barely missed being drenched. He watched the rain through the door for a few moments, and another flash of lightning lit the dim courtyard. The crack of thunder followed, shaking the glass in the door. Philip backed away from the storm and headed up the stairs to the lounge. He hoped the room would be insulated enough that he'd be able to focus. He thought the lounge might be empty, but it seemed like his best shot at being around other people.

He was pleased to see he wasn't the only one who'd had that idea. David was sprawled out on the sofa. The fluorescent lights were turned off, and David was reading by the light of the floor lamps in the room. One was positioned over him at the side of the couch, and the other stood watch in the corner —a sentry over the back of an under-stuffed arm chair. He smiled when he saw Philip come through the doorway.

"Hey." David sat upright and swung his feet to the floor so that Philip could take a seat. "How was your trip home?"

"It was good," he replied simply. He took the seat beside David on the couch. "My brother's on drugs, but he doesn't think it's a problem. My parents are keeping an eye on him." Philip could still hear faint cracks of thunder, but they weren't as jarring as they had been in the lobby.

David's eyebrows raised. "That sounds... complicated." In the low light, David's long cheeks looked more gaunt and hollow, and they reminded Philip of Kam. Now *everything* reminded Philip of Kam.

Philip nodded and sighed. "How about yours?"

"I enjoyed the time with my sister. I got to see my grandparents." He was being more reserved than usual as he closed the book. "Do you want to talk about your brother?"

Philip frowned. He pulled his bag onto his lap. He shook his head and pulled out the book he had tried to read in his room. "I don't think so. Maybe later." He forced a weak smile. "Thanks, though."

David nodded. "Of course. I'll be here if you change your mind." He reopened his own book and they sat in silence, reading together. Having company helped, even though the room was quiet.

After a lengthy pause, Philip sighed and closed what he was reading. "I might have changed my mind," he said quietly. "Is that offer to talk still open?"

David closed his book too, and moved the blanket so it would cover Philip's legs as well. "Always," he replied softly. "What's on your mind?"

"Kam, my brother." The explanation wasn't necessary, but David nodded along. "He thinks he's in control of his life and that our parents are overreacting. And maybe he is, and they are—but it seems excessive that he'd need to self-medicate to get to sleep every night, or that he'd need to pop pills to get through his days off."

David nodded. "Did he use while you were there?"

Philip shook his head. "I don't think so. He smoked marijuana to sleep, but that's normal for him. He didn't take anything else. Apparently some guy he works with gets hydrocodone for an old back injury and he gave Kam a few pills. That was what got him started." Philip sighed. "He kept trying to reassure me that it's not a big deal and that he doesn't need help, but when I asked him about his habits, it sounds like he might." Philip raised his attention from his hands in his lap to David's face. "What can I do?"

David looked serious for a moment. "Well, you are a little limited in how you can help," he admitted. "You're far away, and you can't help your brother if he won't help himself."

Philip nodded.

"You'll have to keep in good contact with him, and let him know you love and support him. Your parents have come at this aggressively, so you'll have to take a different approach."

"And then what, I just wait for his life to fall apart?"

"While praying for him," David replied with a nod. "He probably won't realize he needs help until he starts facing the consequences of his actions. Those aren't going to happen right away."

Philip nodded and worried the hem of the blanket with his fingers. "It's hard. I don't want him to get hurt." Before David could reply a heavy wind beat the hard rain against the window. Though it was muffled, there was a distinctive howl as the weather intensified.

"The Lord will see him through," David assured him. "And so long as you keep in touch, he won't have to go through these trials alone."

16

CHAPTER 16

Philip was tense as he waited in the train terminal, thoughts drifting to the last times he'd seen Kam. He swallowed the lump in his throat when he remembered how much he'd struggled when they needed to share a bed. He took a deep breath and held it for a count of four. As he released the exhale, his memory flashed to the reoccurring dream that haunted him over that break. As he thought of being a jungle cat, he picked at the skin around his parched nail beds. He glanced up at the board every few minutes. It proclaimed when Kam's train was due, and just like his dream, the time never seemed to get closer.

"It'll be fine," he murmured in a whisper to himself. "It's just Kam."

Philip knew it was a lie, though. His brother had *never* been *just* Kam.

Three nights prior, he had walked into the lounge and was surprised to hear the phone ringing. He hadn't been certain the line could even take incoming calls.

"Hello?" he'd asked into the receiver.

"Philip, thank God." Kam's voice was clear as day on the other end. "I need your help."

The problem had spilled from him immediately; Kam wasn't in a position to beat around the bush. Kam had gotten fired from his job at the restaurant. He had applied to other places, but nowhere was biting. That had been just under a month ago.

His friends and roommates had floated him some cash in the beginning, but he had exhausted all their goodwill. He was getting kicked out of the house he was living in. He had nowhere to go.

"I can't go back to Mother and Father until I'm clean," he explained. "I can't handle *them* and a detox."

Philip understood that, but he didn't know what he could do. He certainly didn't have the money to pay Kam's rent.

"If I can get there, can I stay with you?" Kam asked, abruptly. The question sent Philip's heart rate to the moon. "I'll get off the drugs, all of them. I just need to be somewhere safe while I do it."

A minute passed in silence while Philip processed the request. The faint static in the line let Kam know the call was still going, so he kept silent. He didn't want to make it worse.

"Yeah," came Philip's eventual reply. "Yeah. If you can get here, you can stay with me."

That had been it. Kam had excitedly gotten the details for the closest train depot—he couldn't afford a plane ticket, but the train was cheaper—and he said he'd find a way. He asked Philip to call him back the next night to finalize all the details. In a daze, Philip had agreed and hung up the phone.

After that call, he'd struggled to actually do the studying he'd come to the lounge for in the first place. When he went to bed, his sleep was uneasy. He was torn. He wanted to help Kam. If his brother wanted to be off drugs for good, then *of course* he would do whatever it took to get him there.

But a smaller part, a selfish part, saw this as an opportunity. Kam would be dependent on him, and Philip had never had that kind of power over another person before.

He worried about what might happen if he let that small, hungry piece of himself take over. He'd always had to resist a certain flavor of temptation where Kam was concerned. He was worried that balancing two types might be too much.

Philip hissed in pain as the finger he'd been picking at began to bleed. The stinging was calmed when he stuck his fingertip into his mouth. With his digit between his lips, he caught sight of a familiar head of hair exiting the train car. Seeing Kam, though he looked worn and tired, brought a smile to Philip the way it always had.

"Philip!" Kam's voice rang out, and Philip got to his feet. He yanked his hand from his lips and shoved it roughly into his pocket.

"Hey," he greeted his brother warmly. Kam had a heavy backpack over his shoulder, and he was carrying an overloaded duffel bag as well. He crossed the terminal and dropped the duffel at Philip's feet and then he swept his younger brother into a bone-cracking hug. Philip returned the hug with one arm.

"Have you eaten?" Philip asked, trying to pry out of the hug. Kam held him a moment longer.

"No, I haven't," Kam admitted when they parted. He picked up the duffel again and started with Philip toward the exit.

"Let's get settled in and get you something to eat."

Kam smiled. "Thanks, Philip. For all of this." He looked at his brother for a moment after they settled into a taxi, but then he focused his gaze out the window. "Once we've eaten, I was hoping you could take me to the church you go to on Sundays."

"Yes, of course."

"Thanks. I'll need to go by a few churches to find support group meetings, but I thought I'd start with one."

Philip raised an eyebrow. "You're really serious about getting better, aren't you?"

Kam nodded. "Yes, I really am. I took my last doses earlier today so I wouldn't get sick on the train."

Philip smiled. "I'm proud of you, Kam. It will be hard, but you can do it."

"We'll find out," Kam replied. He sounded exhausted already.

After a short taxi ride, they arrived at campus. Philip led the way into the building and up the stairs. When they got into Philip's room, Kam set his bags down next to the bed.

"We can unpack after you've eaten," Philip offered. Kam nodded, and together, they descended the stairs and headed to the cafeteria.

Kam unloaded his clothes into the drawers Philip had emptied for him in his dresser. Philip had taken a seat on the bed and was reading a book for one of his classes. Kam was very focused on his task, and was quieter than Philip had ever known him to be. Philip was trying to focus on his book, but having Kam in such close proximity in a space that had only ever been his was jarring. The room was too small for the both of them.

After dinner, Philip had taken Kam to the church as he'd asked. Kam had made note of all the AA and NA meetings scheduled for the next month. He planned to go to four in the next two weeks. Philip had also shared the location of a few other churches that Kam could visit to get their schedules, and he had eagerly written all the details down.

"You can do this, you know," Philip said quietly, into his book.

"Huh?" Kam asked, looking up at his brother.

"Getting through this. You can do it," Philip repeated a little louder before he closed his book around the bookmark. "You're strong, and I'll be right here with you."

Kam smiled and approached the side of the bed. He gave Philip a firm hug around his shoulders. Philip froze for a moment before he raised his arms to hug Kam back. He swallowed and tried to relax through sheer force of will.

As Kam rubbed Philip's back, the younger brother felt some tension ebb from his body. It was nice, holding Kam like this. Before he could linger too long on that thought or even begin to really savor it, Kam let him go. Philip smiled up at him.

"Thank you, Philip."

"You're welcome, Kam."

Even as he said the words, he wondered if he would regret them.

17

CHAPTER 17

Just as they had at their parents' house, the two young men had slept with their backs together and remained that way through the first few nights.

But the further Kam got from his last fix, the more restless his sleep became. Instead of lying still on his left side, he would shift, struggling to get comfortable and feel at ease while his body cried out for the pills. Eventually, he would fall asleep, but Philip could never be sure what position they'd wind up in throughout the night, or how his body would react.

He woke before his alarm one morning to find his brother curled up around his arm. Kam's head rested on Philip's shoulder. He looked beautiful in the dim light. At peace. Philip had reached up to softly stroke Kam's shaggy blond-brown hair, and Kam had nestled in closer without waking up.

Philip felt a tightness in his chest and a lump in his throat. This was wrong, but it felt so good. So *right*. Philip leaned forward and placed a feather-light kiss to his brother's forehead. Then he placed another one on his cheek. Then his other cheek. Kam stirred a little, but he didn't wake. Philip was playing with fire, but he was too far gone to stop.

When he leaned in to kiss Kam again, he captured his lips, and that was when Kam's eyes snapped open. His eyebrows furrowed into a glare, and that was when Philip jolted awake. He was relieved and mortified to find that Kam was still snuggled against him, fast asleep. Blissfully unaware of his brother's depraved imagination.

Philip debated reaching out to stroke his hair, but the alarm sounded which roused Kam from his peaceful slumber.

"Oh shit, I'm sorry. I think I drooled on your shoulder," Kam apologized.

"Don't worry about it," Philip replied, stretching his arms as Kam got to his feet.

It seemed like Kam took the reassurance to heart, because the next night, Kam cuddled beneath Philip's arm to find comfort enough to fall asleep. It took Philip extra time to relax with his brother snuggled up to him so close. When he woke the next morning, Philip found he was curled around Kam's back.

He got up quickly, and quietly gathered his clothing. He made his way down the hall to take a bracing cold shower before Kam woke up.

This *couldn't* continue.

That night, he'd have to sleep elsewhere.

An hour after Philip had drifted off into a fitful sleep on the sofa in the lounge, he was jarred awake. He still felt off and restless, just as he had before he'd fallen asleep. He tossed the light throw blanket that had been covering him to the floor. He kicked his feet and scowled at the way the coarse cushions felt against his bare heels.

Philip rolled onto his left side facing the sofa, and then onto his right. Then he sat up and picked the blanket off the floor. He stood and covered the sofa with it.

That was better, at least. He shuddered, as if by shrugging his shoulders, he could shed his cotton button-up or denim trousers. He huffed a sigh and frantically began unbuttoning his shirt. Suddenly, he had broken out in an unpleasant, sticky perspiration all over his body.

He threw his shirt to the floor at his feet and hastened to unfasten his pants as well. Some small part of his brain questioned the wisdom of sleeping naked in a public lounge, but it couldn't overpower the instinct that forced him out of his remaining clothes.

Once he was nude, Philip sat on the sofa atop the blanket. He was panting and still covered in that unpleasant dampness. It felt like he'd just ventured outside into impossible humidity. He ran his fingertips across the blanket on either side of him.

But then he was moving. He was on his feet, pacing back and forth from one wall to the other. Restless, restless, restless didn't begin to do the feeling justice. He'd torn off his clothes, but he wanted to tear off his skin!

Now, there was a thought. He paused his pacing to study his fingers in the dim light from the hallway. His fingertips felt almost itchy with a tingle that ran up his forearm and all the way to his shoulder. It all felt like too much. Even the light from the hall felt too bright in the darkness.

He reached up to touch his forehead, to stroke the damp skin, but he jerked his fingers back.

Beneath his fingertips, where his skin should be, he felt hair—soft, silky hair that was maybe an inch long. He patted the rest of his face. He felt his cheeks, his nose, his chin, all covered in thick hair. What was happening?

He clasped a hand over his mouth, lest he shout something profane to the heavens, and he felt vicious teeth protruding from between hair-covered lips. When he finally cried out, terrified, his voice was deep and throaty and feral.

Then Philip was tumbling forward. He reached out toward the carpet to catch himself, but instead of fingers, he saw large, clawed paws. He realized that he had not felt his knees hit the floor. When he looked down, he saw clear as day that muscular feline haunches stood there.

Philip's startled cry became a warning growl in his throat.

The restlessness had faded away, replaced by something more familiar. His mind was racing, and he struggled to conjure an explanation for this or a name for what he was feeling. Philip was still struggling to come up with either when he heard... a motor? Words were so hard now.

Philip inclined his head toward the door, cracked open to the hallway. The sound of the machine was muffled, as though its source was underwater, but it was still so impossibly loud. What *was* that?

He stepped toward the door, moving as easily on four legs as he ever had on two. His paws were silent as he moved down the hall and across the tiles. Philip felt so incredibly strong now. Every movement of his legs felt deliberate and controlled. He was molten steel, and every movement was smooth and liquid.

When he got to the end of the hall near the stairwell, he heard the machine more clearly. There was a mechanical whirring coming from the floor below. He had to stop that sound. His paws carried him quickly as he descended. The door to the first floor was slightly ajar, so all it took was a nudge of his head to fully open it.

The machine was deafening. Philip saw the source—the overnight janitor was pushing a floor waxer across the tile with his back toward the stairs.

Philip lunged before he had time to think better of it.

His claws connected first and sank deeply into the man's shoulders and back. Philip barely saw the tan fabric of the man's uniform turn maroon before his powerful jaws embedded in the back of his neck. Philip felt the muscle split as blood sprayed from the wounds. The blood was in the air and in Philip's fur and in his mouth and down his throat. It was everywhere. He'd dragged the man to the ground before he could blink, and his strong jaws made quick work of his spinal cord. He felt a satisfying pop as it severed.

Philip yanked hard on the back of the man's neck and came away with a mouthful of meat and skin and tissue. The taste was metallic and salty and more powerful than anything he'd tasted with his human tongue.

He chewed and swallowed and dug his claws deeper into the unmoving flesh. Philip growled deep in his throat, and he heard the man's heart now that the machine had switched off. The blood pulsed out in spurts, and Philip recoiled from the spray. It was wet, and he didn't like the way it threatened to obscure his vision. He blinked a few times, clearing it as best he could without fingers.

Philip released his claws and took a step back, leaving the janitor's remains in a mangled heap. Blood was spreading in a steady circle from the shape the man made on the glistening floor. The massive black cat yawned.

He was tired. Now that the waxer wasn't running, he could finally get some rest.

18

CHAPTER 18

Philip's hazel eyes struggled to stay open, crusted with sleep. He raised his hand to rub the remnants away, and was surprised to see his arm was bare instead of covered by the long-sleeved shirt he'd laid down in. He glanced down to his unclothed chest. He was covered by a light blanket, which he peered under. He jerked it down again when he saw he was totally bare.

He sat up, gathering the blanket at his waist to keep himself covered. He glanced around the room and was somewhat relieved to see his clothing strewn about the floor. He was less comforted by the open door to the lounge. He stood, the blanket wrapped around him to protect his modesty from imagined prying eyes, and he closed the door. Then he gathered his clothing so that he could hurriedly get dressed.

He folded the blanket and put it under his arm so he could take it to wash. It was only then that he started to consider just how he had ended up naked in the lounge to begin with.

(He couldn't help but feel grateful that he hadn't stayed in his room. Ending up unclothed in bed with Kam would have surely ended worse.)

The sofa was barely comfortable enough to sit on, let alone try to sleep. He remembered tossing and turning and feeling overheated.

And then he slowly remembered his dream.

Philip had been a dark feline, a hunter on the prowl. He shook his head, but the bloody images still lingered. What could have possibly made him dream such a horrible thing? He'd dreamt of being a cat before, of hunting before, but *never* like this. He glanced at the clock on the wall and frowned. He didn't have time to linger on it—he needed to get moving if he wanted to be on time for class. He still needed to go back to his room to change and check on Kam.

Philip headed straight for the stairwell and down the flights of stairs to the ground floor. He made a line directly for the exit, not bothering to leave through the lobby. Once he was outside, he quickened his pace. He didn't want to have to explain why he had taken the blanket from the lounge, especially since Eileen had been the one to put it there.

When Philip got to his room, Kam was still sleeping peacefully. He dropped the blanket into his basket for washing and started collecting fresh clothes for the day. Philip had just bent to untie his shoes when Kam rolled over and opened his eyes.

"Morning," he greeted Philip with a yawn. He had been less perky during his detox.

"Good morning," Philip returned as he stepped out of his shoes. "Sleep well?"

"Not especially," Kam replied, rolling over so his back was to Philip.

He missed you, Philip's mind supplied unhelpfully. He pushed the sentiment down.

"You?"

"No," Philip answered honestly. "I had a weird nightmare." He was unbuttoning his shirt when Kam rolled back over to look at him.

"Oh? What about?"

Philip shrugged out of his shirt and dropped it into the basket, buttoning up its replacement. "I dreamed I turned into a jungle cat and tore a man to pieces." Kam's eyes widened.

"Jesus." That earned Kam a frown from Philip. "Why can't you just dream about going to class naked like the rest of us?" That made Philip laugh, especially given the state he woke up in. He dropped his pants and stepped out of them. He was glad that Kam kept his eyes on his face.

"When have I *ever* been normal, Kam?" His brother grinned at him, and Philip finished getting dressed.

"That's part of your charm."

"Uh-huh." Philip sat on the end of the bed by Kam's feet so he could put on his socks and shoes. "Make sure you tell everyone else that. I don't think they got the memo."

"I'll be sure to do that, right after my NA meeting." Kam rubbed his eyes and sighed. "It's going to get easier, isn't it?"

"Of course."

Kam smiled. "That's exactly what I wanted to hear, thanks."

After breakfast, Philip ventured out to his first class. He was surprised to see flashing blue lights across the courtyard. A small crowd had gathered outside the lounge building. A knot of dread began to form in his stomach. Philip saw David among the gathered students, so he crossed the lawn to speak with him.

"What's going on?" he asked. David turned to face him and shrugged.

"I was going to go up and call my sister before class, but they won't let anyone in. An ambulance is parked around the other side of the building." Philip watched the police holding the line of people back. He swallowed hard.

"Do you want me to save you a seat in class?"

David shook his head.

"I want to see what all this is, but if you'd let me copy your notes later, I'd be grateful."

The building's double doors swung open suddenly, and several EMTs came through with a gurney. There was a form on it covered with a blood-stained sheet, and Philip swallowed again.

David bowed his head and closed his eyes, offering a prayer for the unknown departed. Without another word, Philip turned away and headed toward his class. His stomach was churning, and he barely made it to the bushes outside the lecture hall before he regurgitated his breakfast. The sight of the body had reawakened the more gruesome parts of his dream. His toast, and everything else, was far less pleasant the second time around. He avoided looking at the mess, choosing to ignore it like the rest of his problems.

He wiped his mouth on the back of his hand and stood more or less upright. It was a small miracle that no one had witnessed him losing his meal. He straightened up fully and headed inside. He'd find out more from David later.

David never made it to the lecture. He was also absent from their second class, and then the third. Philip was relieved when David settled in beside him just in time for their last lecture of the day. The older man looked pale when he took his seat.

"Did you find out any more?" Philip asked. He was trying to stay casual, but his heart was thrumming in his chest.

"Something killed the janitor."

Philip's throat went dry.

"*Something*?" he croaked.

"Yeah. I talked to a couple of cops after I saw the Fish and Wildlife people leave." David shook his head. "They said it was brutal. The worst animal attack they'd seen."

Fortunately, if he got sick again, there would only be stomach acid to contend with. "Inside?" Philip asked.

David nodded.

"Yeah. They don't lock that building at night, and he was on the ground floor. They don't know if something *got in* or if *someone let it in*. Lord have mercy." David shuddered. "It's scary to think about. Can I borrow all the notes I missed today?"

"Of course." Philip retrieved his notebooks from his bag, though it was hard to grip them with sweaty palms. "Let me know if you have any questions. I put the reading assignments at the end." He'd managed to distract himself by focusing on the lectures and his need to take good notes for David.

David smiled. "Thanks, Philip."

When it was time for class to start, Philip was left to sit in silence, and he didn't have the excuse of David to keep him on task. He struggled to pay attention to the lecture and push down his disjointed thoughts. Why would he dream of turning into a creature and attacking the janitor the night the man was *actually* attacked?

He thought of the book of Isaiah. There was a parable of a hungry man who dreamed of eating, but then awoke to find he was still hungry. In the verse, the comparison was made between nations attacking Jerusalem and that dream. The verse had always been taught as a reminder to trust in God and of the folly of opposing his will.

Wanting to avoid Kam and temptation had led him to sleep in the lounge in the first place. He swallowed. Was his brother the lure he couldn't avoid? That *couldn't* be. God wouldn't encourage—

David nudged Philip with his elbow. Philip hadn't written anything in several minutes. Rather than being spurred to write again, he set his pen down on the tabletop. David raised his eyebrows, but kept scrawling his own dutiful notes. Philip knew David would share his notes later, so he tried to make some sense of his dream instead.

He struggled to remember everything he'd imagined the night before. Unlike most dreams, it seemed that the more time that passed, the more he recalled. The details were coming back to him in a slow, steady stream. He could hear the hum of the waxing machine. He could smell the cleaning products from the bathroom. He could see the janitor who he barely recalled from his waking hours, there as clear as day...

It felt so *real*.

19

CHAPTER 19

It was Sunday, and Philip had started his day with services, just like always. When he'd gone back to the dorm, he collected his laundry and his homework to take down to the washing machines. He didn't like to do chores on Sunday, but he needed the distraction, the routine of it. Besides, he'd need clean clothes to see the week through, and he hadn't had a chance to get to them the day before. He had spent most of the day arguing with Kam. Philip had made the mistake of telling his brother about his dream and what he thought it meant. Talking about nightmares with Kam used to be a safe process, one of the few he could rely on throughout his childhood. Then again, he hadn't tried to convince his older brother his childhood nightmares were *prophetic*. That was where the conversation had gone awry.

"What are you talking about?" Kam had asked, exasperated.

"My dream played out exactly like the police said the creature attacked the janitor."

"Well, yeah," Kam grumbled. "You dreamed of an animal attack and the guy was attacked by an animal. There are only so many options."

Philip rolled his eyes. "Actually, there are a lot of ways it could have happened."

"Really? I'm thinking *guy is there, animal attacks guy,* and *guy dies.* That's really all you've got to work with."

"My dream was more specific than that."

"Just because your dreams are morbid doesn't mean you're psychic, Philip. Your dreams have *always* been morbid."

"I didn't say I was psychic."

"It doesn't mean you're channeling God, either."

Philip felt his jaw getting tight just remembering the conversation. That wasn't how talks with Kam were meant to go, especially when they were about things that bothered him. Kam had always made him feel better in the past, not worse. The fact that this conversation hadn't gone according to plan had him feeling terribly.

In the staircase, Philip passed one of his classmates. They smiled and greeted one another, but Philip wasn't in the mood to chat. He hadn't been in a good mood since the night the janitor had been killed, and the fight with Kam had only made it worse. If he left his thoughts idle for too long, they always seemed to circle back to that horrible dream.

From the dream of the janitor, it wasn't a far fall to recalling his childhood. He'd see the clawed-up man and then, in a flash, he'd see his parents laying bloody on the floor of their caravan. Each time the thought occurred to him, his stomach lurched.

Philip closed his eyes and took a deep breath, and then another. He needed help. He was studying scripture eight hours a day, five days a week. That was not to mention his homework and regular services, but it wasn't the same as getting counseling from Pastor Andrew. Since talking with Kam hadn't relieved any of the tension he felt, he needed to try something else. Glancing at his neglected clean laundry, he sighed and resolved to get the next best thing.

The phone rang four times before Father answered. He sounded gruff, as he usually did on the phone, until he recognized Philip's voice.

"You're calling early," he said. "Your mother went to the grocery store when we got home from church. She won't be back for a while."

"That's alright," Philip replied, holding tight to the receiver. "I wanted to talk to you."

"Oh?" Father wasn't the one who got to talk to Philip week after week. "Is everything alright with Kam?"

Philip carded his fingers through his wavy, dark hair. *That* was a loaded question. He was glad his father couldn't see him. His eyes were focused on the corner of the room, and he fiddled with the hem of his sleeve.

"Yeah," he replied. "Kam's staying out of trouble."

"Good," Father said. "What's on your mind?"

"A man was killed here a few nights ago. Some kind of animal attack. I didn't know him, but it was one of the staff. And the night it happened, I dreamed about it. I was in the same building, so I don't know if maybe some part of me heard something and imagined the rest...?" Kam had floated that as a suggestion when Philip had implied he might have had a spiritual dream.

"Is that what you think?" Father asked doubtfully.

"At first, when I heard what happened, I thought it might have been a vision. It all felt so real, and everything I dreamed lined up with what the police said happened."

Father made a noise of acknowledgment on the other end of the line.

"What?" Philip asked.

"Have you spoken to anyone at the church about it?"

Kam had conveyed some strong feelings about Philip's theory that his dreams were from a higher power, and after the less-than-helpful discussion, Philip was concerned the pastor at his church might be similarly inclined. Philip swallowed. He was a couple years out from his last hospitalization, but he remembered all too clearly what it was like. He couldn't go back—he *wouldn't* go back. He bit his lower lip hard to ground himself in the present moment.

"If you think you're having visions, you should really talk to a pastor," Father suggested.

"Do *you* know anything about religious dreams?"

"I have a few books in the attic on interpreting signs," Father replied. "If you're determined to avoid talking to your pastor or someone in your program about it, I can send what I have to you." The older man didn't do much to conceal the judgment in his tone.

"That would be great." Philip pretended he didn't notice. "I'm the youngest person in the program, the only one who didn't go to college, and now I'm trying to help my big brother get sober. Forgive me for not wanting to add *the guy who thinks he's having visions* to my resume." His tone was a little short.

Father made a small grunt of acknowledgment, but he didn't laugh. Philip thought he might be able to get a chuckle, and it was disappointing when he couldn't.

"How are you and Mother doing?"

"Better now that we know you're keeping an eye on Kam."

"Well, you knew I'd do that." It had been part of why his parents had 'let it slip' that Kam had been struggling. They both knew it. "He's doing well."

"Good." Father sounded tired. "You've always been good for him."

"I've always tried to be, even when I was struggling myself. He helped me a lot, too."

"Yeah." The reply rang empty. Philip's chest felt tight and his cheeks felt warm. He hated that his parents thought he was the good son when he was the one with Hell-worthy secrets.

"I'm going to go," Philip said to break the silence. "I need to see what Kam's up to and put some laundry away."

"I'll send you those books tomorrow."

"Thank you."

"Goodbye, Philip."

"Bye, Father."

When he hung up the phone, Philip sat in silence for a moment. He didn't feel better for having spoken to his father. Still, he was glad to know that some resources were on the way. That felt like a plan forward.

Back in his room, he was relieved to see Kam had returned. Philip had been worried the argument might be sufficient to push his brother away from him. He was embarrassed when he saw Kam was putting *his* laundry away.

"You don't have to do that," Philip said, crossing the room to take the folded shirt from Kam's hands. Kam tugged it back from him.

"It's the least I can do. You washed, dried, and folded everything that was in the basket, including my things." He inclined his head at Philip. "You didn't take my clothes out, did you?"

"No, but..."

"No buts," Kam replied. "I brought us some lunch." He pointed to a paper bag on top of the dresser. Philip knew Kam well enough to know this was a peace offering.

"You didn't—"

"If you say I 'didn't have to do that' one more time when I'm trying to help you, I'm going to smack you." Kam was smirking, and Philip snorted a laugh.

"Alright. Alright. You win. Thank you. I can thank you, can't I?" His tone lilted playfully.

"I will allow it." Kam's grin faltered when he spoke next. "How are our parents?"

Philip's smile dimmed too. They hadn't talked about their parents much since Kam had arrived. The tightness in his chest was moving down his torso and into his gut.

"They're fine. Father's going to send me some books he thinks might help me understand my dream." He didn't need to explain what dream he was referring to.

"Good. That's nice of him." Kam sounded sincere.

"He asked about you." That wasn't entirely true, but the way Kam's shoulders relaxed when he said it made Philip happy he'd lied.

"Did you talk to Mother?"

"No, she was at the store. I'll call back later this week during the day to talk to her. You can call with me if you want." He knew Mother would actually ask about Kam, and that it would ease her nerves to hear both of her sons. She'd be relieved to know he was doing well. Philip thought it would be good for Kam to hear her, too.

"I might. It depends on when you go." He placed a few folded pairs of pants in the appropriate drawer before he looked at Philip. "I found another church nearby with

165

meetings. I can go to at least one a day, some more than that if I need to."

He hadn't spoken much about the pull of his addiction with anyone, much less Philip. Philip took a seat on the edge of the bed.

"That's great!" he said, the tense feeling in his chest relaxing a little. "How are you liking the meetings you've been to so far?"

"It depends on the group," Kam admitted. "Some of them are heavy on the program. They preach, sorta. The readings they do have been on the religious side. I expected that. The steps mention God, but they say that can be any power outside yourself that motivates you." Kam shrugged and turned to face Philip. "You know I'm trying, right?"

The question caught Philip off guard. His eyebrows drew together. "Of course I know you're trying. You wouldn't be here if you weren't trying." Philip's heart was in his throat. "I *know* you're trying, Kam."

"I wasn't expecting things to fall apart so quickly after I moved out. I was using before you left, so it's not like it was because of you, I just..." His voice trailed off and he shook his head. "I'm gonna do better."

Philip swallowed. He had needed to hear that it wasn't his fault, and now that he had he felt like he might cry from relief. He blinked his eyes several times, until he didn't feel tears threatening to fall.

"You are," Philip agreed. His voice sounded more certain than Kam's did, despite the emotion in it. "You're already making some great strides. You came out here with me so you're not around all the old haunts and temptations. You're going to meetings—"

"And I want to start working," Kam interjected. Philip frowned. "Look, I know you aren't making a lot. I know our parents are helping, but I don't want you all to have to support me."

"Let us help you," Philip replied, shaking his head. "You're under enough stress just trying to stay out of trouble. You don't need to add a job into the mix." Plus, working was how he'd made the friends that got him into this mess, but Philip didn't want to say that.

From the way Kam was looking at him, they were both thinking it.

"Alright," Kam conceded, raising his palms up in defense. "I won't work."

"Good," Philip said. He forced a strained smile across his lips and looked at Kam. "Now, how about we have that lunch?"

"It's just sandwiches," Kam replied, grabbing the bag and taking a seat on the edge of the bed.

"Sandwiches sound great," Philip insisted. "So, tell me about the meeting."

20

When Philip got home from his last class on Thursday, a box was sitting on the bed with his father's handwriting on the label. He cut into it hurriedly and looked over the titles as he pulled them out. Most of the books were by religious leaders—things his father had picked up over the years on his own, as books for his Bible study group, or even for the church-sponsored book club he had been a part of.

True to his word, there were several books about interpreting signs from God and the gift of prophecy. At the bottom of the box, there were a few journals as well. The first two were filled with Father's handwriting, his notes and annotations about the books. The final journal gave Philip pause. He didn't recognize the handwriting as he flipped through a few pages. He turned to the front inside cover, and his blood ran cold.

This journal belongs to Ashley Porter.

His birth mother.

He couldn't recall the last time he'd heard her name. He turned more deliberately through a few of the pages. Each entry was in pen, in her careful, feminine hand. He turned back to the first entry.

It was dated the year before his parents died.

'Dear Journal,

We just got into Athens. We haven't been this far west in a while. I think folks are gonna wear their tongues out telling us we're in for a dry heat.

We're camped near a little lake, so the kids have been playing in it when me or Nate can watch them. If we stay here long, we might be able to teach them to swim, wouldn't that be something?

Philip has been so patient with Melissa lately. She's at the age where all she wants to do is follow her big brother around. I feel guilty sometimes that their only skills are circus-themed and that they only have each other to play with, but they'll pick up more skills and friends as they get older. Besides, juggling might come in handy one of these days. I just have to be careful that the sword swallowers don't get their hooks in them.

That's all for now. I need to help Nate get ready for the next show.

Wish me luck,

Ashley'

• • •

Philip swallowed. How long had it even been since he'd thought of his mother? Of Melissa? He shook his head and turned the page. He wanted to feel guilty for reading his mother's diary, even though she was long dead, but the feeling was struggling to take root. This was the closest he'd ever get to knowing her.

The thought sunk to the pit of his stomach.

'Dear Journal,

Philip is getting so tall now. Martha has been helping me add inches to all his pants so he won't be walking around in high waters this fall. We're lucky it's hot. His shorts come up a little high, but it's nothing anyone is going to judge a child for.

I'm glad that Melissa is still such a tiny little thing. Martha's handy, but I don't know that her sewing machine could handle a double growth spurt.

Tonight after the show, she and Andy said they'd watch the kids so Nate and I can go out together. When was the last time we both got to go out? I'm glad I have the sewing to keep me busy, otherwise I'd be fussing over my outfit or my hair. Not like it'll matter. I'll have to wait till after the show to get ready, and my hair's always a frizzy mess, after.

I'm hoping Melissa will behave for them. She's older now and doesn't cry as much. I think she'll be fine with Martha and Andy. She doesn't always need Mom and Dad in her line of sight now.

I'll let you know how our little date night goes. For now, I've got more sewing to do!

Ashley'

Philip's lips curled into a small, weak smile. His mother's life sounded simple, but she sounded happy. He wondered how she could get from planning date nights with his father and mending her children's clothes to suicidal in a year's time, but he didn't know that he wanted to learn the answer.

Philip sat down on the mattress and went to the next entry.

'Dear Journal,

Date night was *just* what I needed. We let it go too long without one, and we won't be making that mistake again soon. We dressed up and went to a little dive bar nearby. It wasn't too late, so the kitchen was still open. We got beers and burgers and danced together until the band stopped playing. We were having so much fun and we were so loose together. It was nice.

There was a younger couple at the table next to us that was watching us while we ate and even when we danced. They were in their early twenties, I guess. They were drinking a lot heavier than we were, and the girl kept smiling at us so wide. Nate thought maybe they had come to the show and recognized us from that, but I didn't think so. There's a different kind of look that people give you when they run into you out in the wild after seeing you perform.

This wasn't that.

I knew it for sure when she approached me in the bathroom. I was looking in the mirror, fixing my lipstick when she came in the room. She smiled that same big grin at me and then she said hey, introduced herself, and then started flirting with me! I couldn't believe it—'

Neither could Philip. His eyebrows raised as he studied the page.

'She told me that she and her boyfriend had been watching us all night. I played it cool, but said we had noticed. She blushed and asked if they could come over to our table when she was done in the bathroom. I told her they could and left. I had to tell Nate!

I knew her guy would be watching, so I strutted back to the table. I was very calm and collected. When I told Nate, he couldn't believe our luck. Usually when we want to swing, we have to work a lot harder, but you know all about that.'

Philip couldn't believe what he was reading.

'So the girl comes out and sits down with us. She waves her fella over, and then we all start chatting...'

Philip wanted to stop reading. *This* wasn't exactly what he'd been looking for when he had decided to read about his mother, but something compelled him to press on. He skimmed the details about the rest of the encounter at the bar, landing in the middle of the next page.

'The change slipped over me quick, just like it used to. While Nate kept both of them busy, I pulled away. Next thing I knew, I was a cat. I crawled back up onto the bed, and when the girl rolled over to pay me some attention, I bit her throat before she could scream."

Philip drew back from the page. That was too much. She was so *casual*. It reminded him of his dream. He didn't believe it was a coincidence, but what else could it be? Had his mother shared her fantasy with her children? Had he forgotten her delusion until overhearing the creature attack? Were his mother's delusions just dreams? She had to believe them. Who would write lies in a diary?

He skimmed the rest of the page. She talked about eating the girl alive as his birth father began to transform. She sounded so enthusiastic. In the entries about her family, she'd sounded normal, hadn't she? In her entries about this violent hallucination, she sounded *delighted*. It made Philip's stomach heave.

Was this the kind of thing that led to his parents killing themselves? Was he at risk now that he'd started having similar dreams?

He couldn't handle this, any of this. He wanted to understand the dream, his vision. He did want to figure out what was happening, but he didn't want to sink deeper into it, especially without knowing what it was.

Philip wondered if Father had known the journal was in the box when he'd sent it. Did he know what was *in* the journal? He couldn't have. He would have destroyed it for mentions of swinging alone, much less detailed descriptions of murder.

Philip picked up one of his adoptive father's journals. He flipped through the first quarter of it and only saw references to scripture and quotations from one of the books in the box. He took small comfort in knowing that not everything had gone insane.

He knew he'd have to revisit his mother's journal again, but he wanted a clear head when he did it. Now that he knew what the entries contained, he needed to be careful to keep himself separate from them. He'd read through the journal later with a notebook of his own so he could make notes of the similarities between his mother's writing and his own experience. He'd also want to have something to eat before he read on, because he didn't think he'd be able to eat afterward.

He swallowed and made a plan. Kam would be back soon. Philip resolved to look at the journal after dinner.

21

CHAPTER 21

Philip collapsed into a heap on the end of the bed, the box of books abandoned on the floor by his bare feet. "How am I supposed to deal with the fact my parents were mental, Kam?" He ran a hand through his unkempt hair. "You know the trouble I've had. I was in and out of facilities my whole childhood. How do I cope with the fact my parents were dangerous fruitcakes, and I'm headed down the same path?"

Kam studied Philip from beside him on the mattress. "You had *one nightmare*, Philip. One nightmare doesn't make you a dangerous fruitcake. It certainly doesn't make you a murderer."

"You don't *understand*. It felt so real. *So* real. It was like I could see it happening." He swallowed. "I could *taste it*, Kam."

"So it was a vivid nightmare," Kam countered. "You dreamt the taste because you've tasted blood. Who hasn't? One bloody nose or lost tooth and any six-year-old could dream that taste in their mouth." His brother shook his head. "I'm not convinced."

Philip chuckled bitterly. "You weren't there." He swallowed again. "There's something I haven't told you."

"*What* didn't you tell me?"

Philip took a breath and held it, his eyes closed. "I undressed in the dream before I changed. I woke up naked in the lounge."

Both of Kam's eyebrows had raised. "So you got overheated and stripped, and then you had a bad dream. I'm not hearing a compelling case here. You sleepwalked some when you were a kid, and this is less convincing than that." He shrugged his shoulders. "So what?"

Philip laughed incredulously. "Do you hear yourself?"

"Do you hear *yourself*?" Kam countered. "You read a few journal entries and decide after one bad dream that you're an axe murderer? Come on now, Philip. I know you better than that." He gave Philip's shoulder a playful shove. "You're a good guy. Good guys don't kill janitors in their sleep."

"Crazed mental patients might," Philip replied sharply.

"You're not a crazed mental patient," Kam said evenly. "You're *in seminary,* for Christ's sake." He raised a hand apologetically. "Pardon the expression."

Philip shook his head, but he was smiling a little. "You really aren't worried about this, are you?"

Kam shook his head. "I've known you for a long time. You've had struggles, sure, but you've been through a lot. Anyone who went through what you did would have had trouble. But you aren't your parents. And that even assumes that your mom was telling the truth about hurting people." Philip shook his head again, and a lock of hair fell into his eyes. Before he could reach for it, Kam did. He swept the hair behind Philip's ear with his index finger before he dropped his hands back into his lap. "Just because it was real to her doesn't mean it was *real*." Kam sighed. "Your parents killed themselves, Philip. It's not like you thought they were well-adjusted before all this." Philip cracked a little smile, which seemed to encourage Kam to continue. "I will admit, though, it's a little fucked up that the first time you lightened up was when I mentioned a double suicide." That got Philip to chuckle, and Kam grinned. "There he is." He gave Philip's shoulder a squeeze.

"Thanks for talking me down off the ledge," Philip sighed. "It just swept me up in all those old fears from when I was a kid."

"Anytime," Kam replied. "Besides, I owe you."

"Owe me?"

It was Kam's turn to sigh as he leaned in a little. "You're the one person in my life who doesn't make me feel like a massive fuck-up."

When he looked at Philip, he smiled again. Philip was finally watching him rather than gazing at the spot he'd been focused on in the middle distance. Kam was still smiling when he leaned toward Philip and pressed their lips together.

Philip went rigid at first. He was frozen, his arms tightly trapped by his sides. His lips were more responsive. When they parted slightly from his surprise, he felt Kam's tongue, and Philip's eyes closed at the gentle touch. When he couldn't see his brother anymore, he relaxed. He felt himself kissing back suddenly, and he felt Kam's hand on his hip.

When the pair separated, Kam was still smiling and Philip's cheeks were flushed.

"You know, I had a whole apology speech planned for if I ever did that." Although his words were flowing slowly, they were even, and he kept his eyes locked on Philip's. "I figured I'd blame the drinking or the drugs, or whatever I thought I could say that would keep you from hating me." Kam's tone was almost apologetic, which matched his earnest expression.

"I could never hate you," Philip replied softly, and then he closed the distance between them for a rough kiss of his own. Philip didn't have experience—not like Kam obviously did, but he was eager.

Kam grinned into the kiss and pulled Philip over sideways onto the bed. He let his hands roam over Philip's chest and arms. Philip's hands were less adventurous. They first held onto Kam's waist, before Philip allowed himself to paw up Kam's back.

Kam kissed down Philip's chin and along his jaw. His lips brushed Philip's neck, and then he pulled back. "May I?" he asked, fiddling with the buttons on Philip's shirt.

Philip's mind was pure electricity. He'd been daydreaming about this moment since he was a teenager. His thoughts were racing, but it was like a TV switching between static channels rather than anything coherent. His guilt was a dark, swirling knot in his stomach, but he could push it down, for now.

He nodded, but Kam shook his head.

"I need to hear you say it."

"Yes," Philip replied, his voice a raspy whisper.

That was enough encouragement for Kam. He began unbuttoning Philip's shirt from the bottom, one button at a time. Philip couldn't take his eyes off his brother.

Kam, too, was studying Philip with rapt attention. When the shirt was unfastened, he slipped his fingers beneath it on either shoulder and slid it back and down Philip's arms. The younger man scrambled out of it, and Kam grinned.

"Well, you're impatient, aren't you?" There was a hint of teasing in his voice, but it was familiar. Philip didn't find it intimidating.

"Do you blame me?" he asked. Kam shook his head, his fingers gliding from Philip's shoulders down to his chest.

"No. It's just cute, is all." He lowered his lips to kiss along Philip's collarbone. Philip's eyes fluttered closed, and he exhaled in a breathy sigh. He felt his cock twitch to life in his trousers, but he was too wrapped up in the sensations to try to will it away.

After several more minutes of kissing, Philip's erection was straining inside his pants and pressing firmly against Kam's thigh. The younger man gasped when Kam reached down and palmed it through the fabric. Philip whimpered against Kam's neck where he'd been kissing him.

Kam growled into Philip's shoulder. "I knew you'd be repressed, but I never imagined you'd be this *needy*. I love it."

179

He passed his judgment immediately, so Philip wouldn't be left to wonder. The younger man whined again when Kam stroked the length of him through his clothing. Kam groaned in response and made a move with both hands toward Philip's zipper. "May I?" he asked again, his fingers paused.

"Please," Philip begged. The guilt in his stomach was a yawning pit, but the heat in his core made it possible for him to ignore it.

Kam made quick work of Philip's remaining clothing and tugged the pants and underwear down to his knees. When he finally wrapped his fingers around Philip's boldness, Kam was still fully clothed, but he didn't seem to mind.

Philip shuddered at the touch. His eyes rolled back. He didn't touch himself, he never had, so even Kam's dry palms felt like magic. "Oh, Kam..." he moaned softly, his hands batting uselessly at the taut torso beside him. He pulled at the waist of Kam's tucked-in shirt and slipped his fingers beneath the hem. His fingertips all but sizzled when they touched Kam's stomach.

Kam slid his thumb across the head of Philip's cock to gather the moisture that had beaded there. He gave Philip a deep, lingering kiss before he drew back.

"Let me taste you," he said. "Please."

"Yes." Philip didn't hesitate, shame be damned. Kam grinned and kissed him, first on the mouth and then on the side of his neck. He continued trailing kisses down Philip's body, his hands still teasing exposed bits of flesh as he did.

Philip took a deep breath and held it when Kam's lips met his pubic bone. Kam laughed, washing Philip in hot, damp breath. "Don't forget to breathe," he reminded Philip, and then he dropped his head and ran the tip of his tongue the length of Philip's shaft.

Philip's fingers knotted in the bedspread. The heat of Kam's willing tongue was almost too much. Then it came again, and Philip had to exhale the breath he'd held.

"Don't hold back, okay?" Kam murmured, his breath still scorching against Philip's skin.

Then he sank down over Philip, his tongue flicking back and forth as he reached further depths. He reached out to where Philip's hand still grasped the duvet and gently pried his fingers loose. Kam guided Philip's hand to the back of his head, and immediately, Philip's fingers tangled in Kam's hair. He exerted a little pressure, guiding Kam just where he was discovering he liked. Philip moaned, his voice ragged. Kam groaned too, the head of Philip's cock deep in the back of his throat. The younger man felt the vibrations to his core. The all-consuming shame was a distant memory in the wake of the glorious warmth.

He was panting and desperate. Kam gave Philip's hips a squeeze of encouragement, and he groaned again with Philip deep. That pushed the younger man over the edge. He tensed, his hand coming to a stop on the back of Kam's head. The elder man kept bobbing, swallowing down each pulse. Tears welled in Philip's eyes as he began to relax. He blinked them away just before Kam raised his eyes to look up at him.

Kam gently withdrew and kissed Philip's hip softly, and then he crawled up beside Philip on the bed. "Hi," he greeted Philip, his voice thick and throaty. "Thank you."

Philip cleared his throat. "You're thanking *me*?"

Kam chuckled. "Yeah. I've wanted to do that for a while."

Philip's eyebrows raised, his hazel eyes wide. That couldn't be true. He was quiet for a moment, and Kam put a hand on his shoulder.

"Are you alright?"

Philip nodded. "Just... processing."

The honest answer made Kam smile. "Alright. Do you want to process out loud?"

Philip was quiet for a moment more, weighing the pros and cons. Finally, he spoke. "That was the first time I ever..." He trailed off.

Kam bit his lower lip and nodded. "I thought it might be. Not a lot of time for sin when you're being so good, I guess."

"No. Not much time for sin at all," he agreed. His tone rang hollow.

"Philip," Kam started. "I was joking. Don't be so literal."

"But it *is* sin," Philip argued. Now that he didn't have the heat of sensation to distract him, the hulking mass of guilt was coming back into focus. *"If a man also lie with mankind, as he lieth with a woman, both of them have committed an abomination; they shall surely be put to death."*

"But you *didn't* lie with a man *as you lieth with a woman*. You haven't *lieth* with a woman," Kam argued, frowning.

"I don't think God operates on technicalities," Philip replied. "Besides, we both know what it's supposed to mean."

"Well, I have no regrets," Kam replied with a shrug. That made Philip smile briefly. It shouldn't have. He felt bad as soon as he felt comforted by the words, but by then, it was too late. "Will you stay here with me tonight?"

Philip nodded, and his arms curled around Kam to hold him tightly. Kam smelled musky and warm when he was this close.

Philip kicked out of his trousers and underwear, and although Kam was still fully dressed, the pair drifted off to sleep together.

A few hours later, Philip stirred. When he woke, he found Kam curled over his back with his arms wrapped loosely around his torso. Philip smiled at the touch and slipped out from Kam's grasp. He got to his feet, quiet in the night. He slipped on a pair of pajama bottoms, and his bare feet padded softly to the bathroom down the hall.

When he'd closed the door behind him, he flicked on the light. He ignored the mirror to walk to the toilet. After he relieved himself, he went to the sink. He turned on the hot water and let it run warm as he stared at himself in the mirror.

As he studied the details of his face, he felt different. Changed. He'd indulged in one of his baser desires. He'd sinned in an almost unimaginable way.

He washed his hands and turned off the water. The sin had to be what it was, why he felt different. It was difficult to describe. It was a deep restlessness that started beneath his skin. It almost felt like itching...

He was scratching at an itch in his very soul, and he wasn't coming close. It spread like wildfire across his extremities. He glanced up into the mirror again, but when he met his own gaze, his eyes were bright and blue. He startled, blinking. When he looked again, his eyes appeared normal.

Philip shook his head. It was late and it had been a long day. No wonder his mind was playing tricks on him.

Philip took a step back from the mirror and reached for the doorknob, and he heard the soft click of hard nails on the tile. He looked down and jolted. Instead of a normal human torso, he saw the slender, fur-covered hindquarters of a black jungle cat.

Philip gave a shout, but it transformed into a feline growl halfway through as the tile rushed up to meet him. He reached out to catch himself, and there were large, clawed paws in place of his hands and fingers.

The transformation was complete.

On instinct, Philip retreated to his bedroom. In the dark, he could see Kam lying beneath the duvet. What was more, he could smell him now. The sweet, warm musk of Kam's scent was still present, but bolder. Beyond that, he could smell the faint scents of sweat and sex. He heard the clock on the wall ticking down the seconds. He heard Kam's deep breaths that weren't quite snoring. Below that, almost too quiet to hear, he heard Kam's heartbeat.

Thud-thud, thud-thud, thud-thud...

Philip was silent as he took a few experimental steps forward toward the bed. Kam's heart was louder now. This wasn't like his last dream with the janitor. That had been wild and unrestrained. He hadn't been able to control himself. Even his transformation had been violent.

This was different.

Kam shifted in his sleep, rolling onto his side. Philip climbed up onto the edge of the bed. He lowered his nose closer to Kam's face and inhaled deeply. He exhaled with a huff, and the breath blew Kam's light hair back from his face.

Kam's eyes blinked open. His features shifted first to bleary confusion, and then to fear. Philip knew it even before Kam's face changed. He could smell it. It was just like the janitor's. It cut through the dark and quiet of the room like a knife and overwhelmed Philip's senses. A low growl rumbled in his chest.

"What the fuck." Kam's voice jarred Philip from the intoxicating swirl of the fear scent.

Philip growled again and bared his teeth. Kam scooted back, and when he did, Philip followed. Kam kept moving back until he fell backward off the bed onto his ass, his legs tangled in the blanket.

Philip followed, standing on the edge of the bed. He looked down at the man sitting below him. The stench of his fear was palpable now.

"Stay back," Kam said, raising a hand toward Philip.

Philip knew that in that moment, he could have torn the man to ribbons. But that wasn't what he wanted.

With a growl, he turned around on the mattress. He padded toward the door and pushed it open with his strong paws and shoulder. Philip wasn't going to hurt Kam, but he had to hurt *someone*, and there was nothing either of them could do to stop it.

Once he was downstairs, the large feline left the building. The chill of the night air made his already sharp senses feel crystal clear. At first, he couldn't see the man who would become his prey, but Philip could smell and hear him. As the cat strode toward the scent of stale human sweat and liquor, a low, rumbling growl emitted from deep within his chest.

The sound was loud in his ears, but it couldn't stifle the shuffling, drunken steps of his prey. The man was walking—shambling more like, diagonally down the sidewalk. He was moving slowly, but that was less due to any pointed deliberation on his part and more a desire to stay upright despite the swimming of his head.

It was too easy.

Philip pounced, his claws extended. Fabric and skin tore. Flesh rended from the bone. Blood sprayed when claws and teeth nicked an artery, and still, Philip kept going. The fear was so salient, he could taste it along with the metallic bite of the man's blood.

The man's heart raced faster and faster, fueling the spray until it became weak. Philip growled with disapproval when his prey stopped struggling. He raised his head to listen, but all he heard was the sound of distant, discordant traffic. He let out a small, grumbling growl and wandered back towards campus.

22

CHAPTER 22

Philip awoke blearily. He'd overslept and was running late for class. He hurried to dress and decided to forgo brushing his teeth in the interest of saving a few precious minutes. He pulled on his shoes and hastened to tie them before he reached for the door.

When he pulled the door open, he recoiled. Instead of the hallway outside his dorm, he was met with an odd room. The floor was a dark hardwood instead of the ancient, gray tile he expected. Where the walls should be, instead there hung heavy velvet curtains. The scarlet fabric seemed to stretch miles high. He couldn't see the rafters or the ceiling. Instead when he looked up, he could only see darkness. There was ambient light enough to see a gray velvet fainting couch and a grandfather clock in the middle of the floor. When he looked back over his shoulder, his bedroom had faded away. In its place was another line of massive curtains. A thick fog, like cigarette smoke, filtered in behind him, swirling at his feet.

When he stepped forward to venture into the room, the fog seemed to follow. It was urging him onward.

He took a few steps into the room and noticed how his footsteps seemed to echo. The couch and the clock moved toward him, but the distant curtains never got any closer. His brow furrowed. This didn't make any sense.

When he finally reached the couch, he was close enough to read the clock face. It was an hour fast. He looked down at the watch on his wrist—it showed the same time. How could he have spent an hour walking to the middle of a room?

The clock chimed loudly, startling him. He was alarmed again when he heard a deep, low growl. He looked around wildly, his arms raised as if he meant to fight off the unseen source of the noise. He caught sight of movement out of the corner of his eye. In the place where the northeast stairwell should have been, a large panther emerged from the curtains. The cat made another low growl, and Philip took a step back.

A tall woman stepped out between the folds of the fabric. As the cat approached him, so did she. Her feet were bare and her long, dark hair was tied back away from her face in a low ponytail. She was dressed simply, in a light blue cotton dress that fell below her knees.

He eyed the approaching cat warily, but the woman smiled brightly at him. Neither creature made a sound as they walked.

"Hello, Philip," she greeted him warmly, as the cat climbed onto the fainting couch at his side. It stretched out lazily and flexed its paws, but its eyes never left Philip. Philip's gaze left the cat so that he could search the woman. She looked friendly, and so, so familiar. He couldn't place her. It felt like he was trying to recall who she was through the dense fog which had followed him.

"Hello," he greeted her cautiously.

"It's good to see you," she replied.

He looked from the woman to the panther and back again. "Do I know you?"

She laughed, a jovial, musical sound. "I should think so," she said. "I'm your mother."

Philip withdrew a step, recoiling from her like she'd burned him. The cat growled its disapproval, low and rumbling.

She raised an eyebrow at him, but kept silent. She had his hazel eyes and dark hair, but was that enough? His memories from childhood were normally clear when he called them to mind, but somehow when he looked at her, her features were too hazy for him to say with any certainty that he believed her.

"You've grown into a strong young man," she observed. As he was studying her, she had been eyeing him in kind. The panther was still sprawling out, its bright eyes fixed on him. He swallowed.

The woman smiled and took a seat beside the cat on the raised arm of the couch.

"I'm here to guide you," she answered. "Now that you've begun to change, there are some things you need to know about our people."

"Our people?" Philip repeated, confused.

"Shapeshifters," she clarified. "We have a special gift, Philip." He frowned at her. Her journal had told him plenty about what she had done with her *special gift*. "You've only just begun to experience this part of yourself."

He folded his arms across his chest and kept his frown rooted in place.

"Why do I change? Why do we," he amended carefully, "change?" Philip swallowed. "What causes it?" Philip didn't know that he believed her, but he was going to ask her as many questions as he could while she was present.

"The gift has been passed down through our family for generations. Your grandparents, great-grandparents, and great-great-grandparents all had it." His jaw was tight. He wanted for any of this to make sense, but it was all so incredible. Everything about the events of the last few weeks was unbelievable. "You need to find others," she explained. "Your desire won't transform you if your lover also has the gift."

That gave Philip pause. So there was a way around it. He wasn't condemned to kill each time he had impure thoughts.

"Can we give the gift?" Philip asked. He knew as soon as he spoke that he'd let too much hope creep into his tone. The woman shook her head.

"No. The only way is to be born with it." She looked apologetic. "There are those who sought to cure the gift with witchcraft or science, but none have succeeded."

Philip pondered that, letting his eyes wander from the large feline to his mother's feet and then back up to her dark hazel eyes.

"Does Melissa have the gift?"

The woman reached down to stroke the panther's muscular haunch.

"She does. Your father and I both did." She stared meaningfully at the cat, and Philip took a few seconds to make the connection. He shook his head.

"The cat is my father?" His words were and were not a question.

His mother made her musical laugh again. "He is. He can resist the urge to kill better than most. He finds his cat form soothing. We both wanted to see you." Philip thought of the times he had transformed, and how quickly he had been compelled to violence. *Soothing* certainly wasn't a word he would have used. "It comes with time," she said, as if she'd heard his unspoken doubts.

Philip nodded but he still felt skeptical. It was all so much.

"You'll find your way." She offered her smile, just as warm as it had been.

It was strange, being comforted by her.

"Thank you," he said quietly.

She nodded. When she opened her mouth next, he heard a loud ringing instead of her voice.

The alarm jolted him harshly awake. He lay on the laminate, tangled in the top sheet. He looked at the clock on his nightstand and reached for the alarm. He was right on time, but his back was screaming.

He turned his head first left and then right, wincing as each vertebra cracked and popped. Slowly, he sat up. His spine was stiff and on fire, and he groaned quietly every time a new muscle objected to movement. When was upright, he could see that Kam was huddled in bed under the blanket. That gave him some small comfort, until he noticed the tears in the fabric. Four slashes ripped through the duvet, and down had seeped from the wounds.

Philip swallowed. He knew he'd had another dream last night, one of his panther dreams. But a dream wouldn't slice holes in his blanket. And of course, there had been the *second* dream with his mother.

He got to his feet carefully, wanting to give his aching limbs time to adjust. He was still naked. He snatched a pair of shorts from the floor by the bed and slipped them on. When he was half-clothed, he sat on the edge of his bed and gently shook Kam's shoulder.

Kam groaned softly in his sleep, and Philip shook him again. Kam opened his eyes and then rubbed them vigorously. He smiled when his blue eyes landed on Philip.

"Hey," he said quietly, his voice thick with sleep.

"I had a cat dream."

Kam raised his eyebrows. "Me, too."

Philip took a handful of down feathers from inside the blanket and held them up. His lips were a tense, thin line. "It wasn't a dream."

Kam sat up abruptly. "Philip, what are you talking about?"

"Did you dream I turned into a cat and cornered you, and then left?"

Kam nodded slowly, his eyes wide. He was confused, and scared, and more than a little groggy.

"After I left here, I went outside. I found a man on the street. He was drunk, and I just..." Philip couldn't bring himself to finish the sentence. "How is this happening?"

"I think you need to see a doctor." Kam spoke slowly, his tone carefully measured. "I had a dream about you turning into a cat because we've been talking about it. That doesn't mean it actually happened."

Philip's jaw tightened. "Then how do you explain this?" Philip asked, sprinkling more down onto the bed like powdered sugar. Kam was quiet. "I dreamt of my birth mother last night. She said *desire* was what brought out the change."

"So what? You think you turn into a panther when you have sex?"

Philip's cheeks warmed and he looked away. He felt foolish. With what he and Kam had done—and yet he still couldn't say it aloud.

"Were you with someone in the lounge?" Kam's voice was curious more than accusatory.

Philip shook his head dramatically.

"No, no. I was alone. I just..." His voice hitched. He'd so far killed two men, but he was afraid to say words. "I wanted *you*," he told his thighs, his fingers knotted in the fabric of the blanket beneath him.

Kam's eyebrows raised again. "You sound crazy, Philip."

"I know," Philip replied softly.

"We could test it," Kam offered in reply. Philip's eyes snapped to him.

"What? What are you talking about?"

Kam sat up straighter and grabbed for Philip with both hands. When he caught him, he pulled Philip close.

"In your dream, she said desire was what made you change," Kam started, lowering his head to kiss Philip's shoulder. "So let's test the theory. If that's what you really think is happening, then I should be able to make you change." Kam slid the fingers of his right hand down Philip's chest, but he stopped just below his navel when he felt Philip flinch.

"But what if I do?" he asked.

"I don't think you will," Kam replied quietly.

"But what if I *do*?" Philip repeated.

"Then we'll figure it out," Kam said with a shrug. "But we can't until we know what we're dealing with."

"What if it only happens at night?" Philip asked. He was trying to resist, but the memories of the good parts of the night were fresh in his mind.

Kam smirked. "Then I'll try again tonight."

Philip raised his eyes from the blanket to meet Kam's gaze. "You're really not afraid?"

Kam exhaled sharply. "Look, Philip, I don't think anything is going to happen." He fluttered his fingertips against Philip's stomach to tease him. "*But* if it does... you didn't hurt me when you had the chance."

Philip swallowed and nodded.

"So no, I'm not afraid of you." He leaned forward and placed a tender kiss to Philip's taut jaw. "Afraid *for* you, maybe. I think your guilt is getting the better of you." His left hand lifted to tangle his fingers into Philip's hair. "To be clear, I mean I'm afraid of your guilt about *me,* not your guilt for having turned into a jungle cat and killed two people. Now kiss me," he ordered.

Philip did as he was told.

Philip watched Kam as he left a trail of kisses across his chest from one side to the other. He raised his hand to lightly stroke Kam's hair. Kam grinned up at him, which made Philip smile as well.

This was so much better than anything Philip had ever imagined. He couldn't have dreamed the way it felt to have Kam on top of him, his lips ghosting across his skin. When

Kam's fingers traced a path down Philip's side, he shivered. Kam chuckled, his lips on Philip's chest.

"I'm going to pretend you're this excited by me, specifically."

Philip exhaled in a light laugh. "You don't have to pretend. This is from you."

Kam grinned and nipped Philip's pectoral. "Is it?" He asked, his tone lilting. Goosebumps broke out over Philip's chest, arms and shoulders.

"*Yes*," Philip replied, his voice throaty. "It's *all* you."

Kam extended his tongue, his eyes on Philip's, and he flicked the tip across Philip's nipple. Philip shuddered and bit his lower lip.

"You're killing me," Philip murmured.

"Well, I've gotta make you *want* it. That's the whole point, isn't it?"

Philip barked a laugh. "I want it," he replied. "I want *you*."

He kissed Philip's chest and down his stomach.

Philip shuddered again and clenched the sheet beneath him. "Kam." His voice was a gasping whine.

Kam slid further down Philip's body, and he kissed along Philip's slender stomach, heading downward. He exhaled, his breath hot against Philip's flesh, and then he licked Philip's hip. Philip exhaled and laughed, breathy.

"What? Does that tickle?" Kam asked before he flicked his tongue out again, and Philip laughed a second time. His torso went tense.

"*Yes*," Philip hissed.

Kam captured Philip's hip in his mouth. Philip growled in his throat and pushed himself a little more upright. "Stop teasing," he rumbled.

"You're not in any position to be making demands," Kam replied.

"I'm not demanding, I'm *begging*," Philip replied, his voice strained. "*Please*."

Kam groaned. "Philip, honey. *Fuck*." Kam dropped his head and ran his tongue the length of Philip's erection before he drew it into his mouth.

Philip moaned and bit hard on his lower lip. He was trying hard to stay still and quiet. Still so he could let Kam work, and *quiet* out of an abundance of concern for their neighbors in the dorm. Kam held onto Philip's hip with his left hand, and his right moved so he could help guide Philip down his throat.

Kam moaned, his eyes raising so he could watch Philip watching him. Philip's lips parted, and he gasped as Kam's tongue slipped across the head of his cock. When Kam saw the reaction, he repeated the motion. Then again. Philip exhaled sharply, a faint whine creeping into his tone.

Philip's heart was pounding in his chest, and his panting breaths were coming rapidly. Kam gave his hip a squeeze and used the grip to raise Philip's hips to meet him. Philip grabbed Kam's head by a fistful of his hair. Kam groaned as he sunk down, his eyes closed as he chased Philip's orgasm.

Kam swallowed down each wave, and he placed a kiss to each of Philip's hip bones before he crawled up Philip's body. He kissed Philip's lips, and then drew back so they could both get some air. When they parted, both men were sweaty and breathless. Philip was panting, and Kam pulled him back across the bed, hugging him close to his chest.

"Now we wait," he whispered quietly, pressing a soft kiss to Philip's forehead.

Philip swallowed. "I can't believe we did that," he murmured softly. "Twice now."

Kam grinned and stroked Philip's hair fondly. "And we'll do it as many times as it takes to reassure you that you're not a monster."

"But I *am*," Philip whispered. "We both are."

Kam frowned. "No. None of that. You can do your Bible thumper routine with everyone else, but not with me."

Philip sniffed, his eyes closing. "It's not a routine, Kam. This is my life. I can't pretend it's not."

"You did a pretty good job of pretending to be alright with things a few minutes ago," Kam teased.

Philip swallowed and shook his head. "That's not funny."

"Neither is you saying we're monsters for how we feel," Kam countered. "We're not blood relations. Yes, we're men, but..."

Philip began to feel the itching, uncomfortable feeling just under his skin that he was coming to recognize. He sat up in bed, pulling away from Kam.

"It's starting," he whispered quietly.

23

CHAPTER 23

Philip felt the changes taking hold in his body, but they were gradual. It felt like an unpleasant irritation, but from under his skin. Philip got to his feet and started toward the door. Kam reached out for him, but let his hand fall when he saw the wild look in Philip's now blue eyes.

Philip slipped out of the room and down the hall toward the stairwell. It didn't matter that he was nude, because before he'd descended a few steps, his legs and hips had sprouted dense fur. His toes and feet melted into paws with vicious claws, and he folded in half so his fore paws could pad across the tile.

His legs moved in silent sync. The sunlight shining in the windows made his ebony fur glisten. In a matter of minutes, Philip was on the ground floor, and he made his way out into the gleaming daylight. There were numerous people outside on the sidewalk and in the courtyard, but Philip ignored them and headed off toward a parking lot at the rear of the building.

Cars were parked neatly into rows, and the cat moved easily between them. The people outside were too engrossed in conversations with one another to pay him any mind.

He emerged on the far side of the lot and cut through an alleyway. When he crossed the street, a dark sedan slammed on its brakes and the driver blared on the horn. The cat's ears tilted back flush against his skull, and he growled, but he didn't stop moving. He continued through the narrow streets to a small park. He heard a few pedestrians on the street exclaim in surprise when they saw him, but once he was in the bushes, it didn't matter.

The park was a long, oval shape, and it had a lake in the center which housed waterfowl in the warm months. Philip's running group had used this trail when they were all struggling to build endurance, before they had branched out to the streets of the surrounding neighborhoods. Now Philip slunk through the brambles on careful paws.

The noise of traffic from the bustling streets was loud in his attuned feline ears. Faintly, he could also hear the rhythmic footfalls of a jogger. From the scent, he could tell it was a woman, and her sneakers crunched against the gravel with her every step. A low growl rumbled in his throat as he got into position.

He didn't have to stalk her long—the woman was running toward him as she made her laps around the pond. He crouched low in the underbrush and shifted his weight across his paws so that he could spring powerfully out when his prey was within range.

She was young and fit, and his mouth watered at the thought of downing her. He shifted his weight again, and then he launched toward the woman, teeth bared. His claws tore through the thin spandex that covered her thighs as his teeth found her soft belly through her hooded sweatshirt.

All he could hear was her screaming as she desperately flailed against him. She tried to hit his face, to dig at his eyes with her frail little human fingers, but it was too late for that. He clawed her middle with his front paws. Her shirt and her skin shredded easily to ribbons. He growled and tried to bite her throat. The woman thrashed again, waving her limbs in an attempt to fend him off, but even with the adrenaline coursing through her veins, she was fading. She had lost a lot of blood, even before the cat's fangs nicked the front of her neck.

Her screams turned to gurgles as air bubbled through the wound in her throat. The cat took a fierce bite and watched the fight fade from her eyes. He reset his grip on her neck and carried her off towards the brambles he'd been hiding in. He'd left a large pool of blood on the trail, but it would seep in between the rocks in time. He could allow himself a moment to enjoy his kill.

Under the coverage of the brush, he bit into the woman's belly again. She had been slender, so there wasn't much skin and fat between him and her delicious entrails. The warmth of her blood felt pleasing as it eased down his throat, and he made a little groan of satisfaction. It was good to indulge his appetite.

Philip awoke curled up in a nest of blankets at the foot of his bed. Kam was sitting on the bed reading when he sat up to stretch.

"Welcome back," Kam greeted him quietly. "You're going to want to take a shower. You're a mess."

Philip swallowed and recoiled. It tasted like he'd licked a dozen pennies, all metallic filth. "And brush my teeth," he grimaced, the memories of his brief time as a panther returning. "Maybe drown myself in mouthwash."

"That bad?"

If he tried, Philip could recall the taste and the feel of the woman's organs between his teeth. "It's worse than you're thinking," he muttered simply.

"Well, that answers it for us. This is real."

Philip nodded. "Yeah." He looked up at his brother, a stern expression pulled across his lips. "Do you want out?"

"No."

Philip had never been more relieved.

When Philip woke for the second time that day, he did so in a panic. His heart was racing and he jolted upright. His entire body was covered in a sheen of sweat. He was in the bed again.

It was true. Kam's words echoed in his memory—it was real. Desire turned him into a monster. He felt the hot tears in his eyes before he realized he was upset. The sound of his whimper caught in his throat and drew Kam out from under the mangled blanket. He peered at Philip before he reached for him.

"Hey," he whispered in a soothing voice. "It's okay. We're gonna figure this out."

Philip shook his head and got to his feet, pulling clothes out of his drawers and yanking them on.

"Hey, Philip... It's going to be okay." Kam was still speaking quietly and placidly, like one might do to a barnyard animal they were trying not to spook.

How could he be so *calm*? How could he have meant it when he said he didn't *want out*?

Philip shook his head and started for the door, searching for his shoes.

Kam silently watched him put on shoes from the bed. "I'll be here when you get back. I won't go to any meetings today."

Philip looked up from where he knelt.

"Go to your meeting," he said firmly.

"I don't nee—"

Philip cut him off. "Go to your meeting. You need to stay on track. I'll be fine."

Kam frowned, but he nodded. "Alright."

Without another word, Philip left. He put his hands in his pockets and kept his eyes turned downward. He made sure not to make eye contact with anyone in the stairwell.

He felt the walls were closing in on him, until he was outside in the courtyard on the grass. It was only then that he felt he could breathe easily. Philip looked around and tried to decide where to go. He didn't want to walk the same path he had as a cat. He didn't want to know if either of the bodies had been found.

He started instead in the direction of the soup kitchen. He wasn't sure of the schedule they ran during the week, but he thought maybe he could lose himself in service. It was difficult to keep his mind clear as he walked. Guilt clawed at his throat and his chest.

There was basic, surface-level guilt that he was missing class— he hadn't skipped a single day of lecture so far. Then there was guilt for having indulged in carnal, bodily pleasures, and further guilt for having done so with another man. The fact that Kam was his brother wasn't lost on him either, no matter their blood.

At the top of the list was the harm he had caused. He had killed two men and a woman, now.

He regretted it all, but the worst part was knowing that even with lives and his eternal soul on the line, he would do it again. He pictured the mangled bodies and then once more, saw his parents' limp forms in his mind's eye. He shuddered and shook his head. He tried to think of something else, anything else. He found that even as he walked down the sidewalk with his eyes on the pavement, the thought of Kam's lips warmed him. Though he knew it was wrong, this was what he had always wanted.

"Hey, Philip!" A familiar voice cut through his disjointed train of thought. Philip looked up to see David smiling, exiting their favorite coffee shop.

"Hello," Philip had raised his eyes to David's shoulder, but he couldn't look him in the eye. His tone was sullen. "Missing class today?"

David's expression sank. "Yeah. I just needed the day. Are you okay?"

Philip felt his throat constrict, and he blinked when the hot tears threatened to flood from his eyes. He cleared his throat to keep his voice from breaking. Then cleared it again. He wasn't confident he could speak without it turning into a sob, so he settled on exhaling sharply and shaking his head.

David slung his arm around his shoulders. "Come on," he said quietly. "Let's go in and talk a little."

Philip didn't think he'd be able to manage it, but he was in no position to argue. He let David lead him into the coffee shop. He stood by as David ordered them both tea. David let go of him only to collect the drinks and add honey to each of them, then he offered one to Philip and put his arm right back around him.

Philip knew this was all meant to be comforting, and it was, but he didn't deserve David's comfort. When they sat together on a plush sofa by the window, he felt his breath hitch and stagger. A few of his tears fell.

Philip sniffed and shook his head. When he spoke, his voice cracked. "Do you think everything can be forgiven?"

David's eyebrows pulled together. "I don't think anyone is beyond saving." It wasn't exactly the answer to what Philip had asked, but it would do.

"Even if they don't repent?"

David swallowed. "Is this about Kam?"

The hot tears streaked Philip's cheeks before he could stop them. How could he answer that?

"It is. In a way." It was an answer that he wasn't happy with, but it was the truth at least.

"I thought he was getting better. He wanted to get off the drugs, didn't he?" David sounded confused.

"He is. He does."

"So what's the problem?"

Philip swallowed and wiped his eyes. "Kam..." His voice broke. He shook his head.

"Is it too much to say?" David asked. Philip nodded. David nodded in reply and patted Philip's shoulder. Philip didn't feel like he could explain his own role. What *he* had done. "We don't have to talk about it," David said. Philip nodded and took a sip of his tea. David followed suit, and after a beat, Philip rested his head on David's shoulder. David didn't stiffen or react, other than to squeeze Philip's shoulders. "It'll be alright, Philip. You'll see him through."

"I'm part of the problem," Philip managed, his head still leaning on David's shoulder. David raised an eyebrow. "A big part of the problem. Most of the problem."

David rubbed Philip's arm reassuringly. "It's not a problem," he said. "*You're* not a problem."

"You don't know—"

"I do," he replied pointedly. "At least, I think I do." He pulled away to look at Philip. "I never talked to you much about the relationship I had before I came here." Philip looked like he meant to interrupt, but David spoke too quickly. "I was with Ben. Benjamin. We were together for two years."

Philip quieted, his eyes going wide. His lips hung a little open. "But that's... But you..."

"I loved him." David was still sitting with his arm around Philip's shoulders. "Does that help?"

"How did you get into the program?" Philip's thoughts were racing.

"I was honest. The administrators and head of the program all know."

"But how's that possible?" Philip asked.

"They don't think acting on same-sex attraction is a sin. It's a different interpretation of the scripture. Didn't you notice they never preached against it here?"

A different interpretation of the scripture. The words reverberated in Philip's thoughts. He swallowed and laid his head on David's shoulder again. He felt tears of relief welling in his eyes.

It didn't absolve him of his panther problem, or of the fact that he was Kam's brother in the eyes of the law, but at least it offered him some reassurance that he might not go to Hell for daring to kiss Kam. Sleeping with him outside of marriage was still a problem, but he'd take one step at a time.

"Thank you, David, for telling me."

"You're welcome. I would have told you sooner, but it never felt like the right time."

"Your timing couldn't have been better."

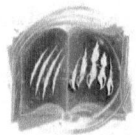

Philip stayed in the coffee shop talking with David for a couple of hours. When he got back to the dorm, he felt marginally better about some of his transgressions. The dorm room was empty when he got back. Philip smiled as he settled in. Kam had made the bed with a different blanket before he left. Philip gathered the clawed blanket and spread it on the floor beside the bed. He picked a flat sheet from the dresser and spread it over the blanket before he tossed his pillow on top of it.

When Kam got back from his meeting, Philip was lying on his makeshift pallet on the floor. Kam inclined his head and raised an eyebrow.

"What are you doing?"

"Laying in the bed I made," Philip replied, smiling up at Kam.

"*I* made *your* bed," Kam said, sitting on the edge of the mattress.

"Not until I get a handle on this."

Kam frowned. "You don't trust me to keep my hands to myself?"

Philip tried to keep his expression neutral, but after a moment, he was grinning. "I trust *you*. I'm the one with a problem."

"We did alright at home."

Philip's lips quirked into a smirk. "We *did*, but that was before you let me kiss you."

"So it's my fault?" Kam teased.

"Yes," Philip nodded. "But I don't mind."

Kam sighed and started unbuttoning his shirt. Philip closed his eyes and exhaled softly. When he reopened his eyes a few minutes later, Kam was peering down at him from the mattress. Philip smiled and sat up. He kissed Kam's cheek.

"I need to see what I can figure out. I don't want to have to kill someone every time we're together. But I'm feeling better than I did."

"Good."

24

CHAPTER 24

When Philip got out of his last class on Friday afternoon he headed straight for his room. He was eager to wash the last remnants of a challenging week off and curl into bed with one of the books he'd borrowed from the library. When he got back to the room he felt uneasy. Kam was sitting hunched over on the floor by the bed, and the room reeked of communion.

"Kam?" Philip said quietly after he dropped his bag to the floor.

Kam didn't look up from the bottle he held by the neck. His cheeks and eyes were red and puffy, and he replied with a muffled sob.

"What's wrong?" Philip fell to his knees in front of his brother and tenderly put a hand on his shoulder. "Did something happen?"

"I happened," Kam replied in a broken, sullen voice. He raised the near-empty bottle and took a swig.

Philip stroked his hand down Kam's shoulder. He rubbed down and then back up, giving Kam's shoulder a squeeze. Kam shook his head, though he didn't shrug away from the contact.

"I've ruined you, and staying sober was too hard, and even before that, I was never good enough. I've *never* been good enough, Philip."

Philip's eyebrows were at his hairline. "One thing at a time." He decided to start with the easiest thing to address first. "What do you mean you've never been good enough?"

"Don't play dumb. You know you've always been the good one, even though I was the oldest. I've never been anything but a disappointment."

Philip was quick to contradict. "You've always been there for me, and you've always been exactly what I needed you to be, even when I didn't know what I needed." Philip wanted to help Kam feel better, but his words were also true. Kam had never let him down in any meaningful way, not when it counted.

"See?" Kam snapped, his bleary eyes locked on Philip. "You think that because I ruined you."

"You didn't *ruin* me," Philip's tone was sharp. He was saying his for Kam, but also for himself.

"Of *course* I did. You were the good one. You're in seminary, for Christ's sake."

Philip inwardly cringed at the profanity, but he gave Kam's shoulder another squeeze.

"I'm *still* the religious one," Philip pointed out. "I didn't drop out of seminary for you, and you haven't asked me to."

"But I want to ask you to," Kam replied. He sounded overcome. "I still think you chose this because it's what *they* wanted. I don't think you ever had a chance to choose for yourself. I don't think you've *ever* chosen *anything* for yourself."

Philip sighed and shook his head. "You're wrong. I chose this. For me." His thoughts were swimming at the idea that Kam, steady Kam, wanted him to leave the program. He didn't have time to examine it. Kam was drunk and needed stabilizing. "And some part of you knows that, which is why you haven't asked me to leave."

"I *kissed* you. I corrupted you. You were *so good* Philip."

"I *wanted* you to kiss me."

"You didn't."

"I *did*." He bit his lower lip. "I chose *you*. I wanted a lot more than a kiss."

"Well, you got it."

"I did." A realization came with the words, and he spoke again before he could second-guess himself. "I don't regret it."

Kam scoffed.

"I don't. Not any of it. I like what we have. Even if it's complicated. Even if no one else understands it. They don't have to."

"Even if it sends you to Hell?"

That gave him pause. "Not everyone thinks it will."

"But what if they're wrong?"

"Then... yes." Philip took a deep, even breath. "Even if it sends me to Hell." His words were slow and steady, and his attention was focused on Kam.

Kam rolled his eyes and moved to take another drink from the bottle, but Philip stopped him with his free hand. Kam frowned, but didn't try again. "I'm not worth going to Hell for. I'm not worth *killing* for."

"You're allowed to be wrong about that," Philip replied. "Just like you're allowed to slip up while you're trying to get sober."

"*You* wouldn't slip up."

"We don't know that. I can't walk in your shoes."

"I *know* it," Kam insisted. "I don't think I can do this. *Any* of this. I'm not strong enough."

"You've been sober every day since you got here. Making one mistake doesn't mean you're a failure. You're human. You *can* do this."

"But it's not just one mistake, is it? I've taken what, fifty drinks from this bottle? That's fifty chances to do the right thing that I've gotten wrong. That's on top of having bought the bottle and brought it here." He sighed, defeated and heartbroken. "That's a lot of mistakes, Philip."

"And you'll probably make hundreds more." Philip decided to take a different tactic. "What's important is that you make more right choices than wrong ones. So you had wine today, fine. If that's all you have and you don't go get more, or go find something else, those are all steps in the right direction."

Kam snorted a laugh. "You're really going to argue that this," he waved the bottle between them, "doesn't matter?"

"It matters, but it isn't the *only* thing that matters. Making some bad choices doesn't mean you can't make good ones."

"*You* were a good one," Kam suggested suddenly, sitting the bottle down beside him on the floor. "You were maybe the best decision I ever made." Kam reached up to cup Philip's cheek instead of the wine. "You've always seen the best in me. *Always.*"

"You've always given me your best," Philip countered. Their eyes were locked together, saying more than either man could put into words. "This doesn't change anything, this is just a mistake. You're trying your best, and I know it's hard."

"It's the hardest thing I've ever done," Kam agreed, tears threatening to fall. "Well," he sniffled and seemed to consider, "maybe not the hardest."

Philip inclined his head. It sounded like Kam wanted to say more. "Oh?"

"The hardest thing was waiting as long as I did to kiss you." He stroked Philip's cheek with his thumb.

"Oh, yeah?" Philip couldn't help but smile. "When did you first want to kiss me?"

Kam dropped the hand from Philip's cheek back into his lap. He took a deep breath and sighed heavily. "It's hard to know the first time, exactly. It was like I woke up one day and you were *more*, and it felt like you always had been."

"What's your best guess, then?" Philip's curiosity had gotten the better of him, but he didn't blame himself.

"That night we snuck out to the neighbor's pool," Kam answered, finally. "The closest I got was telling you I was going to miss you."

Philip blinked. He'd had no idea his brother had felt the same way for so long. "So when we shared a bed on my visits home..."

Kam laughed darkly. "You weren't the only one suffering."

Philip grinned and Kam grinned back at him. "We can get through this," Philip started. "Together."

"Together," Kam repeated as he pushed the bottle aside.

25

CHAPTER 25

Philip woke up on his pallet on the floor at the end of May. The night before had been the last one he and Kam would spend in the dormitory for the academic year. They were slated to go to the train station with all of their clothes and belongings that afternoon so they could spend the summer at home with their parents. Kam stretched and peered over the edge of the bed at Philip on the floor. He leaned down, and Philip leaned up to meet him for a tender kiss good morning.

They had settled into a rhythm together. Philip slept on the floor most nights, but they had plans to share a bed again once they were back home. Philip was more confident that he could keep his libido in check when he had to worry about being overheard by their parents.

Kam had just earned his one-month chip. He was still going to meetings every week. He had recently picked up a job at a grocery store, stocking shelves, so he felt better about being able to contribute. It wasn't enough to live on, but it meant he could treat Philip to meals out every so often while still saving.

The plan had always been for Kam to get clean and independent, but once that happened, it seemed that neither of them were too keen on sending Kam away. Even if Philip was sleeping on the floor, they liked being together.

They shared a glance and a small smile before they got up and dressed. Once they were clothed Kam caught Philip by the hips from behind, hugging him to his chest. "Are you nervous?" he asked, lips close to Philip's ear.

Philip leaned his head back and Kam nuzzled his cheek. "I have faith we'll be fine."

"That's not what I asked," Kam teased.

Philip laid his hands on Kam's on his hips. "I'm nervous," he admitted. "But I'll be with you."

Kam grinned and kissed Philip's neck. "You'll be with me," he agreed.

Over the last few months, Philip had spent a solid portion of his free time in the library studying shapeshifter lore. He had also read his mother's journal cover to cover twice. He didn't feel like he was any closer to finding a solution to his panther problem, but he hoped that the Gardners had more of his mother's journals in the attic.

"We should get breakfast," Kam said.

"Early lunch?" Philip countered.

"*Fine*," Kam huffed, feigning exasperation. "You know if I keep letting you win all the time, they'll know something's up."

Philip turned to face Kam and put his hands on the older man's shoulders. "You *always* let me win," Philip objected. "Always. And you always did."

Kam rolled his eyes.

"Tell me I'm wrong," Philip teased, looking up at Kam through his eyelashes. Kam's lips twitched at the corners.

"I don't want to lie to you," Kam replied, his tone warm and affectionate. Philip grinned.

It was easy for Philip to forget how dangerous this was, how dangerous *he* was, when they were like this. When they were sweet and soft, Philip was tempted to pretend he was normal.

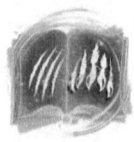

It all came crashing down when they got to the train station. There were police around and inside the station, and the sight of them didn't help Philip's nerves. Ever since his last transformation, there had been a heavier presence of police in the community. Philip knew there was no way the attacks could be tied back to him—he didn't even have a history with big cats the way his parents had—but it still made him feel uneasy every time he saw them sniffing around.

He glanced meaningfully at Kam, who offered him a reassuring smile. They didn't have long to linger at the station. Philip tried to slow his breathing and his racing heart as they waited. Philip pulled out a book that one of his professors had recommended, but his eyes couldn't stay trained on the page. Every few moments, he'd look up to see where the officers were positioned, and then he'd try to focus on the words in front of him once he knew where they were.

When Kam and Philip got on the train, he finally felt some relief. He and Kam got settled onto one of the main cars, and he watched out the window as the train pulled away from the police that were pacing over the platform. He took a deep breath and closed his eyes briefly, willing himself to calm down. They were on their way.

Of course, the closer the train got to home, the more nervous Philip became for *other* reasons. There wouldn't be police at home, but their parents posed a similar threat in his mind. He could tell from the way Kam was fidgeting on the seat beside him that he felt the same. Long swaths of time passed in silence. Philip resumed trying to read again. He'd look at the page, read a passage, and then look out the window. He'd look around the passenger car, people watching until he lost interest in the people around them. Then Kam would catch his eye with a fidget or by stretching his long legs. Occasionally, their eyes would meet, and they would share a small, intimate smile. Their bond was strong and true, and hadn't wavered.

It felt strange to call Kam his *brother*, given everything. Due to the violent transformations Philip underwent anytime he was too aroused, they weren't lovers, really. They had been for a blissful twenty-four hours, but as soon as they realized the risk, they'd cooled down.

But they had remained *something*, even if Philip couldn't put his finger on it. They were closer now than they ever had been. Philip shared his innermost thoughts with Kam, and Kam reciprocated. They were more affectionate now than they had ever been as siblings. In the privacy of the dorm room, they'd often snuggled together on the bed or held hands, or even stolen kisses.

In public, when they met up for coffee or went out for dinner, they were more distant. David had assured Philip that the professors and administrators would accept the same-sex nature of their attraction, so long as they didn't let it slip that they were technically brothers, but Philip still wasn't comfortable. He didn't know if he ever could be.

Kam didn't push. He never pushed. He always asked permission before he did anything he worried might upset Philip, or that might push him towards transformation.

"We can do this," Philip murmured quietly. Kam turned his head to study Philip for a moment.

"I know we can," he agreed. "Part of it is being nervous about Mother and Father. Part of it is being worried about being back in the town where I found my addiction."

Philip nodded. "I'm here for you. Mother and Father will be too. They know you've worked hard."

Kam nodded, and he looked meaningfully at Philip's hand. The younger man gave a slight nod of his head, and Kam took it. He intertwined their fingers, and Philip smiled at the warmth of it.

"I have been working hard. Three months is a long time when you're taking things day by day. I just want to stand on my own two feet without liquor or the pills," Kam said softly.

Philip rubbed his thumb over the back of Kam's thumb. Their eyes met again briefly and they shared another quiet smile. It hurt Philip to think that he'd be losing this if Kam stayed home in the fall.

Over the intercom, the conductor announced that their stop was next. Kam squeezed Philip's hand and then released it.

They didn't see their parents in the station. They followed the signs to the parking lot and spotted their car in short-term parking. Mother and Father had both come, and they were sitting in the front seats of the car. Father had driven, and Mother was watching the stream of passengers flowing out of the station. Her eyes lit up and her smile expanded as soon as she spotted her boys. She waved and said something to Father, and then they were both out of the car and heading toward them.

"Hey!" she called out, waving to them again. Kam and Philip folded her into a group hug. Father stood a few steps away, meeting the young men with a smile and a nod.

"Thank you for coming to get us," Philip said, his arms still swept around Mother's petite frame.

"Of course, boys," she replied, squeezing them both. "How was the train?"

"Long," Kam answered for them. "I feel like I could go straight to bed."

Mother smiled sympathetically. "We'll get you home and let you get some rest."

Philip was the first to withdraw from the hug, but when he pulled away, he was smiling back. "That sounds great."

"Come on then," Father piped in. "Let's get your suitcases loaded up." One went in the trunk, while the other was tethered to the rack on the roof, then the family loaded in. Kam and Philip took the back seat.

Mother kept them all engaged with friendly chat on the whole ride home. She had church gossip, news of volunteering project successes, and other odds and ends to share that didn't require much input from anyone else to keep the lively conversation going. By the time they pulled into the driveway, the brothers were ready to get upstairs and relax.

"Good night, boys," Mother called to them from the base of the stairs.

When they got into their bedroom, Philip was surprised at the sparse furniture for the second time. It had been that way before, but he hadn't expected it to *still* be. He raised his eyebrows and looked at Kam. "What happened to the furniture you took to your old place?"

Kam bit his lower lip. "I sold it, the whole bedroom suite. That was how I got my ticket to come stay with you." He grimaced. "I was in a really rough spot when I headed your way."

Philip put an arm around Kam's shoulders. "You're doing great now." Kam tilted his head to the side so he could lean his temple against Philip's shoulder.

"Thank you. For everything."

"You're welcome, Kam." Philip leaned in and kissed the top of Kam's head. "Let's get ready for bed." He was looking forward to getting to share a bed with Kam again. From the way Kam smiled at him when he straightened up, he could tell the feeling was mutual.

26

CHAPTER 26

Philip was back home for three weeks before he agreed to meet with Pastor Andrew. He saw him each week at services, and they had exchanged a few words about how he was doing and how he had found seminary to be.

"You should come see me," Andrew had encouraged before the end of every conversation. It made sense. He had been Philip's spiritual advisor and counselor for over a decade—it stood to reason that he would want to check in. That was what Philip kept telling himself. Kam tried to reassure him of the same, which was what ultimately got Philip to agree to the meeting.

"I'm worried," Philip told Kam. "I'm worried he'll know. Know I've changed. Know that I'm *trapped in the pit of sin.*"

Kam cocked his head to the side. "He's a pastor, not a wizard. You're being paranoid, Philip."

The retort made Philip laugh, but he had to admit Kam was right. There was no reason to think that Pastor Andrew would know things he shouldn't, or know things that Philip would rather keep secret.

When Kam dropped him off like he used to, he gave the Philip's hand a squeeze before he let him out of the car. It bolstered Philip's confidence before he rapped on the pastor's office door.

"Come in," Pastor Andrew called.

Philip's hands were in his pockets as he crossed the threshold. He was suddenly a frightened little boy again. He lingered in the doorway until Andrew looked up and acknowledged him.

"Philip," he greeted warmly. "Please come in and have a seat. It's so good to see you."

Philip smiled. "It's good to see you, too." He could tell that despite his best efforts, his expression was strained. He took a seat in the chair he was offered. When Andrew met his eyes, Philip tried not to wilt under the intensity of the pastor's attention.

"Well, tell me everything," Andrew said, beaming. "How have your classes been? How have you been keeping busy?"

Philip spoke fondly of his studies, becoming a runner, volunteering, and making friends with David and the other members of his cohort. He felt himself loosening up as he talked. All the while, Pastor Andrew smiled at him and nodded along. It was perhaps the friendliness that put Philip at ease. He was caught off guard when Andrew spoke again.

"Have you kept out of trouble?" It was a simple question. It was probably meant as an *innocent* question. Philip forced a smile across his lips that didn't reach his eyes before he answered.

He even made a noise that he thought sounded like a laugh to seal it. "Of course."

Pastor Andrew smiled, but his smile didn't reach his eyes, either.

"You've had a hard job," he said. "Being your brother's keeper... that's a difficult path to walk."

Philip's smile flickered but didn't fully falter. *Of course* their parents had spoken to the pastor about Kam.

"It's not so bad. He's been the one doing the work."

"As it should be," Andrew said firmly. "He is the one who strayed. He's the one who needs to repent."

Philip narrowed his gaze at Andrew. The pastor raised his eyebrows and his hands as if to calm Philip. "He's working *hard*," Philip said with an edge to his voice. He had always been protective of Kam, but the cat wouldn't let him shrink away this time.

"Of course he is," Andrew replied, his tone soft. "I didn't mean to imply he wasn't."

Philip's jaw was tight. He didn't believe that for a second.

"What's on your mind, Philip?" the pastor asked, his head shifting to the side so that he could study the younger man. "Something seems to be troubling you. If it's not Kam, what are you thinking?"

Philip swallowed. Something *was* on his mind. Several things. But just because Andrew could tell he was thinking something didn't mean he was a safe outlet for those thoughts. Philip averted his gaze from Andrew's eyes to the corner of the ornate desk he sat behind. He tried to think of an approximation of the truth that he could share.

"Someone in my program..." he began. "He's..." Philip struggled to string the words together. "He has a boyfriend," he finished.

Andrew's eyebrows knitted together. "And they *let* him?" Andrew asked, surprised but also irritated. His expression had contorted into something between shock and disgust. "What do your instructors say?"

Philip hoped he looked conflicted. "Nothing, really."

Andrew's lips drew tightly together. "No wonder you're troubled," Andrew said. "Have you or your peers tried to minister to him?"

"He knows the scripture as well as we do," Philip replied. That was the truth, at least.

"That's terrible, Philip," he scowled. "How are you and the other young men in your program supposed to find your spiritual footing with such an overt sinner in your midst?"

Philip bit his lips between his teeth and shook his head, his eyes wide. He could only watch as Andrew worked himself up into a lather of frustration, rifling through papers in the filing cabinet drawer in his desk. After a few moments, he produced several pamphlets about the dangers of homosexuality. When he passed them to Philip across the table, Andrew shook his head.

"I'm sorry, Philip. I feel at least partially responsible for your decision to apply to that school. If I had known..." He shook his head. "It must be so confusing for you to see one of your peers choosing such a sacrilegious life."

Philip took the fliers and nodded. It was all he felt like he could do. It at least settled the question of what Andrew thought of people like him. Philip was disappointed, but wasn't surprised.

"I'll see what else I can put together for you. I'll give you something you can take for yourself and your peers."

Philip nodded again. He forced another unconvincing smile to his lips. "Thank you."

"You're welcome, Philip. I want to see you succeed, and I don't want one wayward young man to poison your future."

Philip felt numb by the time he got back into the car with Kam. He dropped the papers on the dash and heaved a sigh.

"You okay?" Kam asked, studying Philip. The younger man shook his head.

"No. I told Pastor Andrew I knew a gay person," Philip said, gesturing to the papers.

"Why'd you say that? You *know* I'm bisexual," Kam teased.

Philip snorted a laugh. "I didn't mean *you*."

"Well, you can't have said it was *you* or you'd still be in there praying for forgiveness."

Philip rolled his eyes. "I didn't mean *me*, either." Well, he did, but David was an easier scapegoat. "He had... a lot of thoughts."

"Of course he did." Kam huffed as he pulled onto the road. "Don't look at that garbage. You don't need to fill your mind with that trash."

"But I should know what some people think."

"You *know* what they think," Kam replied, his tone firm. "Promise me you won't read that stuff." Kam dropped his right hand onto Philip's thigh, his eyes on traffic. "Don't let them get in your head."

Philip looked at Kam's profile as he drove. His jaw was tight.

"I'm not," Philip replied. He closed his hand over Kam's on his leg. "I'm not," he repeated.

When they got home, Kam gathered the brochures from the dashboard and gave Philip a pointed look as he threw them into the outdoor trash cans. "You don't need to see that shit," Kam said decisively.

"I know," Philip agreed. He bit his lower lip and looked up at Kam. "You're right."

"I know," Kam echoed back to him.

Still, Philip felt uneasy.

Once they were inside, Philip felt his discomfort growing. Mother was away at a women's group meeting and Father was working late, so he seized the opportunity to call David. He got his address book from their bedroom and brought it down to the phone in the living room. Nerves fluttered in Philip's stomach as the phone rang.

Philip smiled so he'd sound more friendly. "Hello. Is David home?"

"Yes, one moment." After a few minutes, there was a rustling again, and then a familiar voice.

"Hello?"

"David!" Philip said, excited. "It's good to hear you! Was that your grandpa?"

"Yeah. It's nice to hear from you. Do you miss me already?"

"Of course," Philip replied with a laugh. "But that's not why I'm calling."

"You're sweet," David chuckled. "What's on your mind?" That was the second time Philip had been asked that over the course of the evening, but this time was less antagonistic than the last.

"I told my pastor, the one I grew up with, about... well, you."

"Oh?" David asked. "I don't suppose that went well."

Philip barked a laugh.

David chuckled again. "You *did* say he was traditional." That was one way to put it. "Are you okay?"

"I'll be fine. Kam threw away the pamphlets he gave me before I could look at them."

David huffed a laugh. "Kam's a wise man."

"How do you do it? How do you handle knowing people hate you?"

David sighed quietly into the receiver. "I remember that it's a problem with them more than with me, and I don't engage with people who feel that way unless I don't have a choice. Remember, everyone in our program—the administrators and instructors—they all accept us."

Philip swallowed at the *us*. David accepted him, too. That was something. "Does it get easier?"

"It does. The more comfortable you get with yourself, the harder it will be for someone else to shake you."

That sounded nice. Philip glanced up when he heard a floorboard creak across the room. Kam was smiling at him, and he couldn't help but smile back. Looking at him, he could believe that things would get better.

"You're the best, David."

"I know," David teased. "You have to go?"

"Yeah," Philip confirmed. "Don't be a stranger."

"You, either."

When Philip hung up the phone, Kam sat on the couch beside him. Philip smiled at him, and Kam leaned in and kissed his neck. Philip inclined his head to the side, exposing more of his skin so Kam had more space to reach. Kam chuckled against his throat, leaning further on his arms so he could reach more easily.

"Brazen," Philip flirted.

"No one's home," Kam murmured. "Besides, we can only go so far." Philip felt a pang of guilt. His face fell, and Kam nipped at his throat with his teeth. "None of that, hon."

"None of what?" He asked, as if he didn't know.

"I. Regret. Nothing," Kam said, punctuating each word with a light bite of Philip's neck. Philip laughed, delighted.

"You're ridiculous."

"Mm-hmm," Kam agreed, sitting up so he could kiss Philip on the lips. Philip brought his hand up behind Kam's head to hold him close. Kam's hair was on the longer side again, and Philip let his fingers tangle between the strands.

Philip was the one to deepen the kiss, and Kam moved so he was more in Philip's lap. The younger man groaned softly into Kam's mouth. They continued for several minutes before Philip pulled back.

"Need to stop?" Kam asked, his eyes wide and hungry. Philip swallowed and nodded, and Kam drew back until he was sitting beside Philip on the sofa again. Philip leaned onto Kam's shoulder and nuzzled it. Kam smiled and gave Philip's hair a fond stroke.

"No regrets?" Philip asked softly.

"None," Kam confirmed, kissing Philip's head tenderly. They stayed like that until they heard their father pull up.

27

CHAPTER 27

Philip was on a mission to see if there were more of his mother's journals in storage. To be thorough, he searched the downstairs, including Father's office, and didn't find anything. That meant the last place he had to look was the attic.

After breakfast, he and Kam headed up the rickety ladder to see what they could find.

"Do you want to open the boxes up here?" Kam asked, peering around the dim space. Philip nodded and passed him a flashlight.

"Yeah, otherwise, we'll have to lug them all down, even the ones we don't want. Just look for any journals or notebooks."

Kam took the flashlight and got to work. Philip used his light to examine boxes on the other side of the room. They both looked through box after box. Nothing in the attic was labeled. They found boxes of Christmas decorations, old sports equipment, and even their parents' old yearbooks. After a few boxes each, Philip was feeling anxious. He was worried that they would go through all of the things in storage and wouldn't find any more journals. When Philip opened another box and found relics of the family's ill-advised croquet summer he heaved an exaggerated sigh. Maybe this was a mistake.

A few moments later Philip peered around Kam and he sighed with relief, instead. He saw the spines of journals and photo albums in the box Kam had just opened. Philip picked up the nearest notebook and flipped it open. His smile broadened when he saw his mother's dainty handwriting.

"Can you take those downstairs?"

Later that day, Kam dropped Philip off at the library with two journals and a notebook under his arm. Philip aimed to see what other materials their local library had on werewolves and the like. It was sure to be different from what he'd read in the library at school.

It was Saturday, so the library was a little crowded, but he still found a seat at a table that was far enough from where children had gathered for story time. He settled in with the journals first. There was a line waiting at the desk for librarian help, and he didn't want an audience when he made his odd research request. He opened the first journal and began to read, but he kept an eye on the librarian.

It took an hour, but once the desk was clear, Philip approached with more than mild apprehension. His librarian at college had assured him that all libraries should have someone familiar with the odd and macabre on staff, but what if this was the exception? He was desperate to learn anything that could help him with his condition. He didn't want to have to wait until the fall to resume his investigation.

Philip's back was straight and his smile was forced as he greeted the young woman behind the desk. "Hello," he chirped, doing his best impression of a normal person with a normal reason to use the library. "I'm hoping you can point me in the direction of books or materials that will help me with a research project."

The woman smiled up at him, her dark, natural curls bobbing when she nodded. "Of course. What are you looking for?"

Hope. *A cure.* A reason to keep going.

All answers he couldn't speak aloud.

"Books about shapeshifters. Werewolves. That sort of thing." The woman—Harriet, judging by her name tag—furrowed her brow. Philip was tempted to apologize for the strangeness of his request, but she cut him off before he could.

"Fiction or folklore?" Philip realized he had misinterpreted her expression as frustration when it was concentration instead.

"Folklore, if you have it," he answered. "Do you have much?"

Harriet smiled, her brown eyes light. "We do! If you don't have a specific region in mind, you might focus on Louisiana."

Philip cocked his head to the side as she typed something into the computer beside her. "Oh?"

She jotted down a few things on the pad in front of her and then got to her feet. "Follow me, please." She went around the desk and led Philip to the stacks. "The stories from that region are remarkably consistent. We don't have a lot of the collection here, but we have an interlibrary loan system with a few of the local universities. There was a professor at one of them that studied the roles of cryptids and loup-garou myths in the context of the societies they originated from. I audited a few of his courses. It was really interesting stuff. He actually retired to New Orleans."

Philip nodded. It was as good an angle as any, and narrowing his focus might help to make his research less overwhelming. "That's very interesting."

"Isn't it?" she asked, handing him two of the books she had collected. "See if those will get you what you need." Then she handed him her neat, handwritten note. "If not, you can try the others on this list. I can also let you know what we can get from the other libraries, if you end up needing them."

Philip smiled at her, genuinely this time. "Thank you, Harriet. You've been a big help." He took the books she gave him and her list back to his table. Harriet returned to her desk just in time to help another patron.

I have to figure this out, Philip thought. He couldn't spend his life afraid to experience pleasure out of fear of the consequences.

Philip settled in and began reading as much as he could about the loup-garou. After couple of hours, Kam returned to keep him company. Philip decided then to switch back to the journals they had found in the attic. He read Kam an entry in a hushed whisper so as not to disturb the other patrons.

"Dear Journal,

Philip made his performance debut! He's a natural. I've never seen someone as comfortable in front of a crowd as he was. I couldn't believe it.

He's nine and so he's much too young to be a part of *our* show, but Martha made him a cute little outfit out of some scraps. John and Willy thought it would be fun to add a little juggler to the clown act. I asked Philip if he wanted to give it a try, and he said sure. He's the bravest little thing.

He marched right out to the center ring and started juggling by himself as more and more clowns funneled in, and then he was tandem juggling with John, and I couldn't stop smiling.

He did so well! I'm so proud of my little guy."

When Philip finished reading the entry aloud Kam cocked his head to the side.

"Can you still juggle?" He whispered.

"I don't know," Philip answered honestly.

"We'll have to give it a try when we get home."

Philip turned the page and started reading the next entry.

. . .

"Dear Journal,

Date night was *magnificent*. Our best in a long while. We found this terrible little hole in the wall biker bar a few miles away from the fairgrounds. It was wall to wall with big, muscular guys. There were a couple of girls, but they were all wrapped up in their husbands or boyfriends and didn't want to play.

Nate had the idea that I should try to get the attention of a couple of the guys who were playing pool, because he's a genius. I sidled up to a couple of rough-looking types and asked if I could join their game. Nate was watching me from the bar, nursing a beer. They let me play with them, and I flirted a little bit with both of them. I had them show me how to shoot a couple of trick shots—you know the routine.

These guys started getting really friendly. They were the type that liked any kind of female attention. The taller one asked about why I wasn't with Nate. I told them that he didn't mind sharing, and that he liked to watch me having fun. It was then that he sent the waitress over with a round of beers for the three of us. His timing was perfect. That got them excited, which I hoped it would.

The fellas started getting a little more bold, a little more handsy, and I was doing my best to brush up against them every chance I got. Finally I told them that I wanted to get out of there, and I asked if they lived nearby. It turned out they were roommates and lived a few blocks from that bar in the middle of nowhere. They had walked over, so me and Nate left with them on foot. I was flirting up a storm and taking turns kissing them, and by the time we got to their place, they were half ready to go.

We go to the tall one's room and they brought in a chair for Nate, and it's all I can do to not laugh at loud at how perfect it was. I held it together, though, and then me and these two guys started putting on a *show*. I almost hated to kill them. They really knew how to treat a girl. To tell you the truth, I don't think this was the first time they played together. They didn't touch each other, but I've got a sixth sense about these things.

So before too long, they filled me up from both ends, and I can tell Nate has almost creamed his pants just from the watching."

Philip scowled and exhaled sharply. He felt deeply uncomfortable, and it wasn't lessened when he raised his attention from the journal to the wide-eyed look Kam was giving him. His jaw was tight when he spoke. "What?

"She didn't hold anything back, your mother."

"I guess she never thought anyone would read these..." Philip muttered.

Kam raised his eyebrows in a challenge. "Or she wanted them to."

Philip drew back, his expression as mask of horror. "What?"

Kam's expression shifted into something more sympathetic. "Would you really be surprised to learn that your circus-performer parents were exhibitionists?"

Philip's whole face went red and he closed his eyes, as if not seeing Kam could quell his second-hand shame.

"Come on," Kam coaxed. "Please don't leave us on your Dad creaming his pants."

"*Almost*," Philip corrected. He still looked miserable and flushed, but he continued.

"Practically before the shorter one pulled out, Nate was on him. His claws cut right through all that muscle, and blood was spraying everywhere. The tall one screamed as Nate started chowing down on his friend. He grabbed me and we ran out into the living room. I think he meant to take me somewhere else, like maybe his buddy's room, but we didn't make it that far. I got him so good he just about split in two.

I can't remember a time when I've had so *much fun*! There was a couple down in Jacksonville, those girls we shared down in Savannah, and then the brothers in St. Louis – but this had all those times beat. I enjoyed every part of it. Plus, once we got home, Nate had to stake his claim, if you know what I mean. I told him I didn't want to wait so long before we hunt together again."

"Your mom was *wild*," Kam whispered when Philip paused at the end of the story. "Your dad, too."

"When I was skimming the journals when I got here, I saw at least a dozen entries like that. They liked having sex with strangers and murdering them."

"Hell of a hobby."

That got a chuckle out of Philip. He was still pink in the cheeks and ears, but talking through the entries with Kam made the pill easier to swallow. He turned the page and read on.

"Dear Journal,

Nate is nervous. I am too, but he's taking it much more seriously than I am. We're still in that small town just outside of Baton Rouge where we had our last date night. The cops came sniffing around the last night of our run, and aren't letting us leave for our next stop. They interviewed everyone, but they were especially eager to talk to Nate and me because of the big cats. They told the boss that they were investigating an animal attack, but they never gave us any particulars. We know they had to be checking into the bikers, though.

When we were interviewed, they took us in, separately. We both admitted we went to the bar. Better to admit as much of the truth as you can than get caught in a lie that's easy to disprove.

This was the second time in three months that cops have come calling. They asked the boss about where we were last and where we were headed next. Nate doesn't like how suspicious they were, but like I told him they can't prove anything. Even if they locked us up, they couldn't make us change.

Besides, that's why we don't have date nights at every stop anymore. We have been careful. We only go out every two or three months. There are usually at least six towns in between one kill and the next. Nate still isn't buying it, though. He wants to stop hunting.

Stop hunting.

Can you imagine?

I can't let that happen. I'd rather die than give up our life together, or end up in a cage.

We have a plan, though. Until we get out of town, there'll be cops camped out watching for big cats where they shouldn't be—like nobody would have noticed them getting out and wandering into town."

"What do you think the plan was?" Kam asked.

"Well, it wasn't much longer after this that they..." Philip trailed off and cleared his throat. "They didn't live much longer after that."

"Jesus," Kam muttered with a frown.

Philip shot him a disapproving look, though it was more a habit than any real displeasure at the swearing.

"I'm just saying, you've gotta really love murder-hookups if you'd rather kill yourself than give them up."

"Especially if you're willing to leave two children behind with nowhere to go." Philip grumbled before he continued reading.

"Dear Journal,

We're back in New Orleans. Every time we come back, I'm amazed by how much it still feels like home. No matter what changes, a lot is always still the same. We took the kids to see the neighborhoods we grew up in. New families have moved into our old houses, but it was good to show them the streets, anyway.

Nate is nervous about the plan, but he doesn't want to go on without me. I told him he can go first. It'll be better this way. We can't spend the rest of our lives on the run or in a cage. The kids are strong. They'll be fine."

At that line, Philip snapped the book shut with the bookmark abandoned on the desk.

"I can't believe she thought *death* was better. That she chose to end it all rather than be there for me and Melissa."

Kam draped his arm around Philip's shoulders and rested his chin on top of his head.

"If they hadn't been so selfish, we would have never met."

Philip opened and closed his mouth several times. He wanted to reply, but his words escaped him. Although he would have preferred not to lose his sister, he couldn't imagine giving up Kam.

"You're right," was what he settled on.

"I'm sorry, though. This has to be hard to hear."

"And that's the last entry in that book. She could have left something for us, a note or an apology, but she didn't. Just these messed-up journals."

"Considering what her journals were like, it might be for the best that she didn't try to leave you anything."

Philip nodded. "You're right."

"Of course I'm right. How about we take a break from all this?" Kam gave Philip's shoulders a squeeze, his arm still curled around him. "I think you've learned all you can for one day."

28

CHAPTER 28

At the end of August, Philip packed up his belongings and planned to head back to seminary. He felt a tightness in his chest every time he actively thought about returning without Kam. While they were staying with their parents, Kam had gotten a summer job, and he didn't want to abandon it. It wasn't a career by any means—as their parents liked to remind him—but it was stable, and Kam wasn't in a position to introduce any more gaps in his employment history.

Philip scheduled leaving in the evening so Kam could be the one to take him to the train station. They were quiet in the car. Kam stroked Philip's thumb with his the whole drive long. As they came to a stop outside the station, Philip looked at Kam in the dark. The corners of his lips twitched into a small, fond smile.

"Thanks for the lift," Philip said quietly.

"Anytime," Kam replied. He was still holding Philip's hand.

"You're going to miss me," Philip teased. "I can't run interference with Mother and Father anymore."

"But you'll call," Kam countered, "and I can write. It'll give you something other than your folklore books and the Bible to read."

"I'd like that." The words *I'll miss you* were on the tip of his tongue, but he couldn't quite get them out. With all they had shared and all he trusted Kam with, the admission still felt too vulnerable. Instead, he took a breath and tugged his hand back. "I'd better get going," was what he said, instead.

Kam nodded, and they both got out of the car. Philip unloaded his massive suitcase from the trunk and grabbed his backpack and duffel out of the back seat. He slipped the backpack on and set the duffel on the suitcase so that he could face Kam unencumbered. He held his arms out, and the taller man swept him into a hug. His palm rested on the back of Philip's head, his fingers tangling softly in his dark hair. They stood there for a moment in silence before they separated.

"Be safe," Kam murmured, his voice a little raw.

"I will. Keep up with your meetings."

Kam produced his chip key chain, he hadn't faltered again. "I will," he assured him.

Philip smiled and slung the long duffel strap over his shoulder. "I'll call you when I get in."

Kam nodded. Their eyes met and lingered for a moment before Philip cleared his throat. "I'll see you."

"See you," Kam echoed, giving Philip a wave.

When he was on the train and settled, Philip had to blink back tears that stung his eyes.

Settling back into his old routine, the one he'd had before Kam came to stay, was difficult. Philip spent more and more time in the lounge with David and the others because his room felt far too empty, now that he was alone.

Philip shifted to volunteering at the soup kitchen two nights a week plus Saturdays, just to keep his loneliness at bay. David went with him sometimes, but more often than not, he just worked with the other volunteers. He was on a first-name basis with several of the patrons, and it did his heart good to see them week after week.

They celebrated birthdays and new jobs, and some of the children shared when they got good grades on especially hard projects. The sense of community Philip felt was strong and brought light into his life, but something was missing. The highlights of his days were the nightly phone calls he shared with Kam.

The calls were mundane. Kam would talk about something funny that happened at work or some exchange he'd had with their parents. Occasionally, he would share something that had happened at church since he'd resumed going with them while under their roof, and Philip would feel swept up again, as if he was right back at home.

Sometimes they ran out of things to say and they would just sit in silence together, content to tie up the phone line.

It was Kam that broke first. They were a week out from Thanksgiving, sitting and listening to each other breathe without anything meaningful to say when he finally said what they both were thinking.

"I miss you," he said quietly. "It's hard to be here without you."

"It's hard to be *anywhere* without you," Philip countered. He wet his lips with his tongue. "I know I'll be home soon for Thanksgiving and then for Christmas. Do you think work would give you some time off?"

Kam exhaled sharply. When he spoke again, Philip could nearly hear the relief in his voice. "Yeah. I think I could swing that."

"Could you come back here?" Philip heard Kam take a deep breath again.

"Yeah. I think I can do that. At least for a little while."

Philip's cheeks hurt from his smile. Kam was coming to see him, coming to stay. It would be after the holidays, and therefore after exams, so he'd actually be able to spend some time with him.

"Philip?" Kam's voice on the phone jolted him back to the present. "Are you still there?"

"Yeah," Philip replied, a little dazed from the power of his daydreaming. "Just imagining you getting to visit again."

"Think you'll sleep in bed this time?" Kam was teasing, but Philip gave it some thought.

"Maybe," he answered finally.

"I'd like it if you did," Kam said quietly. Philip couldn't help but smile as he toyed with the spiraling phone cord between his fingers.

"I would too, but I need to be safe."

"I know," Kam was quick to say. "And I want you to be safe. I do. I just... got used to you." They both had. When they were at their parents', the threat of being overheard or discovered kept them out of trouble. Sharing a bed had been nice, and thinking about it now put a lump in Philip's throat.

"I know," Philip replied quietly. "I got used to you, too."

There was so much they weren't saying, that they didn't dare admit to each other. Philip knew he lusted after Kam, and was lusting after him now. As they sat on the phone after more than two months apart, just talking about how they missed one another, he knew it was much more than that.

A small part of Philip had worried their closeness and connection had something to do with Kam's sobriety, that he had just been chasing novelty and sensation after giving up some of his vices. But that wasn't it. That *couldn't* be it. Even after they realized Philip couldn't be intimate, Kam hadn't backed down or pushed him away.

Even now, when they were apart, Kam hadn't wavered. That gave Philip hope that it wasn't only on his side.

Kam *missed him.*

Becca knocked on the door frame. Philip smiled at her. "Need the phone?" he asked.

"Please. It's my niece's birthday."

Philip nodded. "Hey Kam, I have to get going."

"I heard." His voice was honeyed when he replied. "Have a good night, Philip. And remember. Just a few more days until you're home again."

The thought kept Philip warm his whole walk back.

29

CHAPTER 29

One of the books about loup-garous Philip read in the library on his Thanksgiving visit featured two spells, two rituals practiced by medicine men and women. They claimed the rituals suppressed transformations of the creatures. Although Philip knew witchcraft was explicitly forbidden in the Bible, he found his thoughts frequently returned to the passages he'd read. He had hoped there might be a way to control the transformations, but he hadn't anticipated it being witchcraft, even though his mother had suggested as much in his dream. The idea that he could indulge with Kam and not shift shapes was too alluring a prospect to ignore.

As he sat at the desk in their bedroom, he wrote out his thoughts. He believed he was driven by the power of God moving through him, even when he did things God would disapprove of. God's power allowed many impossible things like speaking in tongues, healing like had happened to David, and prophecy. The thought of *prophecy* gave him some pause. The books Father had sent were all about the gift of prophecy, and yet the Bible explicitly forbade divination and mediums.

He wondered if perhaps the intention behind the act could render deviant acts godly. As he wrote the sentiment down, he found that it resonated more strongly. Prophecy and prophetic dreams could be holy when the prophet acted as a conduit through which God could work on Earth. Surely Philip could do the same to inhibit his transformations?

He thought back to sermons Pastor Andrew had delivered when he was a boy. He had spoken of normal, everyday people who had been blessed with the ability to hear God and sense spirits. Those gifts were divine, but sounded pagan to a secular world.

If the Pentecost could take place daily, then surely Philip's work to retain his human shape, made in God's own image, could be a holy practice. He pulled out the photocopy he had made of the first spell and studied it carefully. The first paragraph extolled the virtues of setting intentions which would be carried through the ritual.

Retain human form. Philip wrote the words on the page in front of him three times. It reminded him of the time he had sat down at this very desk and wrote his intentions to rebuke the demons of lust and self-indulgence. He wrote the words a few times more and then read the ingredients he'd need for the spell.

Most of this should be easy to find, he thought. In fact, the majority of the items were herbs Mother kept around the kitchen, and white candles, which they always kept on hand in case of power outages. Philip continued examining the photocopied page. It had everything he'd need to perform his devout version of the ritual. He closed the notebook on the written invocation when he heard Kam opening the door.

Philip believed he had found a way to use the spell without compromising his values, but he wasn't prepared to defend the idea to his brother.

Two evenings later, the last night before he'd head back to seminary, Philip cleared off the desk except for the spell and the ingredients he had collected so he could begin his work. Mother and Father were both out at a church event and Kam had gone to a meeting, so Philip knew he'd have the house to himself. Still, there was no time to lose.

He surveyed his collected supplies. He had a short candlestick, a holder, and a pocketknife, which he had stored in a sandwich bag of salt. The salt was to purify and charge the items in accordance with the ritual's instructions. He'd pilfered a collection of herbs and a small bottle of olive oil from the kitchen.

Finally, he felt ready to start. He pulled out the blade on the tiny pocketknife, and he picked up the candle. Holding both, he tried to clear his mind of any ideas. He focused on his breathing. For several moments he stood there, emptying his tangled thoughts. When his mind was vacant, he turned his attention to the task at hand. *Retain human form,* he thought. He repeated the sentiment several times to himself in his mind and aloud. He kept repeating the short sentence as he began to visualize himself staying human. He imagined every inch of his body, from the soles of his feet to the top of his head keeping human shape and retaining their structure. As he visualized, he began to carve sigils from the ritual instructions into the candle.

Norse runes had nothing on the intricate patterns he tried to replicate with the tip of the small blade. Philip wasn't an artist or a master carver by any stretch of the imagination, but he tried his best with each of the shapes he commanded to the wax. *Retain human shape, retain human shape, retain human shape...* With every new line, he repeated his intention until his body was humming with it. Philip was encouraged that the sensation felt a lot like the way he felt during a rousing hymn or inspiring Bible study. He believed the Holy Spirit was with him as he put the blade down and opened the olive oil.

Philip spread some of the oil across his fingertips. Then, as the spell directed, he rubbed his fingers over the candle from just below the wick to the base. He stroked each sigil in the order they would burn from the top of the candle to the bottom. Once the candle was fully anointed, he wiped his fingers on the rag he'd hung on the back of the desk chair.

He took a pinch from the first jar and sprinkled it down the length of the candle as he rotated it slowly. With every quarter turn, he repeated the mantra *retain human shape.* Once the spice was applied, he took a pinch of the second. Philip replicated the step for each of the four remaining herbs. When that was done, he placed the candle into its stand.

He wiped his fingers on the rag once more and then pulled a lighter out of his pocket. He flicked the flame to life and lowered it to the wick. It was critical, the spell said, for the candle to light the first time the flame touched it, so he held the lighter to the wick until it burned full and bright.

"Retain human shape," he murmured aloud as he laid the lighter on the desk.

The candle flame burned strong and true, which was a good sign, according to the book. Philip's hazel eyes bored into the flame, unblinking, as he muttered the mantra again and again out loud. When the candle burned down past the first sigil, he shifted to thinking the words over and over. He kept his silent meditation over the candle until wax welled on the plate base of the holder. An hour passed, and his mind and body sang with warm vibrations from his casting.

When the candle was nearly ready to burn out, Philip snuffed it out with a thimble, which ended the ritual. When he placed the thimble on the desk, the smoke from the wick spiraled up into the air over his head. The smoke was black, far darker than he would have expected. It was the one thing that gave him pause. Where the mantra had been, a verse appeared in his mind: *He did much evil in the eyes of the Lord, arousing his anger.*

Yet, as Philip cleaned up the evidence of the spell, he didn't feel God's anger. He only felt the warm glow of the words *retain human shape,* which had carved a place in his mind and his heart.

When the desk was clear, Philip knelt by the side of the bed and began to pray.

Kam arrived home shortly after Philip climbed off the floor. Kam greeted Philip with a smile, and when he began to undress for bed, Philip got up to meet him. He approached Kam from behind and curled his arms around to stroke up his chest.

Kam turned in Philip's grip. "Hi," he said before he kissed Philip.

"I want you," Philip murmured quietly when their lips parted.

"But we're at home," Kam countered.

"I don't care."

Kam didn't require further encouragement. He slipped out of his trousers, and Philip did the same before they met again for a heated kiss. Kam guided Philip to the bed and pulled him close. The warmth which had lingered on Philip's skin after the ritual became fiery under Kam's touch. Before long, Kam was stroking them both in one of his large hands.

Philip moaned into Kam's lips as his hands roamed over Kam's stomach. "You want to touch me?" Kam asked.

Philip whispered a breathless, "Yes."

Kam moved his hand so he was only rubbing Philip. When Philip's palm glanced across Kam's head, it was leaking pre-cum already, slicking his shaft as Philip worked Kam eagerly. Kam stifled one of his own groans by capturing Philip's tongue in another searing kiss.

"Close," Philip managed to whimper. He was enjoying himself too much to be embarrassed. Kam picked up his pace and Philip hissed his approval.

"Come on me," Kam instructed, laying on his back on the bed without losing any speed.

"What?" Philip was startled from his enjoyment.

"Give me all your cum," Kam growled. "Paint my belly. *Claim me*." Kam's breathing was ragged. "I want it. *Please*." It was the way Kam's growl descended into broken begging that sent Philip past the point of no return. His hand on Kam stuttered to a stop as he covered Kam's torso. "Fuck, Philip," Kam rumbled. "Don't stop."

Philip's hand jolted back to life and Kam grunted his approval. "Yes, yes, *yes* Philip. Oh *fuck* yes." Kam's teeth dug into his lower lip and his eyes rolled before he closed them.

"Tell me when you're close," Philip said.

"I'm close. *I'm close.* I'm so fucking close, honey." Kam whined. "Make me come all over myself. I want to make a mess. Make me a mess for you."

If he hadn't just climaxed, the words would have spurred Philip's cock to attention. As it was, he only groaned and sped up. Kam whimpered softly.

"That's it. Fuck, Philip." Kam whined. "Yes, *yes*..." His cries faded into unintelligible noises as he shot cum all the way up to his collarbone and sternum, though the majority pooled with Philip's on his belly.

When he finally finished, he pulled Philip down into a kiss. "That was so good," he whispered, breathless.

"Yeah," Philip agreed, nearly speechless.

Kam looked down at the mess they had made and grinned. "That was just what I wanted."

Philip eyed the cum on Kam's torso suspiciously. "Was it?"

Kim smirked and dipped his finger into the puddle of spend that had gathered. He brought it to his lips and flicked his tongue out to lick it. "Yes," he confirmed. "You taste so good, and you made such a mess of me."

Philip's cock twitched at the sight and the words, and he shifted position. "I liked that."

Kam laughed. "Me, too."

Philip leaned over the edge of the bed and picked up his abandoned pajama bottoms. He offered them to Kam. "Here."

Kam took the pants and wiped himself off. "I'm going to take a quick shower before our parents get home."

Philip opened his eyes and looked at the clock. It was 4:30 a.m., and he'd woken feeling agitated. As he climbed naked out of bed and headed toward the bedroom door, he growled under his breath. The change had taken longer to manifest after the ritual, but it was still coming.

He made it down the stairs and to the front door before the transformation started. It felt like his chest meant to split in two when his flesh tore and fur sprouted through the wounds. As he left the house, black-furred cat flesh spread outward from that central point on his body until he was fully covered and crawling on four feline feet.

It was still dark on the streets of his neighborhood. It would be harder to find prey in the suburbs than it had been in the city, but he wasn't worried. He flicked his long, feline tongue across pointed teeth.

When the stalking cat hadn't found someone to bring down by 6:30 a.m., Philip began to feel antsy. This was the longest he had been in his feline form. In two hours, he had trekked across town to a campground, and he was relieved when he saw a series of tents. The holiday hadn't discouraged outdoor enthusiasts. He could tell by listening that the first tent had three people inside. He decided that was too many to take down quietly. The second tent he came across housed a couple, but he wasn't that desperate. Two murders was excessive when one would do.

The third tent had a single occupant who reeked of body odor. The man smelled of sweat and unwashed clothing. It smelled as though he'd spent the week backpacking rather than celebrating, and the resultant scents in the tent were almost too much for the cat to tolerate. Philip crept forward on careful predator paws. He clawed through the vinyl wall of the tent and latched onto the man's throat with his powerful jaws.

Blood sprayed in a wide arc, coating the interior of the tent.

When the man stopped gurgling on his own blood and his racing heart stilled, a blood-soaked cat loped back to where he had come from.

30

CHAPTER 30

The short trips home for holiday breaks passed in a blink, but that was welcome, because it meant January was close. January arrived before Philip knew it, and it marked Kam's two-week visit. The Gardners seemed to suspect nothing when Kam said he was going to pay Philip a visit at school.

"I want to foster the sober connections I made when I was getting started," he had explained. Their parents agreed his sober friendships were important, and they'd encouraged him to go.

Philip arrived at the station twenty minutes before the train was due to arrive. He was all nerves—similar to the last time Kam was expected, but the reasons were all different. It was an excited, happy energy that had him bouncing his leg.

When the train pulled into the station, Philip got immediately to his feet. He paced back and forth across the platform, glancing up at the doors on the cars every few moments.

When Kam finally stepped out, Philip's eyes lit up. When hazel eyes met blue ones, Kam grinned broadly, hurrying toward Philip.

"Hey," he greeted Philip as soon as they were close. Philip replied by wrapping his arms around Kam and hugging him. He buried his face in Kam's chest and held him tightly.

He was holding firm, and relief was washing over him. Philip had known Kam was coming. Kam had assured him that he would be on the train, and Philip had believed him. But now he *was here*, in the flesh. And Philip could hug him and hold him and touch him, and immediately all the apprehension about Kam's arrival and the lingering worry he'd felt about their connection faded away.

"I'm so glad to see you," Philip said, his cheek against Kam's chest. Kam held Philip close, rubbing his hands gently across his back.

"I'm glad to see you, too. I've missed you." Those words sent more relief down Philip's spine. He was still smiling, though he looked more subdued.

"Thank you for coming here," Philip said.

"I'd go anywhere for you," Kam replied quietly, his lips as close to Philip's ear as he could get.

Philip exhaled sharply and moved back so he could look Kam in the eye. "Let's go home."

Once they were in a cab, Philip tried to give Kam a little more space. Still, he reached across the seat for Kam's hand, low and out of view of their driver. Kam smiled at him, and closed his hand over Philip's. Suddenly, Philip was smiling broadly again, and it was difficult to imagine anything was wrong in the universe, or that anything had ever been wrong.

"I thought we could get dinner out somewhere," Philip murmured. "I know they don't feed you on the train."

"That would be great. We can drop my stuff and go. Then you can tell me about how your investigation has been going."

Philip hadn't told Kam much since they last saw one another. He didn't like the idea of sharing details about his condition over the phone. He didn't like the thought of sharing it in public either, but he thought they could go somewhere busy to minimize the likelihood that they'd be overheard.

"I do have a lot to share," Philip admitted. "Between the journals and the time I spent in the library, I've found out a lot."

"Really?" Kam asked. "Does that mean...?" He trailed off and waggled his eyebrows playfully.

"Nothing concrete," Philip replied. "But I would like to run a few things by you."

Kam nodded. "Whatever you need."

When they got up to Philip's room, Kam put down his bags and flopped on the bed.

"What if we skip dinner and just go to bed early?" Kam suggested, smiling fondly up at Philip. "Would that be alright? We could still talk."

He had barely finished his sentence and Philip was already stepping out of his shoes. "That would be fine." He began unbuttoning his shirt. Kam smirked and slipped out of his own shoes. Kam got out of bed and pulled his t-shirt off over his head. They were both down to their underwear before they climbed under the blanket together. Kam laid on his back, and Philip nestled under his arm. "I want to tell you everything, but I don't want to waste time in bed together."

Kam grinned. "Time with you is *never* wasted. Tell me."

"You remember the librarian back home told me to focus on Louisiana lore? While I was there, I learned a lot about loup-garous, which led me to study New Orleans culture and witchcraft. There was a professor back home that studied it all —loup-garous, magic, all sorts of things. I found out through the journals that my parents spent a lot of time in Louisiana. I don't know if that's a sign or a coincidence..."

"Knowing you, I'd expect you to think it's a sign," Kam teased.

Philip chuckled. "You're not wrong." Philip pressed a soft kiss to Kam's chest. "But either way, I've been trying to learn more." He kissed Kam's chest again.

"How's that going?" Kam asked.

"Good, I think. I've just started learning about bayou folk medicine. They have treatments for everything."

"Do you really think there's a cure?"

Philip traced Kam's collarbone with his index finger. He shrugged. "I don't know, but if there is, I'm going to find it."

"I'm sure you will," Kam replied. "I can help you look while I'm here, if you want."

The suggestion made Philip laugh. "But you *hate* studying, and research."

"Yeah, but I care about you," Kam countered. "Plus, we can't pretend that I don't want you cured. My reasons are entirely selfish."

"I wouldn't call it selfish. I want it, too." He let his voice trail off as he traced a line from Kam's throat down to his waistband. He hooked his finger under the elastic and pulled it away from the skin, only to let it snap back against Kam's taut belly. "The *things* I want to do with you..." he murmured, his words barely above a whisper. Then he sighed and looked up at Kam.

Kam's eyes were bright and hungry, and he pulled Philip up and into a kiss before he could object. After a lingering series of kisses, Philip pulled back and huffed an irritated sigh. "Let's just say it would benefit us both if there was a treatment."

Kam nodded.

"So tomorrow evening after my class, you'll come to the library with me?"

"Yes. I can meet you there when you get out at 5:00."

The fact that Kam had memorized his schedule coaxed a smile across Philip's lips.

"We'll figure this out," Kam said. "I promise."

For the next week, Kam met Philip at the library every day after classes were over. He went to meetings during the day, just like he used to, in order to keep busy and feel like he was staying involved with his sober community. Often, he would arrive at the library early and set up at a table they could use. Each day, Philip would trek to the library and he'd smile as soon as he saw the taller man bent over some lore book or jotting notes into one of his notebooks.

Seeing Kam always warmed him, but there was something special about having Kam's support in working toward a treatment. (A cure felt like too much to hope for.) On Thursday, a few days before Kam was scheduled to leave, Philip slid into the seat beside him.

"Hi," he whispered. He depended on the library too much to invite the ire of the librarians or other patrons.

"Hello," Kam replied in his own hushed tones. "I got the books we were working with yesterday."

"Thank you," Philip whispered back. He reached into his backpack and frowned. He began unpacking his things, and the more he drew out of the bag, the more pronounced his frown got. "Oh, no," he murmured. "I left my notebook in the room."

Kam brightened and shook his head. "I thought you might need that." He reached into his own backpack and drew out the composition book Philip had been hunting for. "I noticed you'd let it on the desk. I'm glad I brought it."

Philip's lips parted, surprised, before he brought them together again in a smile. He exhaled a little, making a noise that was barely a chuckle, and shook his head. "You're amazing," he said quietly.

Kam grinned, his cheeks flushing a little at the praise. "You're sweet," he whispered back.

"I mean it," Philip insisted. "I couldn't do all this if it weren't for you."

Kam shook his head. "I'm sure you could. There's someone else out there that you'd be just as attracted to."

Philip rolled his eyes and then shook his head. "I haven't found them yet, and I don't want to."

Kam chuckled quietly. He shot an apologetic look at the librarian, who cleared her throat, staring meaningfully in their direction. "Fine. Let's get to work."

Philip didn't reply out loud, but he gave Kam's thigh a squeeze under the table with his non-dominant hand. He let it rest there while they worked. Kam went quiet too, but he was faintly smiling all the while.

Want to take a dinner break? Philip asked by way of a paper note he slid over the top of Kam's book. Kam nodded, and

Philip let his leg go so that he could repack his things. When they had both gathered up their belongings, Philip took the books they had borrowed back to the reshelving cart.

Once they were outside, they finally spoke aloud again. "What were you thinking for dinner?" Kam asked. Philip shrugged, then stepped close beside him.

"Something simple like soup and a sandwich at Antoine's?" He suggested. Kam nodded.

"That sounds good. I just want something *warm*." Philip grinned and curled his arm around Kam's back, resting his gloved fingers on his hip.

Kam's eyebrows shot up, but he didn't say anything. They were walking down the street near the little mom and pop diner— hardly in the middle of town, but it was still noteworthy that Philip was holding him. This was as close to publicly affectionate as Philip had ever been. Kam slung his arm around Philip's back to mirror his action, and Philip still didn't protest. Kam looked down at his feet so that he could hide his grin in his scarf.

When they were outside the restaurant, Philip tugged on Kam's hip and slowed his own pace. They came to a stop just outside the large, glass door.

"I meant what I said," he muttered quietly, pulling Kam sideways to face him. "I wouldn't be able to do any of this if I didn't have you in my corner."

Before he could reply, Philip surged forward and pressed a kiss to his lips. Kam's arms melted at his sides for a moment before his faculties returned and he held Philip's waist.

The kiss ended as suddenly as it began—the only evidence it had been there at all were the flushed cheeks it left in its wake. "I love you," Philip whispered, as if they were in the library again.

Kam's eyes widened a little, and he didn't reply right away. Philip took the opportunity to guide a stunned Kam into the restaurant and to a table. His plan was that they'd have their soup and sandwiches, and he would ride the high of his confession for the rest of the week.

Kam found he was biting his lower lip throughout the evening, and each time he caught himself, he'd break into a smile.

He didn't reciprocate the declaration aloud, but he insisted that Philip share the bed with him for the rest of his visit.

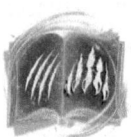

The end of their second year loomed over the entire cohort. What they meant to do after graduating the program and taking their vows became a bigger issue the closer the end of the year crept. David planned to go back to his grandparents' house. He wanted to try to sign on with one of the churches nearby that he had attended as a parishioner. One in particular was encouraging, as the pastor was getting older, and had mentioned to David over the Christmas break that he wanted to retire sooner rather than later. That would be a good place for David.

Philip didn't have such an opportunity. He knew he couldn't bring himself to work closely with Pastor Andrew, given his opinions on gay partnerships. After the kiss he'd shared with Kam outside of Antoine's and the goodbye peck he'd gotten on the train platform, Philip was inspired to find a church where he could be himself.

Part of his research in the last few months had been trying to find religious organizations or churches in and around New Orleans that needed help. So far, his searches had come up empty, but he had started looking on the outskirts of town and in the surrounding areas. He hoped that by the time summer rolled around, that he would have a lead. He just needed somewhere he could go for an internship to get his foot in the door. That was all he needed—an in near New Orleans.

His research into witch doctors and folk medicine was only getting him so far. At a certain point, he knew he would have to go see for himself. The ritual he had performed had delayed the transformation, but hadn't stopped it completely. That meant it was worth trying again. He hadn't mentioned his thoughts explicitly to Kam yet, but once he had a plan, he'd share it.

It was fortunate that his classes were going smoothly. He didn't have to stress as much about his actual studies. He was pleased he could dedicate sufficient time and energy to investigating his transformations and planning his future.

In the spring, Philip finally made some progress planning his summer. He was able to make contact with an administrator with the Louisiana District United Pentecostal Church. As Philip came to understand it, the organization had begun in 1945 as a merger of the Pentecostal Church, Inc. and the Pentecostal Assemblies of Jesus Christ, which had formed the UPC. Just two years after the merger, there had been seventy-four churches in the Louisiana District, and that number had only grown since then.

According to the man Philip spoke to over the phone, the annual camp meeting was also growing every year. He said that if Philip couldn't find a space with one of the dozens of churches, that the camp itself would take him in for a summer of service. Though Philip would have preferred working in a church, he knew beggars couldn't be choosers. Networking with the licensed ministers in attendance would surely benefit him later on.

Once he had a plan, that was when he told Kam. It was a Sunday afternoon. Kam was off work for the day, and Philip had called him to chat before he attended the evening service.

"I have something to tell you," Philip began.

"Oh?" Kam asked.

"I think I'll be going to Louisiana this summer instead of coming home." He paused for a beat, but then pressed on. "You know all my digging keeps pointing me to New Orleans. I think I need to go there."

Kam was quiet for a few more seconds before he cleared his throat. "The whole summer?" he asked. Philip swallowed. He could hear the disappointment in Kam's voice. That made it that much harder to commit to his plan.

"I'm not sure yet. I'm still trying to see what's available. If there's any time I'm not needed, I'd want to come straight home to you." It was the truth, but he didn't know if it would mend the hurt feelings.

"I need you to do what you need to do," Kam said quietly, "whether that's to go to Louisiana or come back here and study more. I wanna support you, no matter what that looks like." Kam swallowed, though it sounded like more still silence on the line. "Just promise me that I can come see you again in the fall if you can't come home this summer."

Philip's relief prompted a loud exhale. "Of course. You're welcome here anytime. As soon as I know the details for the summer, I'll share them with you."

"That's all I can ask," Kam replied quietly. He hesitated for a moment. "I love you, Philip."

It made Philip's chest ache to hear the words for the first time with the full weight of his intention. His chest felt too small to contain his wild, thundering heart.

"I love you, too Kam," he'd replied simply. "More than life itself," he added, when the words didn't feel sufficient.

31

CHAPTER 31

At the end of the semester, Philip boarded a train toward Lake James, Louisiana. The town was a little over three hours by car from New Orleans, but it was in the right state, which he took as a step in the right direction. The church was a relatively small one, but the pastor was eager to have Philip's support working on the few community ministries they had launched.

The pastor, a married man in his fifties, had offered Philip room and board in exchange for his help. Pastor Angus Brown and his wife Edna were happy to have Philip stay with them. They had been married for twenty-three years, and the Lord had never blessed them with children. Both had professed at dinner that first evening to have seen wisdom in the decision —they had so much more time to devote to the community this way! But Philip couldn't help but notice the way Edna's tone of voice changed when she talked about the ministry for the children, or how her eyes got distant and misty when her husband mentioned the 'extra' bedroom Philip would be staying in.

The walls were pale white, but the trim had been done in pastel blue. There were sponge-painted yellow rubber ducks above the corners of the windows and doors inside the room. Philip felt for Edna. He tried to avoid the subject as much as he could, and made sure to compliment her cooking and anything else he could about their home after. She took pride in both and it seemed to make her happy.

That first Saturday when Philip had arrived, Angus had picked him up from the train station in his old sedan, taken him home to meet Edna, and the three of them had a quick lunch before Philip and Angus journeyed on to the church. The church building was a modest size—small when compared to the churches Philip had attended growing up and while in seminary, but large given the size of the town. Once they were inside, Philip realized it was large enough to house most of the population of Lake James.

"Do you usually have a full house?" he'd asked as they walked through the main room. Pastor Brown nodded and ran his fingers along the podium fondly.

There was a younger pastor teaching the Sunday school classes and leading the Bible study group for the youth. Angus didn't need support with the adult sermons, but he said Pastor Edwin could use some help with the youth program. Plus there were a host of volunteer programs that could use a helping hand. There were teenagers from the high school to help with the labor, but the organizing required more time and effort than Angus had to offer. That was where Philip came in. He thought it would offer him some valuable experience in operating a small church with limited resources. He had worked with larger churches and organizations, so this was a chance to do more with something more grassroots. He wasn't sure where he would end up after graduation, so it paid to be flexible.

Plus, he thought he could learn more about the folk magic he'd spent the last year studying. He was a half day's bus ride from New Orleans—closer than he could have hoped.

Running in Louisiana was challenging if not impossible once the sun had risen, but Philip needed to keep up with his routine if he was going to stave off his self-harm urges. It was fortunate that Angus and Edna lived at the end of a country dirt road and there was never much traffic. When Philip left the porch in the morning, it was still dark out. The most he had to fear was turning his ankle by misstepping into an unfilled pothole or twisting his foot on loose gravel. Philip carried a flashlight when he ran, and he'd always had especially good night vision, so he didn't consider either of these concerns to be particularly upsetting. Whenever he ran he usually caught sight of small rabbits sprinting across the fields or under bushes into safety. The trees and fences that lined the road cast long, dark shadows in the early hours. It should have been eerie, being the only one on the road at that hour, but Philip felt at home in the dark.

As long as he woke up early, he could be back at Angus and Edna's before it was too hot and sticky. That meant he could get a shower in before breakfast. He kept his hair short and neat, and if they minded him coming down in the morning with a towel-dried head, they didn't say as much.

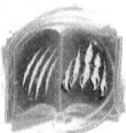

Philip made his calls home from the pay phone at the gas station up the road from the church. He found out his first week with the Browns that Edna liked the eavesdrop, and he didn't want his calls with Kam to be listened in on. He'd call his parents from the landline down in the kitchen, but when he wanted to talk to Kam, he made the walk to the convenience store. It was challenging to catch him at home during the week during the day, but on the weekends, they'd chat until someone else needed the phone or his quarters ran out— usually the latter.

They took to writing each other to offset the infrequency of their communications, but neither one was willing to put anything especially damning in writing. Philip worried that the distance would cause Kam to lose interest or get distracted, but every week, Kam answered the phone like he had run to catch it. The smile that spread across Philip's face after a call with Kam always carried him through the rest of the day. Kam even got to the point he mailed Philip checks to cash for the pay phone quarters, and to help cover Philip's new cola habit. Philip had started saying that he was going to the gas station to buy a soda, as an excuse to make the journey. The Browns were supplying Philip with room and board, but no spending money, so Kam's financing kept them in phone calls, stationery, and postage throughout the summer.

One week at the beginning of August, Kam sent a more substantial check. Philip had blinked back tears when he read Kam's explanation in the letter accompanying it. Kam wanted him to see New Orleans. He had looked into the amount of bus fare that would get Philip from Lake James to New Orleans and back again, and had sent enough for the bus and a motel for a night. Philip knew neither of them could afford for him to stay long, so he wanted to make the most of it.

Philip had been a model guest the whole summer long and hadn't asked for as much as a ride into town the entire time, so Angus was happy to take him to the bus station when he needed the ride. The man was glad that Philip wanted to see more of the state while he was there, because maybe that meant he'd come back.

Angus drove Philip to the bus station Monday morning and agreed to pick him up Tuesday evening. Philip had worked with the small town's travel agent to book the bus, his hotel, and the travel back. He'd explained he wanted to see the French Quarter and the zoo—two tourist attractions that his hosts wouldn't bat an eye at.

Once he arrived in New Orleans, he knew he could look at the Yellow Pages at any pay phone or in his hotel to track down what he was actually after. He didn't exactly want the local switchboard operator to know he was looking for occult practitioners.

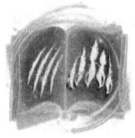

Philip slept the whole bus ride. He yawned and stretched when the bus finally came to a rumbling stop outside the New Orleans station. He had skipped his morning jog and was groggy for his trouble. The seat beside him had ended up empty after a few changes, so he'd stretched his arms and legs diagonally across the seat before he finally got up.

He collected his duffel bag from under the bus and started toward his hotel on foot. According to what the travel agent had marked on his map, it wasn't more than a few blocks away, and he wanted to save his cab fare for when he really needed it.

Once he got to the hotel, Philip checked in and got settled, which consisted of putting his bag on the stand in the room. Then he sat on the edge of the bed and rifled through the bedside table. He passed the Bible and drew out the *Local Sights* pamphlet and a phone book. He knew from the sign by the phone that he could make free local calls, so he hoped to get as much of his reconnaissance done as possible before he left the room to explore on foot.

He took out a notebook and a pen he'd brought and turned to the vague Occult section. He jotted down the names and numbers for the shops with advertisements on the page first—right or wrong, he believed that those who could afford to advertise must be doing well enough for themselves to pay to promote. That seemed like a good sign.

Then he wrote down the names and numbers which had not opted for a full display ad, but which had paid to have their information bold in the directory. There were a few dozen, which gave him some hope. He copied down the plainly listed names and numbers last.

This way, he would have a legible copy of the directory that he could take home with him. He could have tried to get a photocopy made at the library, but it was always hit or miss as to whether or not the copies would be readable. The Yellow Pages were, as the name suggested, on colored paper, and the text was so small. Plus he'd be charged regardless of whether or not he could actually read the copy. He preferred to have a free, handwritten list.

Philip flipped back to the first page of his handwritten directory. He took a deep breath, then picked up the phone and dialed.

Eight calls later, and Philip was getting used to being laughed at, and he was getting a feel himself for when the people he was calling were peddling snake oil. He only had one strong lead on a practitioner who seemed to know anything about loup-garous or any other shapeshifting creature. There had been a couple more promising contacts, but they had either encouraged him to come in person or referred him to a pay-by-the-minute helpline.

The most promising lead had also encouraged Philip to come in, but she had offered resources alongside a paid consultation. The young woman who had answered the phone had apologized that the woman she worked for wasn't available for several months, but she was quick to say the practitioner had authored several books on folk medicine, and she believed that suppressing loup-garou transformations as well as ways to deter the creatures from coming around were covered in those volumes.

The books were available for purchase—he'd just need to come down to their shop or stop at one of the metaphysical shops that carried them around town. After confirming the address from the phone book, Philip had assured her he'd come by in an hour or so.

The young woman had asked where he was staying ("I'm not a psychic, you just don't sound like a local," she had explained). When he told her where, she recommended he visit a few shops "for supplies" before heading home.

"Thank you," he'd said enthusiastically at the end of their call. "You've been a wonderful help."

"If you go to any of those shops and they give you trouble, tell them Nailah sent you."

"Thank you again."

"You're welcome. What's your name? So I'll know you when you come by."

"Philip." He hadn't considered telling her anything but the truth. At this point, he hadn't admitted to anything but having a shapeshifter problem. There was no reason to add further lies to his list of sins.

Philip made a few more calls before leaving, but none were as helpful as Nailah had been. Still, he had taken down their suggestions and made notes of who he could reach out to when he would be in town for longer. Then he took the map he'd marked a few shops on and headed out into the sticky afternoon.

Philip headed straight to Nailah's shop first. When he crossed the threshold, he was greeted by the strong, musky scent of burning incense. Bookshelves lined the walls on the far side of the room, where a woman sat behind a desk. Tables were placed throughout the room with crystals, candles, and small jars on them. Philip couldn't identify the contents from a distance. He could see there were skulls on a few of the higher shelves.

The woman looked up at him when the bell on the door rang. She studied him curiously, not saying a word as he crossed the room toward the shelves of books.

"Hello," Philip greeted her awkwardly, putting the folded map into his back pocket. "Are you Nailah?"

"Philip!" A smile spread over her features when he spoke. "I recognize your voice from the phone. Welcome." She stood and came around the desk to meet him. She was tall, and her patterned dress went nearly to the floor. Her naturally kinky hair was full around her face. "Let me show you the books I told you about."

He smiled at her and followed where she directed.

"I'm sorry for the cool greeting—or I guess, the absence of a greeting. We've had some trouble recently. There's a church down the street that takes issue with us being here. I'm a little wary of strangers in person because of it."

Philip frowned. He had noticed the church on the corner, but both it and the shop seemed well-established. "I'm sorry to hear that."

She shrugged and handed him two books from the shelves. "The boss will just work a little more protection magic. We'll be fine."

He looked at the books in his hands. "So these are where you'd suggest I start?"

"If you need help in a hurry, yes. The best thing to do would be to get an appointment to be seen, but I know you aren't in town for long." She paused for a moment, studying him with her warm brown eyes. "Are you really a loup-garou?" she asked, in a hushed, conspiratorial tone. "I've never met one in person."

Philip chuckled and shook his head. "I don't know if there's a word for what I am, but I'm hoping if your boss can help the loup-garous, she can help me."

Nailah nodded. "I think she can. She's a brilliant woman with incredible powers." She bit her lower lip, studying him. "If you'd like, I'd be happy to help you with any questions you might have about the rituals or processes from the books. If you want to take a look at the books before you go, we sell most of what you'll need." Nailah stepped back around the desk so she could ring up the books.

He passed her cash, and she placed it in a locked drawer in the desk before she smiled up at him. "Let's see what else you'll have to get."

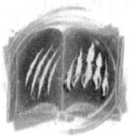

It didn't take long for Nailah and Philip to find the relevant rituals and recipes. Philip was pleased to find that across the two books there were a few.

"From what I've heard, loup-garou transformations are a tricky business. Not every ritual works for every one."

"Is it something that comes up often?"

"More often than you'd think," she replied with a shrug. "New Orleans is where people go to deal with problems like these." She grimaced. "*Problems* isn't really the right word…"

"I'd consider it a problem," Philip agreed with her. He appreciated her sensitivity, but he couldn't think of a better word.

Nailah smiled and nodded. "Where are you headed back to?" she asked. "Do you want to get supplies for a few things and then come back?"

Philip took his turn to grimace. "I'm only in the state for a few more weeks. Do you ship?"

Nailah nodded. "We do. If you like, you can call when you get home and tell me the book and page number you're working from, and I can send you a shopping list's worth."

Philip smiled. "That would be amazing. I'm not sure that I've got room in my bags to travel with a lot of delicate ingredients."

She nodded. "That makes sense."

"I do want to get *something* while I'm here. I'd like to be able to try at least one of these."

"Maybe one of the teas?" she suggested. "They would be easy to mix up and take with you."

Philip nodded. "Yeah. That would be good. How long do these last once they're mixed?"

"It depends on the ingredients and what type of ritual goes along with it. The teas have a fairly long shelf life once you mix them. They can last up to three months without losing potency."

Philip glanced back at the tea ritual. According to the page, he could make six tea bags in a session. Their effects were supposed to last for a month—if they worked, that would be half a year taken care of right away. The idea was thrilling.

"Alright, so one of the teas, then. It doesn't require much equipment to make, and they won't take up much space in my luggage."

Nailah nodded and took the book from him. She reviewed the ingredient list and moved between the tables, collecting items and letting him know what each thing was and what it cost. Philip watched her closely and attempted to commit everything she said to memory.

By the time she was done, he felt confident he was ready to follow the book's recipe. He was one step closer to peace.

After he bought his ingredients, he hurried back to the hotel. He stopped at a pay phone outside of a grocery store on his walk back so that he could call Kam.

"Hello?" Kam answered the phone as he always did in the evening.

"Hey," Philip replied warmly. "I just left a shop. I got some ingredients for a tea that's supposed to help me."

"Oh, yeah? That's great. I'm really glad you got to go and that it was helpful."

"Well, I hope it's helpful. According to the woman in the shop, suppressing transformations can be difficult. The books I bought have several recipes and rituals in them. They don't all work for every person."

"That's really wonderful, Philip. I'm so glad." He paused, and when he spoke, there was a flirtatious smile in his voice. "So when can I visit you to test these out?"

Philip chuckled. He had already given that some thought. "Fall break would be the soonest. I could stay on campus, and you could come to see me."

"It's a date," Kam replied.

Philip smiled at the pay phone on the wall. He wished he could see Kam. "I miss you."

"I miss you, too."

The phone beeped to let Philip know his time was almost over. "I've got to get back to the hotel, but I'll call you when I get back to the Browns'."

"Be safe. I love you, Philip."

"Love you too, Kam," he answered before the line disconnected. He had a lot of hope for the future. It was a glorious thing.

Back in the hotel, Philip spread open his new spell book and all the ingredients that Nailah had sent him with. He felt relatively comfortable with the idea of performing a ritual after the one he'd put together at home, especially since tea bag assembly sounded like an easier process. As he reread the page concerning the spell tea he hoped to make, he wondered how this ritual would perform compared to the last.

First, he laid the empty tea bags out so that he could easily grab each of them. Then he picked up the first bag and began to meditate on the same thought he had before, *retain human shape*. He then poured some black tea into each of the tea bags as a base. Over and over, he repeated the mental mantra *retain human shape*.

He added the other herbs to the bags as a pinch at a time in the order listed in the book. *Retain human shape* was the singular idea which kept him grounded every step of the way.

The tea bags didn't take as long as the candle ritual had. Still, he felt the same ambient warmth he always did that made him think the Holy Spirit was with him. On the phone, he had asked Nailah if she felt the same thing when she was spell casting, and she confirmed she did, though she attributed it to a deep connection with nature rather than the Holy Spirit. Despite her difference of opinion, the shared experience made him feel like he was on the right track.

32

CHAPTER 32

The first semester of his last year of seminary was grueling. It was like he was back in his freshman year—he had little time for anything but his studies. David was buckling down too, and the pair had traded their weekly volunteering for working side by side in the lounge.

In a blink, it was mid-October. Philip was looking forward to a long, four-day weekend. Even more than the time off, he was looking forward to Kam's visit. He'd assembled the tea in his hotel room back in August, but waited to drink it until the Monday before Kam was due to arrive. He drank another dose a few hours before Kam was expected. He was hoping that by doubling up he'd be able to keep his transformations in check.

Philip was late getting to the train station. This time, it was Kam who was sitting and waiting on the platform. He was sitting on a bench, and as soon as Philip entered the doorway, Kam beamed at him. Philip hurried across the room and swept him into a warm hug. He leaned up and kissed Kam's cheek.

"Hey," Kam said, his eyebrows raised. "Everything okay?"

"I'm sorry I'm late. I got caught up studying."

"Aren't you supposed to be on break?"

"I am now," Philip replied, squeezing Kam around the middle. "I was trying to cover as much ground as I could before you got here."

"And now that I'm here?" Kam teased. His arms were wrapped around Philip's waist.

"And now that you're here, I aim to enjoy you."

The words made a playful smirk spread across Kam's lips. "Oh, do you, now?" He chuckled. "Then we'd better get out of this train station."

Once they were in the back seat of a cab, they were quiet. Neither one especially wanted to make chit-chat with the taxi driver. The man behind the wheel seemed content to let the drive pass in relative silence, though he did thank Philip when the young man passed the cash for his fare and tip over the seat.

When they were back in Philip's room, Kam barely had time to set his pack down before Philip had lunged toward him. Kam was slightly taller, but Philip easily pushed him back and toward the wall with an all-but-bruising kiss. Their tongues were intertwined, and their fingers moved freely to unbutton and unfasten every piece of fabric in their way.

"You drank the tea?" Kam asked. He was already breathless when Philip stopped kissing him long enough to slide their shirts off.

"Monday and this morning," he confirmed. He hadn't been due for another dose that morning, the tea bags were supposed to last a month, but he hadn't wanted to take any chances. Plus, the book didn't seem concerned that he would overdose himself.

"You really think it'll work?" Kam asked, his voice fading to a hiss as Philip bit his shoulder.

"I'm hoping." Philip replied. "Praying. At this point, that's all I can do."

Kam chuckled, pulling Philip's belt loose from his trousers. "You think *God* is gonna help you fuck me?"

"He ought to," Philip replied, his expression serious. "I've done a lot of good work for him my entire life. He owes me." Then his lips spread into a playful grin. "And if he's not willing to play ball with me now, he's going to have bigger problems."

"Look at you," Kam teased, tugging on Philip's waistband, "threatening God."

Philip laughed and shook his head. "It has been a long time coming."

"I bet," Kam teased. "Get out of your shoes and pants for me. I want to show my appreciation."

Philip didn't need to be told twice. He first slipped off a shoe and then braced a hand on Kam's shoulders to pull off the other before he stripped himself bare. Kam smirked and removed his remaining garments as well, and then he wrapped his arms around Philip's shoulders and pulled him close. The two kissed feverishly for several minutes before Kam directed them both to the bed. It was Philip who finally broke off to climb down Kam's body. He left a trail of kisses in his wake as he moved toward his lover's waiting cock.

Kam huffed a sigh of contentment as Philip played at taking the lead. He exhaled sharply when Philip's tongue ran the length of him and swept across the ridge surrounding the head. Kam's hand slipped down to stroke through Philip's hair as the younger man found his rhythm. Philip groaned with his lips pressed to Kam's pubic bone, and Kam shuddered from the reverberations rattling through his throat and all the way down. Kam's fingertips caught in some of the longer strands of Philip's hair, but he didn't hold on hard enough to tug him in either direction.

"Philip!" Kam gasped, breathless. Philip grunted in response and bobbed with increasing vigor.

This was the first time Philip had been assertive with Kam, and it suited them both. Philip liked showing that he too could be an active player. In the weeks leading up to this visit, he had walked a delicate balance of trying to concoct this plan for Kam without giving himself over to desire. He didn't want to lose control of himself to the cat. In the time he and Kam had been away from one another, he had tiptoed up to the edge of temptation, and each time he backed carefully away.

To date, Philip's first transformation was the only one he'd made without Kam present, and he aimed to keep it that way. Being tempted *with* Kam was so much more satisfying than getting lost on his own.

Philip dug his thumbs and fingers into Kam's hips as he guided his lover's thrusts back and down his throat.

"Philip," Kam moaned again, his voice verging on breaking. "You've got me so close." Philip gave his hips a squeeze with his right hand before he moved his left to stroke along Kam's shaft, beyond where his lips and tongue could reach. The extra sensation sent Kam gasping and grabbing at Philip's head again. He held the younger man still while he panted and spilled over the edge. When he could finally relax a moment or two later, he pulled Philip up by his shoulders. He encouraged him to crawl back up his body, and then pulled him tight against his bare, sweaty chest.

Philip rested his cheek against Kam's rib cage and listened fondly to his thundering heart. He brushed his fingertips lightly against Kam's skin and smiled when Kam took his hand. "How long have you had *that* up your sleeve?"

Philip chuckled. He didn't move from where he lay. "Since the first time you tried that on me," he admitted. "I've been a little hesitant to try it until now."

"Why?" Kam asked, taking Philip's chin in his hand so he could turn it to face him.

293

"Guilt. Shame. Embarrassment. Take your pick." He shrugged. "But I'm trying to do better." He kissed Kam softly. "You deserve better." The words made Kam smile, and a warmth bubbled up into Philip's chest.

"*You* deserve better, too," Kam purred. "Now lay on your back, it's your turn."

Philip grinned and rolled onto his back. Kam was smiling down at him as soon as he was in position. Philip wanted this —every touch, every kiss, every caress. The guilt still lingered, bubbling in his stomach, but he could enjoy indulgence in the moment. Especially when he was still riding the high of having been able to please Kam, finally.

Kam leaned in and kissed Philip deeply. He was straddling Philip's hips, and as their tongues weaved together, his hand began moving the length of him between their bellies. Philip groaned softly into Kam's lips, still wary of their neighbors in the dorm. He liked being trapped beneath Kam's larger form, his hips unable to buck despite his desperate want.

Philip had enjoyed taking the lead, but he loved being at Kam's mercy. The man knew just what to do to make Philip forget everything else, and he needed that now more than ever.

Philip awoke suddenly and shook his head. *No, this wasn't supposed to be happening.* He pried himself out of Kam's grasp and got to his feet, whimpering. Kam's eyes opened blearily and he scratched his head.

"Philip?" he asked, his voice thick with sleep.

"I'm changing," Philip replied, his tone broken. "It didn't work." He looked down in time to watch fur sprouting along his legs and torso.

"We'll find something that works," Kam promised. "This was just our second try."

Philip wanted to reply, but the transformation stole his vocal chords as he fell forward to land on his paws. A low growl emanated from deep in his chest as the rest of the change overtook him. Kam got to his feet and opened the dormitory door to let Philip out of the room.

Yet again, Philip's lust had gotten the best of him, and he was on the hunt. His thoughts were too swept up by the instincts of the cat—he didn't feel his disgrace anymore. He waited in the stairwell until he heard the security guards leave the lobby. He could hear their polished boots on the tile and the steady thrum of their hearts under their uniforms. It would have been faster and easier to kill security, but Philip had the presence of mind to wait. He didn't want any more violence tied to the school or his program.

His eyes adjusted easily to the dark of the night once he was outside. There was no foot traffic in the courtyard. He craned his neck back and sniffed the air. He could smell people and food in the near distance. He started off in their direction, his paws silent along the concrete sidewalk.

Restaurants along the street had thrown out their garbage after closing for the night, and the remnants of fried things made his feline mouth water—but that wasn't what he was after.

The bar on the corner was still open, and he reached the mouth of the alley beside it as a short redhead stepped outside for a smoke break. She already reeked of cigarette smoke and the sweat from a nearly completed shift. Philip crouched low and crept toward where the woman stood. She was too focused on tapping a cigarette out of her pack to see him. He was just outside of the ring of light cast by the bulb above her head.

When he caught her throat in his jaws, she made a wheezing, gurgling sound. Her hands balled into fists and she hit his strong chest, but it was too late. There was no coming back from a wound like that. Especially not when he yanked his head back and ripped the flesh open with a spurting arterial spray.

He chewed and swallowed the meat that had come free in his teeth. He left a paw print in blood on the side of the pack of smokes that had fallen to the ground. He would have eaten more, but he was stopped by a shrill scream. Another young woman stood in the side doorway for a moment before she yanked it back shut.

Philip had the wherewithal to make a swift exit. By the time he made it back to the courtyard, he could hear the distant sirens. They had been quick—the police and the ambulance must have also been on the prowl.

33

CHAPTER 33

The rest of the academic year passed quickly. Philip was disappointed by the failure of the loup-garou remedy, the second he'd tried, but Nailah had warned him that it was a tricky thing, hadn't she? He wrote her a brief letter and told her about his failures in broad, sweeping terms. He said he'd be back in touch for more supplies in the summer and thanked her again for her help. He didn't put a return address on the letter. He'd reach out to her when he needed to.

While he was still in seminary he started looking back over the other recipes and rituals in his books for another to try. As he pored over the pages, he wondered if any of them would be the cure he needed.

When he wasn't studying his lessons or searching for a remedy, he also spent a fair amount of time writing to the churches in and around New Orleans. When he had visited the city the previous summer, he'd made a list of the churches nearby so that he could contact them later. He wanted to make an effort to reach them now, before it was too late and he didn't have anywhere to go after graduation.

From the beginning of March until the end of May, he had sent out more than a dozen cover letters and resumes. He mailed them along with letters of recommendation from Pastor Brown and some of his professors. He was clear in them that he would be taking his vows and getting licensed at the end of seminary, and was open to any work. He wanted to get in the door anywhere, that was all he needed. Once he had a foot in, he could prove himself with his hard work and devotion. The Browns had told him he would be welcome to return, but surviving on just their room and board would be rough in the long term. Plus, staying with the pastor and his wife would mean he'd have to give up Kam, so it wasn't a viable option.

Although he hadn't heard anything back yet, Philip still hoped to find something a little closer to New Orleans. He thought that in addition to getting started with a church, that he could benefit from having someone like Nailah to support his research. The first two remedies hadn't worked, but he felt that with someone to guide him, that he'd find a solution to his cat problem more quickly. He had been discouraged by the failures initially, but the longer he looked at the books and reviewed the other options, the more he felt sure that a solution *had* to exist—he just hadn't found it, yet.

Their parents and Kam flew in for Philip's graduation. The Gardners both beamed with pride as their younger son showed them around the campus. The four of them even had a dinner out to celebrate the night before the ceremony.

"Philip," Father began, raising his glass. "We couldn't be more proud of you. Completing seminary is a monumental task, and while we never had any doubts, it still means a lot to us that we can be a part of this special accomplishment. We know you'll go on to do great, godly work no matter what the future holds."

Mother raised her wine, and Kam lifted his water. Philip joined them in the toast.

"Thank you," Philip replied graciously, after they had all taken a sip. "It means a great deal to me to have you here, all three of you." He smiled around the table, and he let his eyes linger on Kam. The two men shared a quiet look before he continued. "I couldn't have done it without your support and your faith in me."

The family moved to more idle chit-chat for the remainder of the meal. There was plenty to discuss, between Father's work, Mother's work with the church, and Kam's job. When they left the restaurant, Kam said he'd bunk with Philip for the night, for old time's sake. He explained to their parents he wanted to save himself from spending the night on a pull-out sofa bed in their hotel room.

When the two young men were finally alone in the cab, Philip found Kam's hand.

"I meant what I said at dinner," he said quietly, "about you and all you've done for me. I know I've said it before, but I never could have gotten this far without you. Without your support. Without—" He trailed off. He couldn't put into words all that Kam meant to him.

Kam's eyes were light, and he rubbed the back of Philip's thumb with his. "Well, I wouldn't be where I am now without you either. I owe some of my sobriety to you. You believed in me. You gave me somewhere to go..." He trailed off, too. He gave Philip's hand a squeeze. "Every day is still hard, and I know they'll keep being hard, but it helps me a lot to know you've seen me at my worst and you're still here."

"There's nowhere else I want to be," Philip insisted, his eyes locked on Kam's. He worried his lower lip between his teeth. "Which does lead me to a question."

Kam tilted his head, curious. "What's that?"

"If I find a place to go down in Louisiana... would you come with me?" He averted his gaze to the back of the seat in front of them.

He wanted Kam with him always, he wanted Kam with him *now*, even, but they hadn't talked about it. Plans for the future had always seemed so distant, but with Philip's graduation looming, they were on the cusp of the rest of their lives.

"You want me to come to New Orleans with you?" Kam asked, as if he wasn't sure he'd heard right. Philip managed to look Kam in the eye when he nodded.

"Yes," Philip confirmed. "I want to be *with you*." He let the words sit for a moment before he glanced at the back of the cab driver's head—the old man was doing a good job of paying them no mind. "We can't be together back at home, but Louisiana would be a fresh start." He laid his other hand on top of Kam's. "For both of us."

"You know, I have been saving to get my own place..." Kam started. It was his turn to keep his eyes averted. "...and I'm sure they have grocery stores there that I could work at."

Philip grinned. He could hardly believe what he was hearing. "So you'll come?"

Kam nodded. "Yeah. You figure out where we're going, and I'll be right there."

The thought of living with Kam—really living with Kam—was almost as dizzying as finally graduating. The two chattered about all the places Philip had applied for the rest of the ride back to campus.

Both of them had to take an antihistamine when they got back so they could wind down enough to sleep. They were both filled with excited nerves about the next day, and all the other days ahead of them.

After Philip had collected his diploma, he swore to live a life of discipleship and holiness, swore to serve the church faithfully and diligently, and swore to teach and preach the Word of God. Apart from his public vows, he also swore to learn as much as he could about the rituals and magic that promised him relief and a future.

He was on top of the world.

The letter offering Philip a position arrived two days after his graduation. The Gardners had gone home the day after the ceremony and missed the notice, but Kam had lingered in town to make the most of the plane ticket he'd bought. The pair were enjoying additional time together and imagining what the future might hold. They were delighted when the letter arrived, and they could get a glimpse of what those days might actually look like.

The Spirit's Embrace Church was in New Orleans proper, and they had an opening for a youth leader. Philip called the pastor as soon as he read the offer. The two conversed for a while about the role and expectations before they both agreed it sounded like a good fit.

On the phone, Pastor Michael Lindt revealed he was a lifelong friend of Pastor Angus Brown, and that he had used Philip's letter as an excuse to reach out and catch up with the man.

"He sang your praises," Lindt said. "He said if I didn't offer you this, that he would snap you up for himself."

Philip chuckled, and made a note that he'd need to call and thank Pastor Brown for his endorsement. Getting a position *in* New Orleans was so much more than he had dared let himself hope for.

The two men discussed the logistics of getting Philip and his things to Louisiana. Lindt agreed to wire a small advance to cover the train ticket. He also said he would put Philip up temporarily until he could find an apartment. If all went according to plan, Philip would be in New Orleans within the week.

Philip was grinning when he hung up the phone and recounted the exchange to Kam. They were sitting on the sofa in the lounge, and Philip was holding both of Kam's hands in his lap as he spoke.

"So then I'll come down once you've found us a place?" Kam asked, hopefully.

Philip nodded. "I don't think it will take long. Pastor Lindt seemed confident that I could find something quickly. He knows quite a few landlords in the area, and he said that he'd be willing to make some introductions for me."

It was Kam's turn to grin. "You're really doing it." He released Philip's hand so he could clasp his shoulder. "I'm proud of you, hon."

"Hopefully, a few months from now, all my *problems* will be solved, and we'll be settled in." He enunciated *problems* meaningfully—he'd kept Kam updated on his plans to address his transformations, too. Philip really did think that things were looking up.

"We can only pray," Kam teased.

Pastor Lindt had been right not to worry. Affordable two-bedroom apartments weren't hard to come by, especially with his connections in the city. Within a month of his graduation, Philip was moved into a fresh, spacious apartment within walking distance from the church. Within a few days of that,

Kam was all packed up and ready to move in with him. He'd be driving down in a truck filled with his things in a few days, and he'd tow his car behind it.

One of the first things Philip did when he put down roots was to go back to the shop to see Nailah. She had smiled when he came in, though her expression had flickered when he'd said what he was in town to do. Up until then, he hadn't really mentioned what he did professionally. Still, she sold him the ingredients for the next spell he wanted to try, and she had encouraged him to reach out if he needed anything while he was getting used to the city.

34

CHAPTER 34

After a few weeks, Philip had settled into his life in New Orleans. He rose early each day to run as he had in seminary. He would start before the sun and would herald the morning for his late-sleeping lover. Now that they had a kitchen, Philip would set coffee to brew each morning which usually roused Kam.

Kam would find Philip, showered and freshly dressed, and paging through the latest spell book he hoped could fix him. Every grimoire promised a new resolution, but he had to tread carefully. Every failed experiment was another life lost, and he didn't take that cost lightly.

That morning, Philip was weighing the merits of making a spell jar. He liked the idea that, if it worked, he could renew the ritual by shaking the jar and its contents. Still, he wasn't sold. The ritual work required to create the jar was almost a blend of his tea and candle workings—combining them to create a third magical artifact felt like an acceleration. He had made a reluctant peace with witchcraft, but he still had moments of doubt. He had faith in the Lord, but not himself or his judgment.

"Morning," Kam's half-dressed entrance pulled Philip from the pages. He looked up and caught the groggy kiss Kam pressed to the corner of his mouth. "Find anything good?" he asked as he poured himself a mug of coffee.

"Maybe," Philip answered honestly. "I have to get some things."

Kam nodded absently, yawning. Philip had turned one of their cabinets into an apothecary, already but each ritual had its own demands. "Need any help?" Kam always asked.

Philip shook his head. "I don't think so." His expression quirked into something more playful than serious. "Not until it's time to test."

Kam was drinking his coffee, but Philip could see the smile reach his eyes. "You know I'm always happy to help with *that*," he teased after he'd swallowed.

By the end of the day, Philip had talked himself into trying to make a spell jar. He stopped off at Nailah's shop for the metaphysical components after he finished at the church for the day. He would stop at the corner store near his apartment to purchase a couple of canning jars.

"Hello," Nailah greeted him as he crossed the threshold. "Find something new to try?" She had remained curious about his journey, but she let him explore on his own. She let him know she was interested in his work, but she never pried.

"Spell jars," he explained.

"Ooh, good choice."

"I hope so," he said with a sigh.

"I know it's discouraging," she replied. "But you'll find something."

"I hope so," he replied grimly as he picked a few ingredients. "Not being able to…" He couldn't bring himself to finish the sentence. Admitting his desires aloud to someone else was still too much.

"You will find something," Nailah repeated. It seemed she didn't need to know the particulars of Philip's condition to have her own faith.

"I'll let you know how it goes," he offered. He would, but it wouldn't really be necessary. He had a feeling that if the ritual failed, she would hear about the animal attack before he could come to see her again.

Kam was working, so Philip had a simple dinner by himself. Once he had washed his dishes, he dimmed the lights in the kitchen. He began to spread what he'd need out. Herbs, ingredients, candles, and freshly cleansed jars sprawled across the table next to the open spell book. He took the phone off the hook and sat it on the counter so he wouldn't be interrupted.

The first task was lighting the candles. The short candlesticks would offer some additional light during the ritual, and he would use the wax to help seal the jar. He set his intentions as he brought the flames to life—*retain human shape*. The sentiment rolled over in his mind as he lit the candle on the left and right of his makeshift altar.

He pinched ingredients and herbs carefully into the small jar in front of him. He moved slowly, methodically. He checked and re-checked each step against the book. Then he half-filled the jar with water he'd left outside under the light of the full moon.

Then he wrote his intention out on a scrap of paper. He rolled it tightly before he dropped it into the jar. He took a breath, studying the jar's contents. It didn't look like anything special; it looked like a mess.

This whole thing is a mess, his thoughts supplied helpfully. He returned his mind back to repeating his *retain human shape* mantra as he closed the jar. Then he picked up the candle on the right and tipped it sideways over the lid. Hot wax spread across the lid until it dripped down over the side of the jar.

Everything seemed to be fine at first, but when Philip placed the candlestick back into its holder, both candles blew out and the overhead bulb in the kitchen went dark with a *pop*. He sat blankly in the darkness for a few moments before he got up.

He flipped the light switch in the kitchen once then twice—nothing.

In the limited light, he relied on his feline night vision to find the living room switch. When he flicked that, the bulb overhead sprang to life, and he blinked at the brightness. He then went into the second bedroom and looked at the breakers. According to the switches, nothing was amiss. He switched the breaker marked Kitchen all the way to off, and then snapped it back into the on position.

When he emerged from the bedroom, both the living room and kitchen lights were on.

He wondered if the candle and the lights blowing out was a good sign. When he had performed the previous rituals he'd never had anything magical happen, necessarily. Surely the candles and lights were an omen that *something* had happened. He just hoped it was a *good* sign.

He put the phone back on the hook and sat at the kitchen table. He stared at the jar briefly before he picked it up by the base. He shook it a few times and set it back down on the table.

He'd find out soon enough.

When Kam got home from work an hour later, he found Philip sitting on the couch. He was turning the jar over in his hands, end over end.

"What do you have there?" Kam asked.

"Maybe the solution to all our problems," Philip answered. He stopped turning the jar and offered it to Kam.

Kam took it and examined the contents before he passed it back. "Was it hard to make?"

"Not any harder than anything else." He got to his feet and gave Kam a wry look. "Care to test it out?"

Kam grinned. "Like you even have to ask."

Philip was too anxious to rest. He curled up against Kam's chest in bed, but his eyes never drifted closed for longer than a few seconds. He wasn't *just* fidgety like he usually was before a transformation, he was afraid. There was fear tightening his chest. It coiled around his heart like a snake and restricted his breathing.

He knew he was going to transform. He could feel the harsh itching sensation along his arms and down his spine. It was only a matter of time. The cat was waiting, just under the surface of his consciousness, like it lurked beneath his skin.

Unlike his previous changes, Philip was aware of the cat this time. It felt like it was a separate being. Though he was still in his human shape, he could feel the creature's instincts slipping into focus. He sniffed the air and smelled Kam in bed beside him more strongly than any human should. When he felt his mouth water he got to his feet. If the cat meant to take over, Philip wasn't going to put Kam in danger.

He quickly dressed and headed downstairs. Once he was outside on the street, he realized just how much the cat had taken hold. He could see far into the darkness, not just where the streetlights shone. He could hear the muffled sounds of music and conversations in the bars that were still open. Philip shoved his hands into his pockets and walked away from the activity. He didn't want to risk a kill with an audience. Even with the cat taking control, he had that much presence of mind.

As he walked into the dark, he felt long fangs extending. His lips parted as the teeth lengthened, forcing his mouth open to make room for them. His hearing sharpened further, and he heard the faint sound of a woman crying and the sharp thudding of a fist on a door.

The closer he got, the more clearly he could pick out her words. She was begging for someone to stop, to leave her alone, and to go away. Philip would have frowned, but by the time he rounded the corner, fur had overtaken his feline features. His small ears tilted back as he padded forward, silent in the night. He approached a man who was pounding aggressively on the door of a townhouse.

The fear in the woman's broken voice was all it took for Philip and the cat to strike an agreement. The cat wanted to take its time with this man, and Philip was inclined to let it. Even through the door, he could sense the woman's intense fear. It was sharp and as visceral as any he had tasted when *he* was the threat in the dark.

Philip pounced onto the man's back and dug in with four sets of vicious claws. The man screamed as he fell, and Philip clenched his jaws tightly around the base of his neck. Philip felt the crunch of breaking vertebrae between his powerful jaws. The man wanted to fight, but the severed spinal cord meant he could only shout as Philip drug his claws down along his spine.

The flesh split on each side of the sharp daggers. The evil man would go into shock soon from blood loss, but the cat wanted him to suffer until he did. His tender meat was a feast for the feline until he heard distant sirens. At the sound, he padded further into the darkness.

He'd take the long way home.

35

CHAPTER 35

The next morning, Philip stayed curled up in bed with Kam until the alarm roused them both. He had come home and showered, and then cried until he fell asleep. Whatever the spell jar had done, he didn't want to repeat it. He felt justified in the prior night's kill, more than any of his others, but he felt even guiltier for having taken a more active role than ever before.

When Kam opened his eyes, they went wide when they landed on Philip. "What's wrong?"

"I killed, again," Philip murmured. "It was... worse. I'm getting worse." He had sunken, dark circles around his bloodshot eyes. "Somehow I was more cat and more human than I've ever been." He choked on the words. "I can't keep doing this."

Kam's face fell. "Go see Nailah. Tell her *everything*." Kam pulled Philip tightly to his chest. "It's going to be okay."

Philip wanted desperately to believe that was true.

Philip showered again after he got out of bed, and brushed his teeth twice. When Kam left for work, Philip took off toward the shop. He arrived fifteen minutes before it was due to open, so he took a seat on the stoop. He didn't want to pace, even though he was anxious. He didn't want to do anything that would remind him of the cat.

"Philip?" Nailah called out when she saw him. "What's going on? You're here early."

Philip knew he looked like death warmed over.

"I need your help."

She unlocked the door and let them both into the shop, but she kept the Open sign off and locked the door behind them. Once they were inside, she offered him a stool to sit on, and he tried to tell her everything.

He told her about his birth parents and the way desire unlocked his transformations. Then he told her about the rituals he had attempted, and how the last one had changed his transformations for the worse.

Nailah studied him, her deep brown eyes locked on his as he spoke. Philip was fidgeting and nervous, and Nailah was almost alarmingly calm. When Philip finished telling his story, she finally spoke.

"It sounds like a curse," she said quietly.

"It *feels* like a curse," he agreed.

"And your parents *and* grandparents had it, too?"

"If my dreams can be trusted, yes."

Nailah nodded and raised her fingers to her chin as she thought.

"I think your desire is the way you'll beat this, Philip," she said quietly. "I think you've been trying to *avoid* the desire component, you've been thinking of ways to stay human. What you need isn't the absence of desire, it's to harness it."

Hazel eyes widened.

"What does that mean?"

"You need to *embrace* your desire. *Accept* it. Learn to work *with* it instead of against it, or to spite it." Nailah got to her feet and disappeared into the back room. He knew it was a parlor where Nailah's boss saw her private appointments.

When Nailah returned she was carrying a thin, hardbound book. She offered it to Philip. He took the black book and opened it to the first page. There were no markings on the exterior, but the first several pages were covered in delicate half-inch sigils.

"What is this?" He asked as he turned to the books introduction.

"That book is the crowning achievement of a practitioner who spent decades studying how to use the power of sexual release in ritual magick."

Philip drew back, appalled.

"You're not serious."

"As a heart attack, Philip. I think this is your path forward. It's not the first tool I usually reach for, but I think you have a special case."

Philip turned his attention to the book in his hands. He flipped through the pages past text and diagrams of altars. It all looked very normal until he reached a sketch of a nude woman with her hands bound behind her back. He snapped the book closed and looked up at her.

"I don't know if I can do this."

"Just take the book. Look it over. Spend some time with it." Nailah patted his shoulder. "Do you trust me?"

She had been so kind to him, and had always done her best to help him.

"I do."

"Then give it a try. Read through it, even if you don't try anything. It might inspire you."

"Alright, I'll try."

Philip took the book home and sat with it on the sofa. He was surprised and relieved that the introduction wasn't explicit. It used vague references to wands and cups rather than anything overtly sexual. The closest to profane language used was a broadly reaching mention of 'ecstasy.'

When Kam got home, Philip had read through the introduction and the first two rituals in great detail. His ears were bright pink, but he was pushing through.

"You look better than you did this morning," Kam said, greeting Philip with a kiss. "What did Nailah say?"

"That I need to embrace my desire."

"I like the sound of that," Kam flirted.

Philip rolled his eyes. "I'm serious."

"And I'm not?" Kam teased. He sat next to Philip and peered over his shoulder at the book. "There's talk of a priest and a deacon in there. That sounds like your business."

"What they're up to is less than holy," Philip explained.

"If you need another set of hands to replicate anything you know I'm... *a willing vessel*," Kam paraphrased from the page. "I like the sound of this," he said, pointing. "A *lion-roar of rapture*. How about a panther-roar?"

Philip laughed. "You're incorrigible."

"You love me."

"I do."

When Philip fell to sleep that night, he was swept immediately into a swirling mist. He felt like he had been dipped into a warm bath, but his head was spinning. After several minutes, the mist began to clear, and he was left standing in a long, dark hallway. His mother emerged from a doorway, and his father followed at her heel. As usual, he was in panther form.

"Philip." His mother's tone was sharper than the last time he'd seen her. "You're going down a dangerous path."

He reached toward the wall to steady himself, but the wood buckled and swayed to avoid his touch. He closed his eyes and tried to will his vertigo to stop.

"What are you talking about?" When he opened them again, she was suddenly several paces closer to him.

"That witch is leading you down a bad road. You should leave her."

Philip swallowed the bile that rose in his throat.

"You're wrong. She's going to help me to find a way to stop the transformations."

"You wouldn't need a way to stop it if you paired with another of our kind. You're in New Orleans. It can be easier here. There are more of us. More like you." She glared at him. "Why do you insist on sleeping with your *brother* like some kind of degenerate?"

Philip scowled. "You're one to talk about propriety." His head was still unsteady, but his temper flaring distracted him from the nausea. He knew just what sorts of things his mother liked to get up to. She was in no position to judge him.

"And you're awfully high and mighty for a man who's bedding his brother."

"What business is it of yours?" He snapped. The wall swayed again, and Philip's stomach churned.

"You're my son," the woman growled. "I have a right—"

"You lost your rights when you decided to leave me."

"You know why I left you."

"You *chose*," Philip snapped. "I'm choosing, too."

36

CHAPTER 36

After his rough night of sleep, Philip stayed in bed with Kam rather than getting up to run. Kam woke him with whisper-soft kisses on his forehead and across the bridge of his nose.

Philip was smiling before his eyes opened. "Good morning."

"Good morning. You're going to figure it out today."

"You're confident."

"I have *faith*."

Philip rolled his eyes, but he was still smiling broadly when he climbed out of bed.

When Kam came into the living room, Philip was back on the sofa with the book Nailah had lent him. He wasn't as confident as Kam, but he was determined to learn as much as he could. After his nightmare, he was more driven than ever. His mother had turned against him, but that had to mean he was close.

"The sexual act is a sacrament, and must be accomplished for the love of God. All personal considerations and animal pleasure must be banished entirely," Philip read aloud as Kam approached with his coffee. "Sexual excitement must be suppressed to transform it into its religious equivalent..."

Kam frowned. "I don't like the sound of that, but I suppose if anyone could find a way to drain the enjoyment out of sex, it'd be you."

Philip snorted a laugh. "Oh, really?"

"You've come a long way, but you're still the most fun-averse person I know," Kam said affectionately. "You always have been, hon. Don't worry, it's one of the things I like about you."

Philip continued reading. He glanced up after a few minutes. "If we have to maintain *a reverent attitude without sensual thoughts,* are you still willing to help me?"

Kam took the seat beside Philip. "I will worship you *however* you need."

Philip ignored his burning cheeks and leaned into Kam's side. He didn't reply—he didn't trust himself to maintain the stoic, reverent tone he needed. Kam accepted the contact readily and draped an arm over Philip's shoulder.

By that afternoon, Philip had gone through the entire book, and he had identified a possible way forward. The ritual was for two people to perform—most of them were—and Kam had agreed again to be studious in his participation. After a second pass of the book, Philip felt oddly drawn to the pages. The chant Kam was to recite during the rites was not in any language Philip had ever heard, nor read. Surely that was close enough to speaking in tongues.

Before Philip was ready for the ritual, he had to go see Nailah. He didn't have the tools needed to set up properly.

"I think you were right, but I need some things," was the way he answered her expectant look when he entered the shop. "The book has specific requirements for its altars."

"It does," she agreed. "I may not have everything you need, but I'll point you in the right direction."

"I know you will," Philip agreed. When he told her he trusted her the day before, he realized now that he really meant it. He hadn't known Nailah long, but she was one of the few people who knew and saw all of him.

She guided him to the crimson altar cloth, ceremonial goblet, and rich clove incense that he needed. The knight, Philip, would need to be dressed in a white robe. Kam, who'd play the role of the magician, was to be adorned in blue.

"You don't need to get fancy with it," Nailah explained as she studied the pages he meant to follow. "A bathrobe will do, or even a button-up so long as you let it hang open. *You and Kam* are the key components. The setting is important, but strong intentions can overpower an imperfect setup."

"Thank you." His chest was tight, and the smile he leveled at her didn't reach his eyes.

"Nervous?" she asked, bagging his purchases.

"Every time," he admitted. "Each time I fail, someone pays the ultimate price."

When Philip returned home, Kam was lounging in their bed with the book. While Philip had gone to get their clothing, the altar dressings, and the wine he'd need, Kam had spent the morning trying to commit the incantation to memory. Philip had been worried about the temptation of the alcohol being in the apartment, but Kam had insisted he'd be fine. To cement the point, while Philip got the altar space ready Kam poured out all but what they'd need of the wine. Both of them trusted him, but he had to admit he felt better without the temptation.

Philip spread the altar cloth over the floor in the living room. It was large, bigger than the size of their bed. Then he placed the items they would need. He draped the folded bathrobes he'd purchased for them both on the edge of the sofa.

"I'm going to shower," Philip called from the bedroom doorway.

"Don't be nervous," Kam replied over the cover of the book.

"Easy for you to say," Philip teased.

"Easier for you. You've done spell work before. Some magician I'll be."

"You'll be perfect."

"Sometimes your blind faith plays in my favor," Kam teased back.

In the shower, Philip scrubbed shampoo into his scalp first. He turned the water to a cool temperature and began to rinse his hair before he washed his body, reluctant to let his fingertips touch his skin. He used a cloth to spread the minty soap over every inch of his frame until his skin was tingling in tune with his apprehension.

When he was finished, Kam brought him two towels and the robe from the living room. Kam handed him one towel, which Philip tied quickly around his waist. Kam then knelt to slowly dry his legs from his feet upward. It was affectionate and intimate, but it lacked the heat Kam usually brought to their encounters.

Philip's expression warmed as he realized Kam was *proving* he had nothing to fear. Just as Kam had promised, he was being as reverent as Philip needed.

Kam rose to his feet and toweled off Philip's torso and chest before he dried his arms. When it was time to dry Philip's hair, he draped the towel over him and pulled the younger man in for a chaste kiss.

"I love you," he whispered.

"I love *you*," Philip echoed.

Kam kissed Philip again before he left him to finish drying off. They both needed to ready themselves for the ritual.

Philip left the bathroom with damp hair, making sure the robe was tied securely. He met Kam in the living room, where he was already sitting on the floor wearing his blue robe open. Philip didn't have to ask if Kam was ready; he knew he was.

Philip sat cross-legged beside Kam. Kam then filled the goblet with wine and set the bottle down. He passed the goblet to Philip, who took a shallow sip before he passed it back.

Kam would be the one to serve him, and had an important role to play. Every action taken would need Kam to lead it. It was why he had spent the afternoon studying, though the book was positioned beside them on the red cloth.

Kam lit four candles around them, as well as the incense cone. He watched the smoke drift up from the incense for a moment before he blew it out. Philip watched the flames, and the smoke, and his lover—the magician.

The magician poured oil in his palm and reached for Philip's foot, which he offered willingly. This was what the ritual called for, and there was no way he could imagine Kam could touch him that he wouldn't want.

Kam rubbed each of Philip's toes delicately in turn and then kneaded along his sole to the heel. When he reached the ankle, he extended a hand wordlessly for Philip's other foot. Kam gave it the same careful treatment and then shifted his attention to Philip's original ankle, where he began to work up his calf.

Philip closed his eyes as Kam massaged the muscle up to the knee. It was challenging to keep sensual thoughts from his mind when his lover touched him so tenderly.

Kam sat up on his knees and applied more oil to his palms when he rubbed up Philip's thighs. Philip looked up at Kam with wide eyes and he was met with a serious, somber look. Kam was doing his best to keep carnal thoughts from his mind, too. Philip focused on maintaining deep, steadying breaths, as he had when he ran long distances.

Kam slid his hands up Philip's outer thighs and over his hips under the robe. Philip slipped the fabric off his shoulders and the robe pooled around him on the floor. Kam's fingertips danced along Philip's ribs, up his chest and down his arms.

I love you, Philip thought when their eyes met. Kam smiled at him like he knew. Philip turned so his back faced Kam. This allowed the magician to more readily reach his back and shoulders, and it readied them for the next phase of the ritual. Kam worked his thumbs into the tense muscles and smiled when Philip let out a little satisfied groan.

"That's it, relax," Kam coaxed.

Philip should have chided Kam for speaking normally during the spell, but he was too calm. The purpose of the rubdown was to get him to release tension, and it was working beautifully. He needed to be loose and at ease, and he was much closer to that when Kam finally shrugged his own robe off his shoulders. It fell to the floor around him, and he eased down with his knees on either side of Philip's hips. He wasn't shy—the ritual didn't need him to be. He pressed firmly against Philip's back as he took Philip in hand, and Philip reached back to hold onto Kam's thigh to stay tethered.

Philip exhaled a ragged breath at the touch. It was a struggle to keep his thoughts from going to a sinful, sensual place as

Kam began to stroke him. Kam offered Philip the goblet with his other hand, and he took a deep sip. Throughout the process, Philip needed to drink the full glass of wine, but he could only drink when Kam offered it. He was at his brother's mercy as they conducted the ritual.

Kam's touches were slow and methodical. He wasn't building tension, not yet. He was warming Philip up, easing him into the wealth of sensation which was to follow.

"Tou ehkt blai mah roh..." Kam murmured the chant under his breath. The book was spread out by one of the candles so he could recite the syllables clearly if his memory faltered. *"Hai moh rah moh roh..."* Again, Kam offered Philip the wine. It was the blood of Christ. It was the blessed nectar. It was the promise of release. This time, Philip drank deeply.

"Loo aih moh rah doh ah see aih."

Kam began to move his hand more quickly, and he flicked his wrist the way he knew Philip liked. He *was* building, then. He was driving the knight toward the sun. Philip squeezed Kam's thigh as he began to feel an abundance of warmth and light. Despite his hold on Kam's frame, it was as though he'd lost his tether to his physical form. He had not been overtaken by the drink, nor by the growing sensation in his body, yet somehow, his thoughts swirled and separated.

He was himself warmth, and light, and love, and *power*. Philip felt immeasurably powerful as Kam began to rock them both back and forth in time with his motions. Kam was again murmuring low syllables into Philip's ear, but he couldn't hear them. The room grew dark around them, and only the candles existed for light outside of Philip's own almighty radiance.

"Sei hoo mah foh sah lei..." Kam called the words out in the same careful, even cadence as he sped up their movement. Together, they rocked as the words echoed in that arcane, unknowable tongue. Philip felt himself separate further until he floated above them both. The candles still shone bright in the darkness. As Philip watched from outside of himself, he had to squint at the brightness of his own glowing skin as his body swayed back and forth with Kam.

Independent of his flesh, Philip rose to the ceiling. He saw his lungs through his chest, heaving from the effort. A shimmery sheen had broken out across both of their forms, and the magician's physical being began to emanate his own silvery light in contrast to Philip's gold.

Philip could see Kam was chanting again, but the world had grown silent as he hovered several feet above them. He watched as Kam offered him the wine, and again, his body took it and drank deeply from the ornate cup. Philip felt he had watched himself from outside himself for ages. Time both stood still and stretched on to infinity. Philip was one with all things.

Everything except the scene beneath him was happening slowly, so slowly as he began to sink back toward his physical being. As his spectral form drew closer to his present, human body, he felt incredibly warm, and when he retook his corporeal form, sweat coated his body. He felt the miracle of Kam's touch as an infinite fullness which was at once a perfect, bursting ease and comfort and a vacuous yearning. Philip had and yet he needed in equal, impossible measure. His yearning felt sentient and tangible. When he came with a powerful, explosive shout, his seed spreading over the altar cloth, he saw the cat standing before him in the darkness.

Philip closed his eyes as tears streamed down his cheeks. Kam wiped his hand on the cloth beneath them, and he pulled Philip back toward him. Philip leaned into his lover, his breaths coming in powerful, silent sobs.

"Are you okay?" Kam asked, but Philip was still overcome. He could not put words together to form his experience, to describe what he'd seen or had felt. He brought his lips to kiss Kam's cheeks, and then his lips, and then suddenly, Philip was upon him as if he were again the cat.

The tears had stopped flowing and his breathing had slowed. The emotion had burned out in a spectacular moment of brilliance and only the passionate craving remained. Philip swept his hand through his spend on the altar, and with his slippery palm, he began fondling his lover.

Kam's breath caught and Philip surged forward. Their tongues entwined as readily as they ever had. Philip bit Kam's lower lip hard and both men moaned together as one before Philip crouched and took Kam into his mouth.

Kam's eyes widened as Philip jerked him roughly and suckled the head of his cock. The taste of Kam, covered in his own pre-cum and Philip's seed, was salty and divine.

When Kam, too spilled after a breath, he cried out desperately.

Philip swallowed the release down, then raised up so that he could pull Kam into a tender and loving embrace.

For now, the beast was sated.

37

CHAPTER 37

Philip woke with the aching back and stiff joints he'd come to associate with falling asleep in a heap on the floor. Kam groaned upon his waking, too. The ritual candles had long burned out, and it was dark through the windows, so he knew hours had passed. He got to his feet carefully and crossed into the kitchen.

The moonlight shone in on his bare skin through the window. Philip found it difficult to see in the dark, so he parted the curtains with his hand so that he could pour himself a tall glass of water. He drained the glass and then poured another for Kam.

When he returned to the living room, Kam had crawled up onto the sofa. He took the water readily, and Philip sat beside him.

"How do you feel?" Kam asked after he'd swallowed some of the water.

Philip thought for a moment.

"*Good*," he answered.

"Like you're about to change?"

"No," Philip answered honestly. He felt none of the restlessness or itching discomfort of a pending transformation. "I'm still tired, though."

"Want to go to bed? We can clear the floor tomorrow."

Philip nodded, and the pair ventured into the bedroom together.

When Philip awoke again, it was late morning. He startled when he saw the clock. 11:00 a.m. Well past the time he would have expected to shift. He shook Kam until he woke.

"What's wrong?" Kam asked sleepily.

"I didn't change," Philip whispered, as if saying the words aloud would break the spell.

"What?" Kam sat up. "You're sure?" He ran his hands over Philip's body, searching for any sign that he had transformed in the night and returned.

Philip laughed, a reaction brought on by the shock of it.

"Yeah." He hesitated and then smiled. "*Yeah.*"

Kam pulled Philip into a kiss, tugging him back against the mattress to celebrate.

Philip and Kam lay naked together, cuddled close well into the afternoon, despite the heat. Even after a second round of lovemaking, Philip didn't feel the familiar pull of the cat.

"You know what this means?" Philip asked.

"What?" Kam asked, still a little breathless.

"I need to find Melissa. I can save her from our parents' curse."

Acknowledgments

I can't possibly list all the people who made this book possible, but I'm going to try.

Thank you Linds for sharing the 1982 cinematic masterpiece Cat People with me. On that note thank you Alan Ormsby for writing such an engaging screenplay. Thank you Paul Schrader and Charles Fries for bringing your vision so masterfully to the silver screen. Thank you Natassja Kinski and Malcolm McDowell for performances which made the story that much more compelling.

Thank you Grandma Reedy for letting me work at your kitchen table to get this book ready to go to the editor. I learned a long time ago that spending weeks with you without cell service or internet access is the best way for me to get anything done.

Thank you John for letting me read chapters aloud at various stages of drafting, rewriting, and editing. I'm sure by the time this book comes out you will be incredibly sick of it in all forms, but I'm grateful that you never let on.

Thank you Ana of Sparks Editorial for being an incredible developmental editor. You helped me refine a very rough draft into something I am proud of, and for that I can't thank you enough.

Thank you Amanda Webb for being a willing beta reader, and for always letting me gab about my characters, concepts, and stories. Your friendship is a treasure, your art is spectacular, and I can't wait to read Faith and Ruin.

About the Author

Fox Emm writes genre-defying fiction in rural Virginia or on an island in Maine - both settings are as beautiful and magical as you imagine. When they're not writing they can be found curled up with a book, playing video games, or exploring the great outdoors by foot or kayak.

Download free stories like this one and check out their other works at https://www.FoxEmm.com

Also by Fox Emm

A Remedy Earned

Reclusive healer Vida isn't really a people person. She wants nothing more than to keep treating her friends and neighbors for ailments and injuries. She has tried to stay out of the violent conflict that has rocked her community, with some success.

When she finds a charming talking sword, everything changes. Will Vida find the strength to face her fears? Is the magic sword the key to saving the land?

Find out in this no spice, 43-page novelette.

Bad Neighborhood

In this chilling horror collection, 29 writers and poets have come together to share tales of the grotesque, the supernatural, and more. Their words will pluck you from your comfort zone and leave you for dead, or worse. Have you ever considered where evil bides its time when it's not outside your door? What disturbing locale could make it feel safe? We've all heard that home is where the heart is, but alas, that heart is sometimes racing...

We hope you live in a good neighborhood.

www.ingramcontent.com/pod-product-compliance
Lightning Source LLC
Chambersburg PA
CBHW030519120726
47904CB00005B/1540